Penguin Books
Changing Places

David Lodge is Professor of Modern English Literature
at the University of Birmingham, where he has worked
since 1960. In 1964–5 he held a Harkness Common-
wealth Fellowship to the United States and in 1969 he
was Visiting Associate Professor at the University of
California. He has lectured and addressed conferences in
several European countries. David Lodge is married with
three children. His other novels are *The Picturegoers*,
Ginger, You're Barmy, *The British Museum Is Falling Down*,
Out of the Shelter and *How Far Can You Go?*, which won the
Whitbread Book of the Year Award for 1980, and *Small
World* (1984), a marvellously funny sequel to *Changing
Places* which was shortlisted for the Booker Prize in 1984.
He has also written four books of literary criticism,
Language of Fiction (1966), *The Novelist at the Crossroads*
(1971), *The Modes of Modern Writing* (1977) and *Working
with Structuralism* (1981). For *Changing Places* he was
awarded the Hawthornden Prize and the *Yorkshire Post*
Fiction Prize.

David Lodge

Changing Places

A Tale of Two Campuses

Penguin Books

Penguin Books Ltd, Harmondsworth, Middlesex, England
Viking Penguin Inc., 40 West 23rd Street, New York, New York 10010, U.S.A.
Penguin Books Australia Ltd, Ringwood, Victoria, Australia
Penguin Books Canada Limited, 2801 John Street, Markham, Ontario, Canada L3R 1B4
Penguin Books (N.Z.) Ltd, 182–190 Wairau Road, Auckland 10, New Zealand

First published in Great Britain by Martin Secker & Warburg Ltd 1975
Published in Penguin Books in Great Britain 1978
Reprinted 1978, 1979, 1981, 1982, 1983 (twice), 1984, 1985 (three times), 1986 (twice)
First published in the United States of America by Penguin Books 1978

Made and printed in Great Britain by
Richard Clay (The Chaucer Press) Ltd, Bungay, Suffolk
Set in Monotype Baskerville

For Lenny and Priscilla, Stanley and Adrienne
and many other friends on the West Coast

1. Flying

High, high above the North Pole, on the first day of 1969, two professors of English Literature approached each other at a combined velocity of 1200 miles per hour. They were protected from the thin, cold air by the pressurized cabins of two Boeing 707s, and from the risk of collision by the prudent arrangement of the international air corridors. Although they had never met, the two men were known to each other by name. They were, in fact, in process of exchanging posts for the next six months, and in an age of more leisurely transportation the intersection of their respective routes might have been marked by some interesting human gesture: had they waved, for example, from the decks of two ocean liners crossing in mid-Atlantic, each man simultaneously focusing a telescope, by chance, on the other, with his free hand; or, more plausibly, a little mime of mutual appraisal might have been played out through the windows of two railway compartments halted side by side at the same station somewhere in Hampshire or the Mid-West, the more self-conscious party relieved to feel himself, at last, moving off, only to discover that it is the other man's train that is moving first . . . However, it was not to be. Since the two men were in airplanes, and one was bored and the other frightened of looking out of the window – since, in any case, the planes were too distant from each other to be mutually visible with the naked eye, the crossing of their paths at the still point of the turning world passed unremarked by anyone other than the narrator of this duplex chronicle.

'Duplex', as well as having the general meaning of 'twofold', applies in the jargon of electrical telegraphy to 'systems in which messages are sent simultaneously in opposite directions' (*OED*). Imagine, if you will, that each of these two professors of English Literature (both, as it happens, aged forty) is connected to his native land, place of employment and domestic hearth by an infinitely elastic umbilical cord of emotions, attitudes and values – a cord which stretches and stretches almost to the point of invisibility, but never quite to breaking-point, as he hurtles through the air at 600 miles per hour. Imagine further that, as they pass each other above the polar ice-cap, the pilots of their respective Boeings, in defiance of regulations and technical feasibility, begin to execute a series of playful aerobatics – criss-crossing, diving, soaring and looping, like a pair of mating bluebirds, so as thoroughly to entangle the aforesaid umbilical cords, before proceeding soberly on their way in the approved manner. It follows that when the two men alight in each other's territory, and go about their business and pleasure, whatever vibrations are passed back by one to his native habitat will be felt by the other, and vice versa, and thus return to the transmitter subtly modified by the response of the other party – may, indeed, return to him along the other party's cord of communication, which is, after all, anchored in the place where he has just arrived; so that before long the whole system is twanging with vibrations travelling backwards and forwards between Prof A and Prof B, now along this line, now along that, sometimes beginning on one line and terminating on another. It would not be surprising, in other words, if two men changing places for six months should exert a reciprocal influence on each other's destinies, and actually mirror each other's experience in certain respects, notwithstanding all the differences that exist between the two environments, and between the characters of the two men and their respective attitudes towards the whole enterprise.

One of these differences we can take in at a glance from our privileged narrative altitude (higher than that of any jet). It is obvious, from his stiff, upright posture, and fulsome gratitude to the stewardess serving him a glass of orange juice, that Philip Swallow, flying westward, is unaccustomed to air travel; while to Morris Zapp, slouched in the seat of his eastbound aircraft, chewing a dead cigar (a hostess has made him extinguish it) and glowering at the meagre portion of ice dissolving in his plastic tumbler of bourbon, the experience of long-distance air travel is tediously familiar.

Philip Swallow has, in fact, flown before; but so seldom, and at such long intervals, that on each occasion he suffers the same trauma, an alternating current of fear and re-assurance that charges and relaxes his system in a persistent and exhausting rhythm. While he is on the ground, pre-paring for his journey, he thinks of flying with exhilaration – soaring up, up and away into the blue empyrean, cradled in aircraft that seem, from a distance, effortlessly at home in that element, as though sculpted from the sky itself. This confidence begins to fade a little when he arrives at the airport and winces at the shrill screaming of jet engines. In the sky the planes look very small. On the runways they look very big. Therefore close up they should look even bigger – but in fact they don't. His own plane, for instance, just outside the window of the assembly lounge, doesn't look quite big enough for all the people who are going to get into it. This impression is confirmed when he passes through the tunnel into the cabin of the aircraft, a cramped tube full of writhing limbs. But when he, and the other passengers, are seated, well-being returns. The seats are so remarkably comfortable that one feels quite content to stay put, but it is reassuring that the aisle is free should one wish to walk up it. There is soothing music playing. The lighting is restful. A stewardess offers him the morning paper. His baggage is safely stowed away in the plane somewhere, or if it is not, that isn't his fault, which is the main thing. Flying is, after all, the only way to travel.

But as the plane taxis to the runway, he makes the mistake of looking out of the window at the wings bouncing gently up and down. The panels and rivets are almost painfully visible, the painted markings weathered, there are streaks of

9

soot on the engine cowlings. It is borne in upon him that he is, after all, entrusting his life to a machine, the work of human hands, fallible and subject to decay. And so it goes on, even after the plane has climbed safely into the sky: periods of confidence and pleasure punctuated by spasms of panic and emptiness.

The sang-froid of his fellow passengers is a constant source of wonderment to him, and he observes their deportment carefully. Flying for Philip Swallow is essentially a dramatic performance, and he approaches it like a game amateur actor determined to hold his own in the company of word-perfect professionals. To speak the truth, he approaches most of life's challenges in the same spirit. He is a mimetic man: unconfident, eager to please, infinitely suggestible.

It would be natural, but incorrect, to assume that Morris Zapp has suffered no such qualms on his flight. A seasoned veteran of the domestic airways, having flown over most of the states in the Union in his time, bound for conferences, lecture dates and assignations, it has not escaped his notice that airplanes occasionally crash. Being innately mistrustful of the universe and its guiding spirit, which he sometimes refers to as Improvidence ('How can you attribute *that*,' he will ask, gesturing at the star-spangled night sky over the Pacific, 'to something called Providence? Just look at the *waste*!'), he seldom enters an aircraft without wondering with one part of his busy brain whether he is about to feature in Air Disaster of the Week on the nation's TV networks. Normally such morbid thoughts visit him only at the beginning and end of a flight, for he has read somewhere that eighty per cent of all aircraft accidents occur at either take-off or landing – a statistic that did not surprise him, having been stacked on many occasions for an hour or more over Esseph airport, fifty planes circling in the air, fifty more taking off at ninety-second intervals, the whole juggling act controlled by a computer, so that it only needed a fuse to blow and the sky would look like airline competition had finally broken out into open war, the companies hiring retired kamikaze pilots to destroy each other's hardware in the sky, TWA's Boeings ramming Pan Am's, American Airlines' D C 8s busting United's right out of their Friendly Skies (hah!), rival shuttle services colliding head-on, the clouds raining down wings, fuselages, engines, passengers, chemical toilets, hostesses, menu cards and plastic cutlery (Morris Zapp had an apocalyptic imagination on occasion, as who has not in America these days?) in a definitive act of industrial pollution.

By taking the non-stop polar flight to London, in preference to the two-stage journey via New York, Zapp reckons that he has reduced his chances of being caught in such an Armageddon by fifty per cent. But weighing against this comforting thought is the fact that he is travelling on a charter flight, and chartered aircraft (he has also read) are several times more likely to crash than planes on scheduled flights, being, he infers, machines long past their prime, bought as scrap from the big airlines by cheapjack operators and sold again and again to even cheaper jacks (this plane, for instance, belonged to a company called Orbis; the phoney Latin name inspired no confidence and he wouldn't mind betting that an ultra-violet photograph would reveal a palimpsest of fourteen different airline insignia under its fresh paint) flown by pilots long gone over the hill, alcoholics and schizoids, shaky-fingered victims of emergency landings, ice-storms and hijackings by crazy Arabs and homesick Cubans wielding sticks of dynamite and dime-store pistols. Furthermore, this is his first flight over water (yes, Morris Zapp has never before left the protection of the North American landmass, a proud record unique among the faculty of his university) and he cannot swim. The unfamiliar ritual of instruction, at the commencement of the flight, in the use of inflatable lifejackets, unsettled him. That canvas and rubber contraption was a fetishist's dream, but he had as much chance of getting into it in an emergency as into the girdle of the hostess giving the demonstration. Furthermore, exploratory gropings failed to locate a life-jacket where it was supposed to be, under his seat. Only his reluctance to strike an undignified pose before a blonde with outsize spectacles in the next seat had dissuaded him from getting down on hands and knees to make a thorough check. He contented himself with allowing his long, gorilla-like arms to hang loosely over the edge of his seat, fingers brushing the underside unobtrusively in the style used for parking gum or nosepickings. Once, at full stretch, he found something that felt promising, but it proved to be one of his neighbour's legs, and was indignantly withdrawn. He turned towards her, not to apologize (Morris Zapp never apologized) but to give her the famous Zapp Stare, guaranteed to stop any human creature, from University Presidents to Black Panthers, dead in his tracks at a range of twenty yards, only to be confronted with an impenetrable curtain of blonde hair.

Eventually he abandons the quest for the lifejacket, reflecting that the sea under his ass at the moment is frozen solid anyway, not that that is a reassuring thought. No, this is not the happiest of flights for Morris J. Zapp ('Jehovah', he would murmur out of the side of his mouth to girls who inquired about his middle name, it never failed; all women longed to be screwed by a god, it was the source of all religion – 'Just look at the myths, Leda and the Swan, Isis and Osiris, Mary and the Holy Ghost' – thus spake Zapp in his graduate seminar, pinning a brace of restive nuns to their seats with the Stare). There is something funny, he tells himself, about this plane – not just the implausible Latin name of the airline, the missing lifejacket, the billions of tons of ice underneath him and the minuscule cube melting in the bourbon before him – something else there is, something he hasn't figured out yet. While Morris Zapp is working on this problem, we shall take time out to explain something of the circumstances that have brought him and Philip Swallow into the polar skies at the same indeterminate (for everybody's watch is wrong by now) hour.

Between the State University of Euphoria (colloquially known as Euphoric State) and the University of Rummidge, there has long existed a scheme for the exchange of visiting teachers in the second half of each academic year. How two universities so different in character and so widely separated in space should be linked in this way is simply explained. It happened that the architects of both campuses independently hit upon the same idea for the chief feature of their designs, namely, a replica of the leaning Tower of Pisa, built of white stone and twice the original size at Euphoric State and of red brick and to scale at Rummidge, but restored to the perpendicular in both instances. The exchange scheme was set up to mark this coincidence.

Under the original agreement, each visitor drew the salary to which he was entitled by rank and seniority on the scale of the host institution, but as no American could survive for more than a few days on the monthly stipend paid by Rummidge, Euphoric State made up the difference for its own faculty, while paying its British visitors a salary beyond their wildest dreams and bestowing upon them indiscriminately the title of Visiting Professor. It was not only in these terms that the arrangement tended to favour the British participants. Euphoria, that small but populous state on the Western seaboard of America, situated between Northern and Southern California, with its mountains, lakes and rivers, its redwood forests, its blond beaches and its incomparable Bay, across which the State University at Plotinus faces the glittering, glamorous city of Esseph – Euphoria is considered by many cosmopolitan experts to be one of the most agreeable environments in the world. Not even its City Fathers would claim as much for Rummidge, a large, graceless industrial city sprawled over the English Midlands at the intersection of three motorways, twenty-six railway lines and half-a-dozen stagnant canals.

Then again, Euphoric State had, by a ruthless exploitation of its wealth, built itself up into one of America's major universities, buying the most distinguished scholars it could find and retaining their loyalty by the lavish provision of laboratories, libraries, research grants and handsome, long-legged secretaries. By this year of 1969, Euphoric State had perhaps reached its peak as a centre of learning, and was already in the process of decline – due partly to the accelerating tempo of disruption by student militants, and partly to the counter-pressures exerted by the right-wing Governor of the State, Ronald Duck, a former movie-actor. But such was the quality of the university's senior staff, and the magnitude of its accumulated resources, that it would be many years before its standing was seriously undermined. Euphoric State, in short, was still a name to conjure with in the senior common rooms of the world. Rummidge, on the other hand, had never been an institution of more than middling size and reputation, and it had lately suffered the mortifying fate of most English universities of its type (civic redbrick): having competed strenuously for fifty years with two universities chiefly valued for being old, it was, at the moment of drawing level, rudely overtaken in popularity and prestige by a batch of universities chiefly valued for being new. Its mood was therefore disgruntled and discouraged, rather as would be the mood of the middle class in a society that had never had a bourgeois revolution, but had passed directly from aristocratic to proletarian control.

For these and other reasons the most highly-qualified and senior members of staff competed eagerly for the honour of representing Rummidge at Euphoric State: while Euphoric State, if the truth were told, had sometimes encountered difficulty in persuading any of its faculty to go to Rummidge. The members of that élite body, the Euphoric State faculty, who picked up grants and fellowships as other men pick up hats, did not aim to teach when they came to Europe, and certainly not to teach at Rummidge, which few of them had even heard of. Hence the American visitors to Rummidge tended to be young and/or undistinguished, determined Anglophiles who could find no other way of getting to England or, very rarely, specialists in one of the esoteric disciplines in which Rummidge, through the support of local industry, had established an unchallenged supremacy: domestic appliance technology, tyre sciences and the biochemistry of the cocoa bean.

The exchange of Philip Swallow and Morris Zapp, however, constituted a reversal of the usual pattern. Zapp was distinguished, and Swallow was not. Zapp was the man who had published articles in *PMLA* while still in graduate school; who, enviably offered his first job by Euphoric State, had stuck out for twice the going salary, and got it; who had published five fiendishly clever books (four of them on Jane Austen) by the time he was thirty and achieved the rank of full professor at the same precocious age. Swallow was a man scarcely known outside his own Department, who had published nothing except a handful of essays and reviews, who had risen slowly up the salary scale of Lecturer by standard annual increments and was now halted at the top with slender prospects of promotion. Not that Philip Swallow was lacking in intelligence or ability; but he lacked will and ambition, the professional killer instinct which Zapp abundantly possessed.

In this respect both men were characteristic of the educational systems they had passed through. In America, it is not too difficult to obtain a bachelor's degree. The student is left very much to his own devices, he accumulates the necessary credits at his leisure, cheating is easy, and there is not much suspense or anxiety about the eventual outcome. He (or she) is therefore free to give full attention to the normal interests of late adolescence – sport, alcohol, entertainment and the opposite sex. It is at the postgraduate level that the pressure really begins, when the student is burnished and tempered in a series of gruelling courses and rigorous assessments until he is deemed worthy to receive the accolade of the PhD. By now he has invested so much time and money in the process that any career other than an academic one has become unthinkable, and anything less than success in it unbearable. He is well primed, in short, to enter a profession as steeped in the spirit of free enterprise as Wall Street, in which each scholar-teacher makes an individual contract with his employer, and is free to sell his services to the highest bidder.

Under the British system, competition begins and ends

much earlier. Four times, under our educational rules, the human pack is shuffled and cut – at eleven-plus, sixteen-plus, eighteen-plus and twenty-plus – and happy is he who comes top of the deck on each occasion, but especially the last. This is called Finals, the very name of which implies that nothing of importance can happen after it. The British postgraduate student is a lonely, forlorn soul, uncertain of what he is doing or whom he is trying to please – you may recognize him in the tea-shops around the Bodleian and the British Museum by the glazed look in his eyes, the vacant stare of the shell-shocked veteran for whom nothing has been real since the Big Push. As long as he manages to land his first job, this is no great handicap in the short run, since tenure is virtually automatic in British universities, and everyone is paid on the same scale. But at a certain age, the age at which promotions and Chairs begin to occupy a man's thoughts, he may look back with wistful nostalgia to the days when his wits ran fresh and clear, directed to a single, positive goal.

Philip Swallow had been made and unmade by the system in precisely this way. He liked examinations, always did well in them. Finals had been, in many ways, the supreme moment of his life. He frequently dreamed that he was taking the examinations again, and these were happy dreams. Awake, he could without difficulty remember the questions he had elected to answer on every paper that hot, distant June. In the preceding months he had prepared himself with meticulous care, filling his mind with distilled knowledge, drop by drop, until, on the eve of the first paper (Old English Set Texts) it was almost brimming over. Each morning for the next ten days he bore this precious vessel to the examination halls and poured a measured quantity of the contents on to pages of ruled quarto. Day by day the level fell, until on the tenth day the vessel was empty, the cup was drained, the cupboard was bare. In the years that followed he set about replenishing his mind, but it was never quite the same. The sense of purpose was lacking – there was no great Reckoning against which he could hoard his knowledge, so that it tended to leak away as fast as he acquired it.

Philip Swallow was a man with a genuine love of literature in all its diverse forms. He was as happy with *Beowulf* as with Virginia Woolf, with *Waiting for Godot* as with *Gammer Gurton's Needle*, and in odd moments when nobler examples of the written word were not to hand he read attentively the backs of cornflakes packets, the small print on railway tickets and the advertising matter in books of stamps. This undiscriminating enthusiasm, however, prevented him from settling on a 'field' to cultivate as his own. He had done his initial research on Jane Austen, but since then had turned his attention to topics as various as medieval sermons, Elizabethan sonnet sequences, Restoration heroic tragedy, eighteenth-century broadsides, the novels of William Godwin, the poetry of Elizabeth Barrett Browning and premonitions of the Theatre of the Absurd in the plays of George Bernard Shaw. None of these projects had been completed. Seldom, indeed, had he drawn up a preliminary bibliography before his attention was distracted by some new or revived interest in something entirely different. He ran hither and thither between the shelves of Eng. Lit. like a child in a toyshop – so reluctant to choose one item to the exclusion of others that he ended up empty-handed.

There was one respect alone in which Philip was recognized as a man of distinction, though only within the confines of his own Department. He was a superlative examiner of undergraduates: scrupulous, painstaking, stern yet just. No one could award a delicate mark like B+/B+?+ with such confident aim, or justify it with such cogency and conviction. In the Department meetings that discussed draft question papers he was much feared by his colleagues because of his keen eye for the ambiguous rubric, the repetition of questions from previous years' papers, the careless oversight that would allow candidates to duplicate material in two answers. His own papers were works of art on which he laboured with loving care for many hours, tinkering and polishing, weighing every word, deftly manipulating *eithers* and *ors*, judiciously balancing difficult questions on popular authors with easy questions on obscure ones, inviting candidates to consider, illustrate, comment on, analyse, respond to, make discriminating assessments of or (last resort) discuss brilliant epigrams of his own invention disguised as quotations from anonymous critics.

A colleague had once declared that Philip ought to publish his examination papers. The suggestion had been intended as a sneer, but Philip had been rather taken with the idea – seeing in it, for a few dizzy hours, a heaven-sent solution to his professional barrenness. He visualized a critical work of totally revolutionary form, a concise, comprehensive survey of English literature consisting entirely of questions, elegantly printed with acres of white paper between them, questions that would be miracles of condensation, eloquence and thoughtfulness, questions to read and re-read, questions to brood over, as pregnant and enigmatic as *haikus*, as memorable as proverbs; questions that would, so to speak, contain within themselves the ghostly, subtly suggested embryos of their own answers. *Collected Literary Questions*, by Philip Swallow. A book to be compared with Pascal's *Pensées* or Wittgenstein's *Philosophical Investigations* . . .

But the project had advanced no further than his more orthodox ones, and meanwhile Rummidge students had begun agitating for the abolition of conventional examinations, so that his one special skill was in danger of becoming redundant. There had been times, lately, when he had begun to wonder whether he was entirely suited to the career on which he had been launched some fifteen years earlier, not so much by personal choice as by the mere impetus of his remarkable First.

He had been awarded a postgraduate studentship automatically and had accepted his Professor's suggestion that he write an MA thesis on the juvenilia of Jane Austen. After nearly two years his work was still far from completion and, thinking that a change of scene might help, he applied in an idle moment for a Fellowship to America and for an Assistant Lectureship at the University of Rummidge. To his great surprise he was offered both (that First again) and Rummidge generously offered to defer his appointment for a year so that he would not have to choose between them. He didn't really want to go to America by this time because he had become sentimentally attached to a postgraduate student called Hilary Broome who was working on Augustan pastoral poetry, but he formed the impression that the Fellowship was not an opportunity that could be lightly refused.

So he went to Harvard and was extremely miserable for several months. Because he was working on his own, trying to finish his thesis, he made few friends; because he had no car, and couldn't drive anyway, he found it difficult to move around freely. Cowardice, and a dim, undefined loyalty to Hilary Broome, prevented him from dating the intimidating Radcliffe girls. He formed the habit of taking long solitary walks through the streets of Cambridge and environs, tailed by police cars whose occupants regarded gratuitous walking as inherently suspicious. The fillings he had prudently taken care to have put in his teeth before leaving the embrace of the National Health Service all fell out and he was informed by a contemptuous Boston dentist that he needed a thousand dollars' worth of dental work immediately. As this sum was nearly a third of his total stipend, Philip thought he had found the perfect excuse for throwing up his fellowship and returning to England with honour. The Fellowship Fund, however, promptly offered to meet the entire cost from its bottomless funds, so instead he wrote to Hilary Broome asking her to marry him. Hilary, who was growing bored with Augustan pastoral poetry, returned her books to the library, bought a wedding dress off the peg at C&A, and flew out to join him on the first available plane. They were married by an Episcopalian minister in Boston just three weeks after Philip had proposed.

One of the conditions of the Fellowship was that recipients should travel widely in the United States, and Fellows were generously provided with a rented car for the purpose.

By way of a honeymoon, and to escape the severity of the New England winter, the young couple decided to start their tour immediately. With Hilary at the wheel of a gigantic brand-new Chevrolet Impala, they headed south to Florida, sometimes pulling off the highway to make fervent love on the amazingly wide back seat. From Florida they crossed the southern States in very easy stages until they reached Euphoria and settled for the summer in an attic apartment on the top of a hill in the city of Esseph. From their double bed they looked straight across the Bay at the verdant slopes of Plotinus, location of the Euphoric State campus.

This long honeymoon was the key that unlocked the American experience for Philip Swallow. He discovered in himself an unsuspected, long repressed appetite for sensual pleasure which he assuaged, not only in the double bed with Hilary, but also with simple amenities of the American way of life, such as showers and cold beer and supermarkets and heated open-air swimming pools and multi-flavoured ice-cream. The sun shone. Philip was relaxed, confident, happy. He learned to drive, and flung the majestic Impala up and down the roller-coaster hills of Esseph with native panache, the radio playing at full volume. He haunted the cellars and satirical night-clubs of South Strand, where the Beats, in those days, were giving their jazz-and-poetry recitals, and felt himself thrillingly connected to the *Zeitgeist*. He even finished his MA thesis, almost effortlessly. It was the last major project he ever finished.

Hilary was four months pregnant when they sailed back to England in September. It was raining hard the morning they docked at Southampton, and Philip caught a cold which lasted for approximately a year. They rented a damp and draughty furnished flat in Rummidge for six months, and after the baby had arrived they moved to a small, damp and draughty terraced house, from which, three years later, with a second child and another on the way, they moved to a large, damp and draughty Victorian villa. The children made it impossible for Hilary to work, and Philip's salary was small. Life was riddled with petty privation. So were the lives of most people like the Swallows at this time, and he would not perhaps have repined had he not tasted a richer existence. Sometimes he came across snapshots of himself and Hilary in Euphoria, tanned and confident and gleeful, and, running a hand through his thinning hair, he would gaze at the figures in envious wonder, as if they were rich, distant relatives whom he had never seen in the flesh.

That is why there is a gleam in Philip Swallow's eye as he sits now in the BOAC Boeing, sipping his orange juice; why, despite the fact that the plane is shuddering and lurching in the most terrifying manner due to what the captain has just described soothingly over the public address system as 'a spot of moderate turbulence', he would not be anywhere else for the world. Though he has followed the recent history of the United States in the newspapers, though he is well aware, cognitively, that it has become more than ever a violent and melodramatic land, riven by deep divisions of race and ideology, traumatized by political assassinations, the campuses in revolt, the cities seizing up, the countryside poisoned and devastated – emotionally it is still for him a kind of Paradise, the place where he was once happy and free and may be so once again. He looks forward with simple, childlike pleasure to the sunshine, ice in his drinks, *drinks*, parties, cheap tobacco and infinite varieties of ice-cream; to being called 'Professor', to being complimented on his accent by anonymous telephonists, to being an object of interest simply by virtue of being British; and to exercising again his command of American idiom, grown a little rusty over the years from disuse.

On Philip's return from his Fellowship, newly acquired Americanisms had quickly withered on his lips under the uncomprehending or disapproving stares of Rummidge students and colleagues. A decade later, and a dash of American usage (both learned and vulgar) had become acceptable – indeed fashionable – in British academic circles, but (it was the story of his life) it was then too late for him to change his style, the style of a thoroughly conventional English don, keeping English up. American idiom still, however, retained for him a secret, subtle enchantment. Was it the legacy of a war-time boyhood – Hollywood films and tattered copies of the *Saturday Evening Post* having established in those crucial years a deep psychic link between American English and the goodies of which he was deprived by rationing? Perhaps, but there was also a purely aesthetic appeal, more difficult to analyse, a subtle music of displaced accents, cute contractions, quaint redundancies and vivid tropes, which he revives now as the shores of Britain recede and those of America rush to meet him. As a virgin spinster who, legatee of some large and unexpected bequest, heads immediately for Paris and points south and, leaning forward in a compartment of the Golden Arrow, eagerly practises the French phrases she can remember from school-lessons, restaurant menus and distant day-trips to Boulogne; so Philip Swallow, strapped (because of the turbulence) into the seat of his Boeing, lips perceptibly moving but all sound muffled by the hum of the jet engines, tries out on his tongue certain half-forgotten intonations and phrases: '*cig*arettes . . . prim*a*rily . . . Swiss on Rye to go . . . have it checked out . . . that's the way the cookie crumbles . . .'

No virgin spinster, Philip Swallow, a father of three and husband of one, but on this occasion he journeys alone. And a rare treat it is, this absence of dependents – one which, though he is ashamed to admit it, would make him light-some were his destination Outer Mongolia. Now, for example, the stewardess lays before him a meal of ambiguous designation (could be lunch, could be dinner, who knows or cares four miles above the turning globe) but tempting: smoked salmon, chicken and rice, peach parfait, all neatly compartmentalized on a plastic tray, cheese and biscuits wrapped in cellophane, disposable cutlery, personal salt cellar and pepperpot in dolls'-house scale. He eats everything slowly and with appreciation, accepts a second cup of coffee and opens a pack of opulently long duty-free cigarettes. Nothing else happens. He is not required to cut up anyone else's chicken, or to guarantee the edibility of smoked salmon; no neighbouring trays spring suddenly into the air or slide resonantly to the floor; his coffee-cup is not dashed from his lips, to deposit its scalding contents in his crotch; his suit collects no souvenirs of the meal by way of buttered biscuit crumbs, smears of peach parfait and dribbles of mayonnaise. This, he reflects, must be what weightlessness is like in space, or the lowered gravity of moonwalks – an unwonted sensation of buoyancy and freedom, a sudden reduction of the effort customarily required by ordinary physical tasks. And it is not just for today, but for six whole months, that it will last. He hugs the thought to himself with guilty glee. Guilty, because he cannot entirely absolve himself of the charge of having deserted Hilary, perhaps even at this moment presiding grimly over the rugged table-manners of the three young Swallows.

It is a consoling thought, in the circumstances, that the desertion was not of his own seeking.

Philip Swallow had never actually applied for the Rummidge-Euphoria exchange scheme, partly out of a well-founded modesty as to his claims, and partly because he had long come to think of himself as too trammelled and shackled by domestic responsibilities to contemplate such adventures. As he had said to Gordon Masters, the Head of his Department, when the latter asked him whether he'd ever thought of applying for the Euphoria exchange:

'Not really, Gordon. It wouldn't be fair, you know, to disturb the children's education at this stage – Robert's taking the eleven-plus next year, and it won't be long before Amanda's in the thick of "O" Levels.'

'Mmmmmmner your own?' Masters replied. This habit of swallowing the first part of his sentences made communication with him a stressful proceeding, as did his way of closing one eye when he looked at you as though taking aim along the barrel of a gun. He was in fact a keen sportsman, and the walls of his room bore plentiful evidence of his marksmanship in the form of silently snarling stuffed animals.

The strangled commencements of his sentences, Philip supposed, derived from his service in the Army, where in many utterances only the final word of command is significant. From long practice Philip was able to follow his drift pretty well, and therefore answered confidently:

'Oh, no, I couldn't leave Hilary behind to cope on her own. Not for six months.'

'Mmmmmmmmmnerpose not,' Masters muttered, conveying a certain disappointment or frustration by the way he shifted his weight restlessly from one foot to another. 'Mmmmmmmmmmmmmmmmmmnnnnnertunity, though.'

Straining every mental nerve, Philip gradually pieced together the information that the year's nominee for the Exchange scheme had withdrawn at the last moment because he had been offered a Chair in Australia. It appeared that the Committee concerned was looking rather urgently for a replacement and that Masters (who was Chairman) was prepared to work it for Philip if he was interested. 'Mmmmmmmmnnnnerink about it,' he concluded.

Philip did think about it. All day. With studied casualness he mentioned it to Hilary while they were washing up after dinner.

'You ought to take it,' she said, after a moment's reflection. 'You need a break, a change. You're getting stale here.'

Philip couldn't deny it. 'What about the children, though? What about Robert's eleven-plus?' he said, holding a dripping plate like hope in his hands.

Hilary took a longer pause for thought. 'You go on your own,' she said at last. 'I'll stay here with the children.'

'No, it wouldn't be fair,' he protested. 'I wouldn't dream of it.'

'I'll manage,' she said, taking the plate. 'Anyway, it's quite out of the question for us all to go at such short notice. What would we do about the house, for one thing? You can't leave this place empty in the winter. And there's the fares . . .'

'I must admit,' said Philip, freshening the washing-up water and stirring the suds with gusto, 'that if I did go on my own I could probably save quite a lot of money. Enough to pay for the central heating, I should think.'

The installation of central heating in their cold, damp, multi-roomed house had long been an impossible dream of the Swallows. 'You go, darling,' said Hilary, with a plucky smile. 'You mustn't miss the opportunity. Gordon might not be Chairman of this committee again.'

'Jolly decent of him to think of me, I must say.'

'You always complain that he doesn't appreciate you.'

'I know. I feel I've done him rather an injustice.'

Actually, Gordon Masters had decided to back Philip for the Euphoria Exchange because he wanted to give a Senior Lectureship to a considerably younger member of the Department, a very prolific linguistician who was being tempted by offers from the new universities, and it would be less embarrassing to do so while Philip was absent. Philip was not to know this of course, though a less innocent politician might have suspected it.

'You're sure you don't mind?' he asked Hilary, and was to ask at least once a day until his departure. He was still at it when she saw him off at Rummidge station. 'You're *quite* sure you don't mind?'

'Darling, how many more times? Of course we shall all miss you . . . And you'll miss us, I hope?' she teased him mildly.

'Oh, yes, of course.'

But that was the source of his guilt. He didn't honestly think he *would* miss them. He bore his children no ill-will, but he thought he could manage quite nicely without them, thank you, for six months. And as for Hilary, well, he found it difficult after all these years to think of her as ontologically distinct from her offspring. She existed, in his field of vision, mainly as a transmitter of information, warnings, requests and obligations with regard to Amanda, Robert and Matthew. If *she* had been going to America, and himself left at home minding the children, he would have missed her all right. But if there were no children in the picture he couldn't readily put his finger on any reason why he should be in need of a wife.

There was sex, of course, but in recent years this had played a steadily diminishing role in the Swallow marriage. It had never been quite the same (had anything?) after their extended American honeymoon. In America, for instance, Hilary had tended to emit a high-pitched cry at the moment of climax which Philip found deeply exciting; but on their first night in Rummidge, as they were making up their bed in the flat they had rented in a clumsily converted old house, some unknown person had coughed lightly but very audibly in the adjoining room, and from that time onwards, though they moved in due course to better-insulated accommodation, Hilary's orgasms (if such they were) were marked by nothing more dramatic than a hissing sigh, rather like the sound of air escaping from a Li-lo.

In the course of their married life in Rummidge Hilary had never refused his advances, but she never positively invited them either. She accepted his embrace with the same calm, slightly preoccupied amiability with which she prepared his breakfasts and ironed his shirts. Gradually, over the years, Philip's own interest in the physical side of marriage declined, but he persuaded himself that this was only normal.

The sudden eruption of the Sexual Revolution in the mid-sixties had, it is true, unsettled him a little. The Sunday paper he had taken since first going up to the University, an earnest, closely printed journal bursting with book reviews and excerpts from statesmen's memoirs, broke out abruptly in a rash of nipples and coloured photographs of après-sex leisurewear; his girl tutees suddenly began to dress like prostitutes, with skirts so short that he was able to distinguish them, when their names escaped him, by the colour of their knickers; it became uncomfortable to read contemporary novels at home in case one of the children should glance over his shoulder. Films and television conveyed the same message: that other people were having sex more often and more variously than he was.

Or were they? There had always been, notoriously, more adulteries in fiction than in fact, and no doubt the same applied to orgasms. Looking around at the faces of his colleagues in the Senior Common Room he felt reassured: not a Lineament of Gratified Desire to be seen. There were, of course, the students – everyone knew they had lots of sex. As a tutor he saw mostly the disadvantages: it tired them out, distracted them from their work; they got pregnant and missed their examinations, or they went on the Pill and suffered side-effects. But he envied them the world of thrilling possibility in which they moved, a world of ex-posed limbs, sex manuals on railway bookstalls, erotic music and frontal nudity on stage and screen. His own adolescence seemed a poor cramped thing in comparison, limited, as far as satisfying curiosity and desire went, to the more risqué Penguin Classics and the last waltz at College Hops when they dimmed the lights and you might hold your partner, encased in yards of slippery taffeta, close enough to feel the bas-relief of her suspenders against your thighs.

That was something he *did* envy the young – their style of dancing, though he never betrayed the fact to a soul. Under the pretence of indulging his children, and with an expression carefully adjusted to express amused contempt, he watched *Top of the Pops* and similar TV programmes with a painful mingling of pleasure and regret. How enchanting, those flashing thighs and twitching buttocks, lolling heads and bouncing breasts; how deliciously mindless, liberating, it all was! And how infinitely sad the dancing of his own youth appeared in retrospect, those stiff-jointed, robot-like fox-trots and quicksteps, at which he had been so inept. This new dancing looked easy: no fear of making a mistake, of stepping on your partner's feet or steering her like a dodgem car into another robot-couple. It must be easy, he felt in his bones he could do it, but of course it was too late now, just as it was too late to comb his hair forward or wear

Paisley shirts or persuade Hilary to experiment with new sexual postures.

In short, if Philip Swallow felt sensually underprivileged, it was in a strictly elegaic spirit. It never occurred to him that there was still time to rush into the Dionysian horde. It never occurred to him to be unfaithful to Hilary with one of the nubile young women who swarmed in the corridors of the Rummidge English Department. Such ideas, that is, never occurred to his conscious, English self. His unconscious may have been otherwise occupied; and perhaps, deep, deep down, there is, at the root of his present jubilation, the anticipation of sexual adventure. If this is the case, however, no rumour of it has reached Philip's ego. At this moment the most licentious project he has in mind is to spend his very next Sunday in bed, smoking, reading the newspapers and watching television.

Bliss! No need to get up for the family breakfast, wash the car, mow the lawn and perform the other duties of the secular British Sabbath. No need, above all, to go for a walk on Sunday afternoon. No need to rouse himself, heavy with Sunday lunch, from his armchair, to help Hilary collect and dress their querulous children, to try and find some new, pointless destination for a drive or to trudge out to one of the local parks, where other little knots of people wander listlessly, like lost souls in hell, blown by the gritty wind amid whirlpools of litter and dead leaves, past creaking swings and deserted football pitches, stagnant ponds and artificial lakes where rowing boats are chained up, by Sabbatarian decree, as if to emphasize the impossibility of escape. *La nausée*, Rummidge-style. Well, no more of that for six months.

Philip stubs out his cigarette, and lights another. Pipes are not permitted in the aircraft.

He checks his watch. Less than halfway to go now. There is a communal stirring in the cabin. He looks round attentively, anxious not to miss a cue. People are putting on the little plastic headphones that were lying, in transparent envelopes, on each seat when they boarded the plane. At the front of the tourist compartment a stewardess is fiddling with a piece of tubular apparatus. How delightful, they are going to have a film, or rather, *movie*. There is an extra charge: Philip pays it gladly. A withered old lady across the aisle shows him how to plug in his headphones which are, he discovers, already providing aural entertainment on three channels: Bartok, Muzak and some children's twaddle. Culturally conditioned to choose the Bartok, he switches, after a few minutes, to the Muzak, a cool, rippling rendition of, what is it, 'These Foolish Things' . . . ?

Meanwhile, back in the other Boeing, Morris Zapp has just discovered what it is that's bugging him about his flight. The realization is a delayed consequence of walking the length of the aircraft to the toilet, and strikes him, like a slow-burn gag in a movie-comedy, just as he is concluding his business there. On his way back he verifies his suspicion, covertly scrutinizing every row of seats until he reaches his own at the front of the aircraft. He sinks down heavily and, as is his wont when thinking hard, crosses his legs and plays a complex percussion solo with his fingernails on the sole of his right shoe.

Every passenger on the plane except himself is a woman.

What is he supposed to make of that? The odds against such a ratio turning up by chance must be astronomical. Improvidence at work again. What kind of a chance is he going to stand if there's an emergency, women and children first, himself a hundred and fifty-sixth in the line for the lifeboats?

'Pardon me.'

It's the bespectacled blonde in the next seat. She holds a magazine open on her lap, index finger pressed to the page as if marking her place.

'May I ask your opinion on a question of etiquette?'

He grins, squinting at the magazine. 'Don't tell me *Ramparts* is running an etiquette column?'

'If a lady sees a man with his fly open, should she tell him?'

'Definitely.'

29

bouyant energy

'Your fly's open, mister,' says the girl, and recommences reading her copy of *Ramparts*, holding it up to screen her face as Morris hastily adjusts his dress.

'Say,' he continues conversationally (for Morris Zapp does not believe in allowing socially disadvantageous situations to cool and set), 'Say, have you noticed anything funny about this plane?'

'Funny?'

'About the passengers.'

The magazine is lowered, the swollen spectacles turned slowly in his direction. 'Only you, I guess.'

'You figured it out too!' he exclaims. 'It only just struck me. Right between the eyes. While I was in the john . . . That's why . . . Thanks for telling me, by the way.' He gestures towards his crotch.

'Be my guest,' says the girl. 'How come you're on this charter anyway?'

'One of my students sold me her ticket.'

'Now all is clear,' says the girl. 'I figured you couldn't be needing an abortion.'

BOINNNNNNNNGGGGGGGGGGG! The penny drops thunderously inside Morris Zapp's head. He steals a glance over the back of his seat. A hundred and fifty-five women ranked in various attitudes – some sleeping, some knitting, some staring out of the windows, all (it strikes him now) unnaturally silent, self-absorbed, depressed. Some eyes meet his, and he flinches from their murderous glint. He turns back queasily to the blonde, gestures weakly over his shoulder with his thumb, whispers hoarsely: 'You mean all those women . . . ?'

She nods.

'Holy mackerel!' (Zapp, his stock of blasphemy and obscenity threadbare from everyday use, tends to fall back on such quaintly genteel oaths in moments of great stress.)

'Pardon my asking,' says the blonde, 'but I'm curious. Did you buy the whole package – round trip, surgeon's fee, five days' nursing with private room and excursion to Stratford-upon-Avon?'

'What has Stratford-upon-Avon got to do with it, for Chrissake?'

'It's supposed to give you a lift afterwards. You get to see a play.'

'*All's Well That Ends Well*?' he snaps back, quick as a flash. But the jest conceals a deep unease. Of course he has heard of these package tours operating from States where legal abortions are difficult to obtain, and taking advantage of Britain's permissive new law. In casual conversation he would have shrugged it off as a simple instance of the law of supply and demand, perhaps with a quip about the limeys finally licking their balance of payments problem. No prude, no reactionary, Morris Zapp. He has gone down on many a poll as favouring the repeal of Euphoria's abortion laws (likewise its laws against fornication, masturbation, adultery, sodomy, fellatio, cunnilingus and sexual congress in which the female adopts the superior position: Euphoria had been first settled by a peculiarly narrow-minded Puritanical sect whose taboos retained a fossilized existence in the State legal code, one that rigorously enforced would have entailed the incarceration of ninety per cent of its present citizens). But it is a different matter to find oneself trapped in an airplane with a hundred and fifty-five women actually drawing the wages of sin. The thought of their one hundred and fifty-five doomed stowaways sends cold shivers roller-coasting down his curved spine, and a sudden vibration in the aircraft, as it runs into the turbulence recently experienced by Philip Swallow, leaves him quaking with fear.

For Morris Zapp is a twentieth-century counterpart of Swift's Nominal Christian – the Nominal Atheist. Underneath that tough exterior of the free-thinking Jew (exactly the kind T. S. Eliot thought an organic community could well do without) there is a core of old-fashioned Judaeo-Christian fear-of-the-Lord. If the Apollo astronauts had reported finding a message carved in gigantic letters on the backside of the moon, '*Reports of My death are greatly exaggerated*,' it would not have surprised Morris Zapp unduly, merely confirmed his deepest misgivings. At this moment he

31

feels painfully vulnerable to divine retribution. He can't believe that Improvidence, old Nobodaddy, is going to sit placidly in the sky while abortion shuttle-services buzz right under his nose, polluting the stratosphere and giving the Recording Angel writer's cramp, no sir, one of these days he is going to swat one of those planes right out the sky, and why not this one?

Zapp succumbs to self-pity. Why should he suffer with all these careless callous women? He has knocked up a girl only once in his life, and he made an honest woman of her (she divorced him three years later, but that's another story, one indictment at a time, please). It's a frame-up. All the doing of the little bitch who had sold him her ticket, less than half-price, he couldn't resist the bargain but wondered at the time at her generosity since only a week before he'd refused to raise her course-grade from a C to a B. She must have missed her period, rushed to book a seat on the Abortion Express, had a negative pregnancy test and thought to her-self, I know what I'll do, Professor Zapp is going to Europe, I'll sell him my ticket, then the plane might be struck by a thunderbolt. A fine reward for trying to preserve academic standards.

He becomes aware that the girl in the next seat is studying him with interest. 'You're a college teacher?' she asks.

'Yeah, Euphoric State.'

'Really! What d'you teach? I'm majoring in Anthropology at Euphoria College.'

'Euphoria College? Isn't that the Catholic school in Esseph?'

'Right.'

'Then what are you doing on this plane?' he hisses, all his roused moral indignation and superstitious fear focused on this kooky blonde. If even the Catholics are jumping on to the abortion bandwagon, what hope is there for the human race?

'I'm an Underground Catholic,' she says seriously. 'I'm not hung up on dogma. I'm very far out.'

Her eyes, behind the huge spectacles, are clear and untroubled. Morris Zapp experiences a rush of missionary zeal to the head. He will do a good deed, instruct this innocent in the difference between good and evil, talk her out of her wicked intent. One brand plucked from the burning should be enough to assure him of a happy landing. He leans forward earnestly.

'Listen, kid, let me give some fatherly advice. Don't do it. You'll never forgive yourself. Have the baby. Get it adopted – no sweat, the adoption agencies are screaming for new stock. Maybe the father will want to marry you when he sees the kid – they often do, you know.'

'He can't.'

'Married already, huh?' Morris Zapp shakes his head over the depravity of his sex.

'No, he's a priest.'

Zapp bows his head, buries his face in his hands.

'You feeling all right?'

'Just a twinge of morning-sickness,' he mumbles through his fingers. He looks up. 'This priest, is he paying for your trip out of parish funds? Did he take a special collection or something?'

'He doesn't know anything about it.'

'You haven't told him you're pregnant?'

'I don't want him to have to choose between me and his vows.'

'Has he any vows *left*?'

'Poverty, chastity and obedience,' says the girl thoughtfully. 'Well, I guess he's still poor.'

'So who is paying for this trip?'

'I work nights on South Strand.'

'One of those topless places?'

'No, record store. As a matter of fact I worked my first year through college as a topless dancer. But then I realized how exploitative it was, so I quit.'

'They charge a lot in those joints, huh?'

'I mean exploiting *me*, not the customers,' the girl replies, a shade contemptuously. 'It was when I got interested in Women's Liberation.'

'Women's Liberation? What's that?' says Morris Zapp, not liking the sound of it at all. 'I never heard of it.' (Few people have on this first day of 1969.)

'You will, Professor, you will,' says the girl.

Meanwhile, Philip Swallow has also struck up conversation with a fellow passenger.

The movie over (it was a Western, the noisy soundtrack had given him a headache, and he watched the final gun-battle with his headphones tuned to Muzak), he finds that some of his *joie de vivre* has evaporated. He is beginning to weary of sitting still, he fidgets in his seat in an effort to find some untried disposition of his limbs, the muffled din of the jet engines is getting on his nerves, and looking out of the window still gives him vertigo. He tries to read a courtesy copy of *Time*, but can't concentrate. What he really needs is a nice cup of tea – it is mid-afternoon by his watch – but when he plucks up courage to ask a passing stewardess she replies curtly that they will be serving breakfast in an hour's time. He has had one breakfast already that day and doesn't particularly want another one, but of course it's a matter of the time change. In Euphoria now it's, what, seven or eight hours earlier than in London, or is it later? Do you add or subtract? Is it still the day he left on, or tomorrow already? Or yesterday? Let's see, the sun comes up in the east . . . He frowns with mental effort, but the sums won't make sense.

'Well, blow me down!'

Philip blinks up at the young man who has stopped in the aisle. His appearance is striking. He wears wide-bottomed suede trousers, and a kind of oversize homespun fringed jerkin hanging to his knees over a pink and yellow candy-striped shirt. His wavy, reddish hair falls to his shoulders and he has a bandit moustache of slightly darker hue. On his jerkin, arranged in three neat rows like military medals, are a dozen or more lapel buttons in psychedelic colours.

'You remember me, dontcha, Mr Swallow?'

'Well . . .' Philip racks his brains. There is something vaguely familiar, but . . . Then the youth's left eye suddenly shoots disconcertingly sideways, as if catching sight of an engine falling off the wing, and Philip remembers.

'Boon! Good Lord, I didn't recognize . . . You've, er, changed.'

Boon chuckles delightedly. 'Fantastic! Don't tell me you're on your way to Euphoric State?'

'Well, yes, as a matter of fact I am.'

'Great! Me too.'

'You?'

'Dontcha remember writing a reference for me?'

'A great many references, Boon.'

'Yeah, well, it's like a fruit machine, y'know, you got to keep pulling the old lever. Never say die. Then, Bingo! Anybody sitting next to you? No? I'll join you in a sec. Got to have a slash. Don't run away.' He resumes his interrupted journey to the toilet, almost colliding with a stewardess coming in the opposite direction. Boon steadies her with a firm, two-handed gesture. 'Sorry, darling,' Philip hears him say, and she flashes him an indulgent smile. Still the same old Boon!

A chance reunion with Charles Boon would not, in normal circumstances, have gladdened Philip Swallow's heart. The young man had graduated a couple of years previously after a contentious and troublesome undergraduate career at Rummidge. He belonged to a category of students whom Philip referred to privately (showing his age) as 'the Department's Teddy-Boys'. These were clever young men of plebeian origin who, unlike the traditional scholarship boy (such as Philip himself) showed no deference to the social and cultural values of the institution to which they had been admitted, but maintained until the day they graduated a style of ostentatious uncouthness in dress, behaviour and speech. They came late to classes, unwashed, unshaven and wearing clothes they had evidently slept in; slouched in their seats, rolling their own cigarettes and stubbing them out on the furniture; sneered at the girlish, suburban enthusiasms of their fellow-students, answered questions addressed to them in dialect monosyllables, and handed in disconcertingly subtle, largely destructive essays written in the style of F. R. Leavis. Perhaps overcompensating for their own prejudices, the staff at Rummidge regularly admitted three or four such students every year. Invariably they caused disciplinary problems. In his memorable undergraduate career Charles Boon had involved the student newspaper *Rumble*, of which he was editor, in an expensive libel suit brought by the mayoress of Rummidge; caused the Lodgings warden to retire prematurely with a nervous disorder from which she still suffered; appeared on 'University Challenge', drunk; campaigned (unsuccessfully) for the distribution of free contraceptives at the end of the Freshers' Ball, and defended himself (successfully) in a magistrate's court against a charge of shop-lifting from the University Bookshop.

As Boon's tutor in his third year, Philip had played a minor, but exhausting role in some of these dramas. After an examiners' meeting lasting ten hours, nine of which were spent in discussion of Boon's papers, he had been awarded a 'low Upper Second' – a compromise grudgingly accepted by those who wanted to fail him and those who wanted to give him a First. Philip had shaken Boon's hand on Degree Day in joyful expectation of never having anything to do with him again, but the hope was premature. Though Boon had failed to qualify for a postgraduate grant, he continued to haunt the corridors of the Faculty of Arts for some months, giving other students to understand that he was employed as a Research Assistant, hoping in this way to embarrass the Department into actually making him one. When this gambit failed, Boon at last disappeared from Rummidge, but Philip, at least, was not allowed to forget his existence. Seldom did a week pass without a request for a confidential assessment of Mr Charles Boon's character, intelligence and suitability for some position in the great world. At first these were usually teaching posts or postgraduate fellowships at home and abroad. Later, Boon's applications took on a random, reckless character, as of a man throwing dice compulsively, without bothering to note his score. Sometimes he aimed absurdly high, sometimes grotesquely low. At one moment he aspired to be Cultural Attaché in the Diplomatic Service, or Chief Programme Planning Executive for Ghana Television, at the next he was prepared to settle for Works Foreman, Walsall Screw Company, or Lavatory Attendant, Southport Corporation. If Boon was appointed to any of these posts he evidently failed to hold them for very long, for the stream of inquiries never ran dry. At first Philip had answered them honestly; after a while it dawned on him that he was in this way condemning himself to a lifetime's correspondence, and he began to suppress some of the less creditable features of his former student's character and record. He ended up answering every request for a reference with an unblushing all-purpose panegyric kept on permanent file in the Department Office, and this testimonial must have finally obtained Boon some kind of graduate fellowship at Euphoric State. Now Philip's perjury had caught up with him, as such sins always did. It was deuced awkward that they should both be going to Euphoric State at the same time – he fervently hoped that he would not be identified as Boon's original sponsor. And at all costs Boon must be prevented from enrolling in his own courses.

Despite these misgivings, Philip is not altogether displeased at finding himself on the same plane as Charles Boon. He awaits the latter's return, indeed, with something like eagerness. It is, he explains to himself, because he is bored with the journey, glad of company for the last, long hours of this interminable flight; but, truthfully, it is because he wants to show off. The glory of his adventure needs, after all, a reflector, someone capable of registering the transformation of the dim Rummidge lecturer into Visiting Professor Philip Swallow, member of the academic jet-set, ready to carry English culture to the far side of the globe at the drop of an airline ticket. And for once he will have the advantage of Boon, in his previous experience of America. Boon will be eager for advice and information: about looking left first when crossing the road, for example; about 'public school' meaning the opposite of what it means in England, and 'knock up' meaning something entirely different. He will also frighten Boon a little with the rigours of American graduate programmes. Yes, he has lots to say to Charles Boon.

'Now,' says Boon, easing himself into the seat beside Philip's, 'let me put you in the picture about the situation in Euphoria.'

Philip gapes at him. 'You mean you've been there already?'

Boon looks surprised. 'Sure, this is my second year. I've just been home for Christmas.'

'Oh,' says Philip.

'I guess you must've visited England many times, Professor Zapp,' says the blonde, whose name is Mary Makepeace.

'Never.'

'Really? You must be all excited then. All those years of teaching English Literature, and now you finally get to see where it all happened.'

'That's what I'm afraid of,' says Morris Zapp.

'If I get the time I'm going to visit my great-grandmother's grave. It's in a village churchyard in County Durham. Don't you think that sounds idyllic?'

'You going to have the foetus buried there?'

Mary Makepeace turns her head away and looks out of the window. The word '*Sorry*' rises to Morris's lips, but he bites it back. 'You don't want to face facts, do you? You want to pretend it's just like going to the dentist. Having a tooth extracted.'

'I've never *had* a tooth extracted,' she says, and he believes her. She continues to gaze out of the window, though there is nothing to see except cloud, stretching to the horizon like an endless roll of roof insulation.

'I'm sorry,' he says, surprising himself.

Mary Makepeace turns her head back in his direction. 'What's eating you, Professor Zapp? Don't you want to go to England?'

'You guessed it.'

'Why not? Where are you going?'

'A dump called Rummidge. You don't have to pretend you've heard of it.'

'Why are you going there?'

'It's a long story.'

It was indeed, and the question put by Mary Makepeace had exercised many a group of gossiping faculty when it was announced that Morris Zapp was the year's nominee for the Rummidge–Euphoria exchange scheme. Why should Morris Zapp, who always claimed that he had made himself an authority on the literature of England not in spite of but *because* of never having set foot in the country, why should he of all people suddenly join the annual migration to Europe? And, still more pressingly, why did a man who could have gotten a Guggenheim by crooking his little finger, and spent a pleasant year reading in Oxford, or London, or on the Côte d'Azur if he chose, condemn himself to six months' hard labour at Rummidge? Rummidge. Where was it? What was it? Those who knew shuddered and grimaced. Those who did not went home to consult encyclopedias and atlases, returning baffled to confer with their colleagues. If it was a plot by Morris to further his career, no one could give a satisfactory account of how it would work. The most favoured explanation was that he was finally getting tired of the Student Revolution, its strikes, protests, issues, non-negotiable demands, and was willing to go anywhere, even to Rummidge, for the sake of a bit of peace and quiet. Nobody dared actually to test this hypothesis on the man himself, since his resistance to student intimidation was as legendary as his sarcasm. Then at last the word got round that Morris was going to England on his own, and all was clear: the Zapps were breaking up. The gossip dwindled away; it was nothing unusual after all. Just another divorce.

Actually, it was more complicated than that. Désirée, Morris's second wife, wanted a divorce, but Morris didn't. It was not Désirée that he was loth to part from, but their children, Elizabeth and Darcy, the darlings of Morris

39

Zapp's otherwise unsentimental heart. Désirée was sure to get custody of both children – no judge, however fair-minded, was going to split up a pair of twins – and he would be restricted to taking them out to the park or a movie once a month. He had been all through that routine once before with his daughter by his first wife, and in consequence she had grown up with about as much respect for him as for the insurance salesman whom he must have resembled to her childish vision, turning up on her stoop at regular intervals with a shy, ingratiating smile, his pockets bulging with candy dividends; and this time it would cost him $300.00 per visit in fares since Désirée proposed moving to New York. Morris had been born and brought up in New York, but he had no intention of returning there, in fact he would not repine if he never saw the city again: on the evidence of his last visit it was only a matter of time before the garbage in the streets reached penthouse level and the whole population suffocated.

No, he didn't want to go through all that divorce hassle again. He pleaded with Désirée to give their marriage another chance, for the children's sake. She was unmoved. He was a bad influence on the children anyway, and as for herself she could never be a fulfilled person as long as she was married to him.

'What have I done?' he demanded rhetorically, throwing his arms about.

'You eat me.'

'I thought you liked it!'

'I don't mean that, trust your dirty mind, I mean psychologically. Being married to you is like being slowly swallowed by a python. I'm just a half-digested bulge in your ego. I want out. I want to be free. I want to be a person again.'

'Look,' he said, 'let's cut out all this encounter-group crap. It's that student you found me with last summer, isn't it?'

'No, but she'll do to get the divorce. Leaving me at the

Dean's reception to go home and screw the baby-sitter, that should make an impression on the judge.'

'I told you, she's gone back East, I don't even know her address.'

'I'm not interested. Can't you get it into your head that I don't care where you keep your big, fat circumcised prick? You could be banging the entire women's field hockey team every night for all I care. We're past all that.'

'Look, let's talk about this like two rational people,' he said, making a gesture of serious concern by turning off the TV football game he had been watching with one eye throughout this argument.

After an hour's exhausting discussion, Désirée agreed to a compromise: she would delay starting divorce proceedings for six months on condition he moved out of the house.

'Where to?' he grumbled.

'You can find a room somewhere. Or shack up with one of your students, I'm sure you'll have plenty of offers.'

Morris Zapp frowned, foreseeing what an ignominious figure he would cut in and around the University, a man turned out of his own home, washing his shirts in the campus launderette and eating lonely dinners at the Faculty Club.

'I'll go away,' he said. 'I'll take six months' leave at the end of the quarter. Give me till Christmas.'

'Where will you go?'

'Somewhere.' Inspiration came to him, and he added, 'Europe maybe.'

'*Europe? You?*'

Slyly he watched her out of the corner of his eye. For years Désirée had been pestering him to take her to Europe, and always he had refused. For Morris Zapp was that rarity among American Humanities Professors, a totally un-alienated man. He liked America, Euphoria particularly. His needs were simple: a temperate climate, a good library, plenty of inviting ass around the place and enough money to keep him in cigars and liquor and to run a comfortable modern house and two cars. The first three items were, so to speak, natural resources of Euphoria, and the fourth, the money, he had obtained after some years of strenuous effort. He did not see how he could improve his lot by travelling, certainly not by trailing around Europe with Désirée and the kids. 'Travel narrows,' was one of the Zapp proverbs. Still, if it came to the crunch, he was prepared to sacrifice this principle in the interests of domestic harmony.

'Why don't we all go?' he said.

He watched the emotions working across her face, lust for Europe contending with disgust for himself. Disgust won by a knockout.

'Go fuck yourself,' she said, and walked out of the room.

Morris fixed himself a stiff drink, put an Aretha Franklin LP on the hi-fi and sat down to think. He was in a spot. He had to go to Europe now, to save face. But it was going to be difficult to fix things at such short notice. He couldn't afford to go at his own expense: though his salary was considerable, so was the cost of running the house and supporting Désirée in the style to which she was accustomed, not to mention alimony payments to Martha. He couldn't apply for paid study-leave because he had just had two quarters off. It was too late to apply for a Guggie or a Fulbright and he had an idea that European universities didn't hire visitors as casually as they did in the States.

The next morning he called the Dean of Faculty.

'Bill? Look, I want to go to Europe for six months, as soon after Christmas as possible. I need some kind of a deal. What have you got?'

'Where in Europe, Morris?'

'Anywhere, Bill.'

'England?'

'Even England.'

'Gee, Morris, I wish you'd asked me earlier. There was a swell opening in Paris, with UNESCO, I fixed up Ed Waring in Sociology just a week ago.'

'Spare me the narrow misses, Bill, what have you got?'

There was a rustling of papers. 'Well, there is the

Rummidge exchange, but you wouldn't be interested in that, Morris.'

'Just give me the dope.'

Bill gave it to him, concluding, 'You see, it isn't your class, Morris.'

'I'll take it.'

Bill tried to argue him out of it for a while, then confessed that the Rummidge post had already been given to a young assistant professor in Metallurgy.

'Tell him he can't have it after all. Tell him you made a mistake.'

'I can't do that, Morris. Be reasonable.'

'Give him accelerated promotion to Associate Professor. He won't argue.'

'Well . . .' Bill Moser hesitated, then sighed. 'I'll see what I can do, Morris.'

'Great, Bill, I won't forget it.'

Bill's voice dropped to a lower, more confidential pitch. 'Why the sudden yearning for Europe, Morris? Students getting you down?'

'You must be joking, Bill. No, I think I need a change. A new perspective. The challenge of a different culture.'

Bill Moser roared with laughter.

Morris Zapp wasn't surprised that Bill Moser was incredulous. But there was a kind of truth in his answer that he wouldn't have dreamed of admitting except in the guise of a palpable lie.

For years Morris Zapp had, like a man exceptionally blessed with good health, taken his self-confidence for granted, and regarded the recurrent identity crises of his colleagues as symptoms of psychic hypochondria. But recently he had caught himself brooding about the meaning of his life, no less. This was partly the consequence of his own success. He was full professor at one of the most prestigious and desirably located universities in America, and had already served as the Chairman of his Department for three years under Euphoric State's rotating system; he was a highly respected scholar with a long and impressive list of publications to his name. He could only significantly increase his salary either by moving to some god-awful place in Texas or the Mid-West where no one in his right mind would go for a thousand dollars a day, or by switching to administration, looking for a college President's job somewhere, which in the present state of the nation's campuses was a through ticket to an early grave. At the age of forty, in short, Morris Zapp could think of nothing he wanted to achieve that he hadn't achieved already, and this depressed him.

There was always his research, of course, but some of the zest had gone out of that since it ceased to be a means to an end. He couldn't enhance his reputation, he could only damage it, by adding further items to his bibliography, and the realization slowed him down, made him cautious. Some years ago he had embarked with great enthusiasm on an ambitious critical project: a series of commentaries on Jane Austen which would work through the whole canon, one novel at a time, saying absolutely everything that could possibly be said about them. The idea was to be utterly exhaustive, to examine the novels from every conceivable angle, historical, biographical, rhetorical, mythical, Freudian, Jungian, existentialist, Marxist, structuralist, Christian-allegorical, ethical, exponential, linguistic, phenomenological, archetypal, you name it; so that when each commentary was written there would be simply *nothing further to say* about the novel in question. The object of the exercise, as he had often to explain with as much patience as he could muster, was not to enhance others' enjoyment and understanding of Jane Austen, still less to honour the novelist herself, but to put a definitive stop to the production of any further garbage on the subject. The commentaries would not be designed for the general reader but for the specialist, who, looking up Zapp, would find that the book, article or thesis he had been planning had already been anticipated and, more likely than not, invalidated. After Zapp, the rest would be silence. The thought gave him deep satisfaction. In Faustian moments he dreamed of going on, after fixing Jane Austen, to do the same job on the other major English novelists, then the poets and dramatists, perhaps using computers and teams of trained graduate students, inexorably reducing the area of English literature available for free comment, spreading dismay through the whole industry, rendering scores of his colleagues redundant: periodicals would fall silent, famous English Departments be left deserted like ghost towns . . .

As is perhaps obvious, Morris Zapp had no great esteem for his fellow-labourers in the vineyards of literature. They seemed to him vague, fickle, irresponsible creatures, who wallowed in relativism like hippopotami in mud, with their nostrils barely protruding into the air of common-sense. They happily tolerated the existence of opinions contrary to their own – they even, for God's sake, sometimes changed their minds. Their pathetic attempts at profundity were qualified out of existence and largely interrogative in mode. They liked to begin a paper with some formula like, 'I want to raise some questions about so-and-so', and seemed to think they had done their intellectual duty by merely raising them. This manoeuvre drove Morris Zapp insane. Any damn fool, he maintained, could think of questions; it was *answers* that separated the men from the boys. If you couldn't answer your own questions it was either because you hadn't worked on them hard enough or because they weren't real questions. In either case you should keep your mouth shut. One couldn't move in English studies these days without falling over unanswered questions which some damn fool had carelessly left lying about – it was like trying to mend a leak in an attic full of dusty, broken furniture. Well, his commentary would put a stop to that, at least as far as Jane Austen was concerned.

But the work proceeded slowly; he was not yet halfway through *Sense and Sensibility* and already it was obvious that each commentary would run to several volumes. Apart from the occasional article, he hadn't published anything for several years now. Sometimes he would start work on a problem only to remember, after some hours' cogitation, that he had solved it very satisfactorily himself years before. Over the same period – whether as cause or effect he wasn't sure – he had begun to feel ill-at-ease in his own body. He was prone to indigestion after rich restaurant meals, he usually needed a sleeping-pill before retiring, he was developing a pot-belly, and he found it increasingly difficult to achieve more than one orgasm in a single session – or so he would complain to his buddies over a beer. The truth was that these days he couldn't count on making it even once, and Désirée had less cause for resentment than she knew over the baby-sitter last summer. Things weren't what they used to be in the Zapp loins, though it was a dark truth that he would scarcely admit to himself, let alone to anyone else. He would not publicly acknowledge, either, that he was finding it a strain to hold his students' attention as the climate on campus became increasingly hostile to traditional academic values. His style of teaching was designed to shock conventionally educated students out of a sloppily reverent attitude to literature and into an ice-cool, intellectually rigorous one. It could do little with students openly contemptuous of both the subject and his own qualifications. His barbed wisecracks sank harmlessly into the protective padding of the new gentle inarticulacy, which had become so fashionable that even his brightest graduate students, ruthless professionals at heart, felt obliged to conform to it, mumbling in seminars, 'Well, it's like James, ah, well the guy *wants* to be a modern, I mean he has the symbolism bit and God is dead and all, but it's like he's still committed to intelligence, like he thinks it all *means* something for Chrissake – you dig?' Jane Austen was certainly not the writer to win the hearts of the new generation. Sometimes Morris woke sweating from nightmares in which students paraded round the campus carrying placards that declared KNIGHTLEY SUCKS and FANNY PRICE IS A FINK. Perhaps he *was* getting a little stale; perhaps, after all, he would profit from a change of scene.

In this fashion had Morris Zapp rationalized the decision forced upon him by Désirée's ultimatum. But, sitting in the airplane beside pregnant Mary Makepeace, all these reasons seemed unconvincing. If he needed a change, he was fairly sure it wasn't the kind that England would afford. He had neither affection nor respect for the British. The ones he had met – expatriates and visiting professors – mostly acted like fags and then turned out not to be, which he found unsettling. At parties they wolfed your canapés and gulped your gin as if they had just been released from prison, and talked all the time in high, twittering voices about the differences between the English and American university systems, making it clear that they regarded the latter as a huge, rather amusing racket from which they were personally determined to take the biggest possible cut in the shortest possible time. Their publications were vapid and amateurish, inadequately researched, slackly argued, and riddled with so many errors, misquotations, misattributions and incorrect dates that it was amazing they managed to get their own names right on the title page. They nevertheless had the nerve to treat American scholars, including even himself, with sneering condescension in their lousy journals.

He felt in his bones that he wasn't going to enjoy England: he would be lonely and bored, all the more so because he had taken a small provisional vow not to be unfaithful to Désirée, just to annoy her; and it was the worst possible place to carry on his research. Once he sank into the bottomless morass of English manners, he would never be able to keep the mythic archetypes, the patterns of iterative imagery, the psychological motifs, clear and radiant in his mind. Jane Austen might turn *realist* on him, as she had on so many other readers, with consequences all too evident in the literature about her.

In Morris Zapp's view, the root of all critical error was a naïve confusion of literature with life. Life was transparent, literature opaque. Life was an open, literature a closed system. Life was composed of things, literature of words. Life was what it appeared to be about: if you were afraid your plane would crash it was about death, if you were trying to get a girl into bed it was about sex. Literature was never about what it appeared to be about, though in the case of the novel considerable ingenuity and perception were needed to crack the code of realistic illusion, which was why he had been professionally attracted to the genre (even the dumbest critic understood that *Hamlet* wasn't about how the guy could kill his uncle, or the *Ancient Mariner* about cruelty to animals, but it was surprising how many people thought that Jane Austen's novels were about finding Mr Right). The failure to keep the categories of life and literature distinct led to all kinds of heresy and nonsense: to 'liking' and 'not liking' books for instance, preferring some authors to others and suchlike whimsicalities which, he had constantly to remind his students, were of no conceivable interest to anyone except themselves (sometimes he shocked them by declaring that, speaking personally on this low, subjective level, he found Jane Austen a pain in the ass). He felt a particularly pressing need to castigate naïve theories of realism because they threatened his master-work: obviously, if you applied an open-ended system (life) to a closed one (literature) the possible permutations were endless and the definitive commentary became an impossibility. Everything he knew about England warned him that the heresy flourished there with peculiar virulence, no doubt encouraged by the many concrete reminders of the actual historic existence of great authors that littered the country – baptismal registers, houses with plaques, second-best beds, reconstructed studies, engraved tombstones and suchlike trash. Well, one thing he was *not* going to do while he was in England was to visit Jane Austen's grave. But he must have spoken the thought aloud, because Mary Make-peace asks him if Jane Austen was the name of his great-grandmother. He says he thinks it unlikely.

Meanwhile, Philip Swallow is wondering more desperately than ever when this flight is going to end. Charles Boon has been talking at him for hours, it seems, permitting few interruptions. All about the political situation in Euphoria in general and on the Euphoric State campus in particular. The factions, the issues, the confrontations; Governor Duck, Chancellor Binde, Mayor Holmes, Sheriff O'Keene; the Third World, the Hippies, the Black Panthers, the Faculty Liberals; pot, Black Studies, sexual freedom, ecology, free speech, police violence, ghettoes, fair housing, school busing, Viet Nam; strikes, arson, marches, sit-ins, teach-ins, love-ins, happenings. Philip has long since given up trying to follow the details of Boon's argument, but the general drift seems to be concisely summed up by his lapel buttons:

LEGALIZE POT
NORMAN O. BROWN FOR PRESIDENT
SAVE THE BAY: MAKE WATER NOT WAR
KEEP THE DRAFT CARDS BURNING
THERE IS A FAULT IN REALITY — NORMAL
   SERVICE WILL RETURN SHORTLY
HAPPINESS IS (just IS)
KEEP GOD OUT OF AMERICA
BOYCOTT GRAPES
KEEP KROOP
SWINGING SAVES
BOYCOTT TRUFFLES
FUCK D*CK!

In spite of himself, Philip is amused by some of the slogans. Obviously it is a new literary medium, the lapel button, something between the classical epigram and the imagist lyric. Doubtless it will not be long before some post-graduate is writing a thesis on the genre. Doubtless Charles Boon is already doing so.

'What's your research topic, Boon?' he asks, firmly interrupting an involved legal disquisition on some persecuted group called the Euphoria Ninety-Nine.

'Uh?' Boon looks startled.

'Your PhD – or is it an MA?'

'Oh. Yeah, I'm still getting a Master's. That's mostly course work. Just a little baby dissertation.'

'On what?'

'Well, uh, I haven't decided yet. To tell you the truth, Phil, I don't have too much time for work, academic work.'

At some point in their conversation Boon has begun calling Philip by his first name, using moreover the contraction he has always detested. Philip resents the familiarity, but can think of no way of stopping him, though he has declined the invitation to address Boon as 'Charles'.

'What other kind of work are you doing?' he asks ironically.

'Well, you see, I have this radio show . . .'

'The Charles Boon Show?' Philip inquires, laughing heartily.

'That's right, you know about it?'

Boon is not laughing. The same old Boon, barefaced liar, weaver of fantasies. 'No,' says Philip. 'Do tell me.'

'Oh, it's just a late-night phone-in programme. You know, people call up and talk about what's on their mind and ask questions. Sometimes I have a guest. Hey, you must come on the programme one night!'

'Will I get paid?'

''Fraid not. You get a free tape-recording of the programme and a coloured photograph of the two of us at the mike.'

'Well . . .' Philip is unsettled by the particularity of the account. Could it conceivably be true? Some campus radio system perhaps? 'How often have you done this programme?' he asks.

'Every night, that is morning, for the past year. Midnight till two.'

'Every night! I'm not surprised your studies are suffering.'

'To tell you the truth, Phil, I'm not too bothered about my studies. It suits me to be registered at Euphoric State – it allows me to stay in the country without getting drafted. But I don't really need any more degrees. I've decided my future's in the media.'

'The Charles Boon Show?'

'That's just a beginning. I'm having discussions with a TV network right now about starting an experimental arts programme – 's'matter of fact, I'm flying at their expense, they sent me over to look at some European programmes. Then there's *Euphoric Times* . . .'

'What's that?'

'The underground newspaper. I do a weekly column for them, and now they want me to take over the editorship.'

'The editorship.'

'But I'm thinking of starting a rival paper instead.'

Philip looks searchingly at Boon, whose left eye jumps abruptly to port. Philip relaxes: it is all a pack of lies after all. There is no radio programme, no TV show, no expense account, no newspaper column. It is all wish-fulfilment fantasy, like the Rummidge Research Assistantship and the career in the diplomatic service. Boon has certainly changed – not only in appearance and dress: his manner is more confident, more relaxed, his speech has lost some of its Cockney vowels and glottal stops, he sounds not unlike David Frost. Philip has always supposed he despised David Frost but now realizes that in a grudging kind of way he must respect David Frost quite a lot, so sickening has it been to entertain, even for a moment, the idea that Charles Boon is successfully launched upon a similar career. An extraordinarily plausible fibber, Boon, even after years of close acquaintance he could take you in, it was only the vagrant eye that gave him away. Well, it would make a good story for his first letter home. *Who should I meet on the plane but the incorrigible Charles Boon – you remember him, of course, the Parolles of the English Department, graduated a couple of years ago. He was all dolled up in the latest 'gear', with hair down to his shoulders, but as full of tall stories as ever. Patronized me like mad, of course! But he's so transparent, you can't take offence.*

His train of thought, and Boon's continuing monologue, are interrupted by an announcement from the captain that they will be landing in approximately twenty minutes, and he hopes they have enjoyed the flight. The instruction to fasten safety belts is illuminated at the front of the cabin.

'Well, Phil, I'd better get back to my seat,' says Boon.

'Yes, well, nice to have met you again.'

'If there's anything I can do for you, Phil, just call me. My number's in the book.'

'Yes, well, I have been to America before, you know. But thank you for the offer.'

Boon waves his hand deprecatingly. 'Any time, day or night. I have an answering service.'

And to Philip's astonishment, Charles Boon gets up and walks, unchallenged, past a hovering stewardess, through the curtains that conceal the First Class cabin.

'I guess we must be over England, now,' says Mary Makepeace, staring out of the window.

'Is it raining?' Zapp asks.

'No, it's very clear. You can see all the little fields, like a patchwork quilt.'

'It can't be England if it's not raining. We must be off course.'

'There's a great dark smudge over there. That must be a big city.'

'It's probably Rummidge. A great dark smudge sounds like Rummidge.'

And now, in the two Boeings, falls simultaneously the special silence that precedes an airliner's landing. The engines are all but cut off, and the conversation of the passengers is hushed as if in sympathy. The planes begin to lose height – clumsily, it seems, in a series of lurching, shuddering drops, as though bumping down an enormous staircase. The passengers swallow to relieve the pressure on their eardrums, close their eyes, finger their passports and vomit-bags. Time passes very slowly. Each person is alone, temporarily, with his own thoughts. But it is hard to think connectedly, swaying and lurching here between heaven and earth. Philip thinks of Hilary smiling bravely and the children waving forlornly on Rummidge station as his train drew away, of an essay that he has forgotten to return to a student, of the probable cost of a taxi from the airport to Plotinus. The future seems frighteningly blank and he has a sudden spasm of homesickness; then he wonders whether the plane will crash, and what it would be like to die and whether there is a God, and where did he put his luggage tickets. Morris Zapp debates whether to stay in London for a few days or go straight to Rummidge and know the worst at once. He thinks of his twins playing secretively in a corner of the yard and breaking off their game reluctantly to say goodbye to him and how Désirée had refused to make love the night before he left, it would have been the first time in months, and remembers the first girl he ever had, Rose Finkelpearl the fish-monger's daughter on the next block, and how puzzled he'd been when his second girl also reeked faintly of fish, and wonders how many people at the airport will know what this charter has come to England for.

The planes yaw and tilt. A wall of suburbs suddenly rears up behind Mary Makepeace's head, and falls away again. Cloud swirls round Philip Swallow's plane and the windows are slashed with rain. Then houses, hills, trees, hangars, trucks, skim by in recognizable scale, like old friends seen again after a long separation.

Bump!

Bump!

At exactly the same moment, but six thousand miles apart, the two planes touch down.

2. Settling

Philip Swallow rented an apartment in the top half of a two-storey house high up on Pythagoras Drive, one of many classically named but romantically-contoured residential roads that corkscrewed their way up and around the verdant hills of Plotinus, Euph. The rent was low, by Euphoric standards, because the house stood on what was called a Slide Area. It had, in fact, already slid twelve feet towards the Bay of Esseph from its original position – a circumstance that had caused the owner hurriedly to vacate it, leasing the accommodation to tenants too indigent, or too careless of life, to complain. Philip fell into neither of these categories, but then he had not learned the full history of 1037 Pythagoras Drive until after signing the six months' lease. That history had been related to him on the first evening of his occupancy by Melanie Byrd, the prettiest and most wholesome-looking of the three girls who shared the ground-floor apartment, as she kindly explained to him the controls of the communal washing machine in the basement. At first he had felt exploited, but after a while he grew reconciled to the situation. If the apartment was not, after all, *surprisingly* cheap, it was still cheap; and as Melanie Byrd reminded him, there was no truly safe place to live in Euphoria, whose unique and picturesque landscape was the product of a huge geological fault running through the entire State. It had caused a major earthquake in the nineteenth century, and a repetition of this disaster before the end of the twentieth was confidently predicted by seismologists and local millennial sects: a rare and impressive instance of agreement between science and superstition.

When he drew back the curtains in his living-room each

morning, the view filled the picture window like a visual *tour de force* at the beginning of a Cinerama film. In the foreground, and to his right and left, the houses and gardens of the more affluent Euphoric faculty clung picturesquely to the sides of the Plotinus hills. Beneath him, where the foothills flattened out to meet the Bay shore, was the campus, with its white buildings and bosky paths, its campanile and plaza, its lecture rooms, stadia and laboratories, bordered by the rectilinear streets of downtown Plotinus. The Bay filled the middle distance, stretching out of sight on both sides, and one's eye naturally travelled in a great sightseeing arc: skimming along the busy Shoreline Freeway, swerving out across the Bay via the long Esseph Bridge (ten miles from toll to toll) to the city's dramatic skyline, dark downtown skyscrapers posed against white residential hills, from which it leapt across the graceful curves of the Silver Span suspension bridge, gateway to the Pacific, to alight on the green slopes of Miranda County, celebrated for its redwood forests and spectacular sea coast.

This vast panorama was agitated, even early in the morning, by every known form of transportation – ships, yachts, cars, trucks, trains, planes, helicopters and hovercraft – all in simultaneous motion, reminding Philip of the brightly illustrated cover of a *Boy's Wonder Book of Modern Transport* he had received on his tenth birthday. It was indeed, he thought, a perfect marriage of Nature and Civilization, this view, where one might take in at a glance the consummation of man's technological skill and the finest splendours of the natural world. The harmony he perceived in the scene was, he knew, illusory. Just out of sight to his left a pall of smoke hung over the great military and industrial port of Ashland, and to his right the oil refineries of St Gabriel fumed into the limpid air. The Bay, which winked so prettily in the morning sun, was, according to Charles Boon and other sources, poisoned by industrial waste and untreated effluent, and was being steadily contracted by unscrupulous dumping and filling.

For all that, Philip thought, almost guiltily, framed by his living-room window and seen at this distance, the view still looked very good indeed.

Morris Zapp was less enchanted with his view – a vista of dank back gardens, rotting sheds and dripping laundry, huge, ill-looking trees, grimy roofs, factory chimneys and church spires – but he had discarded this criterion at a very early stage of looking for furnished accommodation in Rummidge. You were lucky, he had quickly discovered, if you could find a place that could be kept at a temperature appropriate to human organisms, equipped with the more rudimentary amenities of civilized life and decorated in a combination of colours and patterns that didn't make you want to vomit on sight. He considered living in a hotel, but the hotels in the vicinity of the campus were, if anything, even worse than the private houses. Eventually he had taken an apartment on the top floor of a huge old house owned by an Irish doctor and his extensive family. Dr O'Shea had converted the attic with his own hands for the use of an aged mother, and it was to the recent death of this relative, the doctor impressed upon him, that Morris owed the good fortune of finding such enviable accommodation vacant. Morris didn't see this as a selling point himself, but O'Shea seemed to think that the apartment's sentimental associations were worth at least an extra five dollars a week to an American torn from the bosom of his own family. He pointed out the armchair in which his mother had suffered her fatal seizure and, while bouncing on the mattress to demonstrate its resilience, contrived at the same time to reflect with a mournful sigh that it was scarcely a month since his beloved parent had passed to her reward from this very bed.

Morris took the flat because it was centrally heated – the first he had seen thus blessed. But the heating system turned out to be one of electric radiators perversely and unalterably programmed to come on at full blast when you were asleep and to turn themselves off as soon as you got up, from which time they leaked a diminishing current of lukewarm air into the frigid atmosphere until you were ready to go to bed again. This system, Dr O'Shea explained, was extremely economical because it ran on half-price electricity, but it still seemed to Morris an expensive way to work up a sweat in bed. Fortunately the apartment was well provided with gas burners of antique design, and by keeping them on at full volume all day he was able to maintain a tolerable temperature in his rooms, though O'Shea evidently found it excessive, entering Morris's apartment with his arm held up to shield his face, like a man breaking into a burning house.

Simply keeping warm was Morris Zapp's main preoccupation in his first few days at Rummidge. On his first morning, in the tomb-like hotel room he had checked into after driving straight from London airport, he had woken to find steam coming out of his mouth. It had never happened to him indoors before and his first thought was that he was on fire. When he had moved his baggage into the O'Shea house, he filled the micro-refrigerator with TV dinners, locked his door, turned up all the fires and spent a couple of days thawing out. Only then did he feel ready to investigate the Rummidge campus and introduce himself to the English Department.

Philip Swallow was more impatient to inspect his place of work. On his very first morning he strolled out after a delicious breakfast of orange juice, bacon, hot cakes and maple syrup (maple syrup! how delightful it was to recover such forgotten sensations) to look for Dealer Hall, the location of the English Department. It was raining, as it had been the previous day. This had been a disappointment to Philip initially – in his memory Euphoria was bathed in perpetual sunlight, and he had forgotten – perhaps he had never known – that it had a rainy season in the winter months. It was, however, a fine, soft rain, and the air was warm and balmy. The grass was green, the trees and shrubs were in full leaf and, in some cases, flower and fruit. There was no real winter in Euphoria – autumn joined hands with spring and summer, and together they danced a three-handed jig all year long, to the merry confusion of the vegetable world. Philip felt his pulse beating to its exhilarating rhythm.

He had no difficulty in finding his way to Dealer Hall, a large, square building in the neoclassical style. He was prevented from entering it, however, by a ring of campus policemen. Quite a lot of students and staff were milling about, and a long-haired youth with a KEEP KROOP button in the lapel of his suede jacket informed Philip that the building was being checked out for a bomb allegedly planted during the night. The search, he understood, might take several hours; but as he was turning away it ended quite suddenly with a muffled explosion high up in the building and a tinkle of shattered glass.

As Morris Zapp learned much later, he made a bad impression on his first appearance in the Rummidge English Department. The Secretary, young Alice Slade, returning from her coffee break with her friend Miss Mackintosh of Egyptology, observed him doubled up in front of the Departmental noticeboard, coughing and wheezing and blowing cigar ash all over the floor. Miss Slade had wondered whether it was a mature student having a fit and asked Miss Mackintosh to run and fetch the porter, but Miss Mackintosh ventured the opinion that he was only laughing, which was indeed the case. The noticeboard distantly reminded Morris of the early work of Robert Rauschenberg: a thumb-tacked montage of variegated scraps of paper – letterheaded notepaper, memo sheets, compliment slips, pages torn clumsily from college notebooks, inverted envelopes, reversed invoices, even fragments of wrapping paper with tails of scotch tape still adhering to them – all bearing cryptic messages from faculty to students about courses, rendezvous, assignments and books, scribbled in a variety of scarcely decipherable hands with pencil, ink and coloured ball-point. The end of the Gutenberg era was evidently not an issue here: they were still living in a manuscript culture. Morris felt he understood more deeply, now,

what McLuhan was getting at: it had tactile appeal, this
noticeboard – you wanted to reach out and touch its rough,
irregular surface. As a system for conveying information it
was the funniest thing he'd seen in years.

Morris was still chuckling to himself as the mini-skirted
secretary, looking, he thought, rather nervously over her
shoulder from time to time, led him down the corridor to his
office. Walking along the corridors of Dealer Hall was like
passing through some Modern Language Association Hall
of Fame, but he recognized none of the nameplates here
except the one on the door Miss Slade finally stopped at:
MR P. H. SWALLOW. That rang a distant bell – but, he
recalled, as the girl fumbled with the key (she seemed very
jumpy, this chick) it wasn't in print that he had encountered
the name, merely in the correspondence about his trip.
Swallow was the guy he was exchanging with. He recalled
Luke Hogan, present Chairman of Euphoric's English Department, holding a letter from Swallow in his enormous
fist (a handwritten letter, again, it came back to him) and
complaining in his Montana cowboy's drawl, 'Goddammit,
Morris, what are we gonna do with this guy Swallow? He
claims he ain't *got* a field.' Morris had recommended
putting Philip down to teach English 99, a routine intro-
duction to the literary genres and critical method for
English majors, and English 305, a course in novel-writing.
As Euphoric State's resident novelist, Garth Robinson, was
in fact very rarely resident, orbiting the University in an
almost unbroken cycle of grants, fellowships, leaves of
absence and alcoholic cures, the teaching of English 305
usually fell to some unwilling and unqualified member of the
regular teaching staff. As Morris said, 'If he makes a fuck-up
of English 305, nobody's going to notice. And any clown
with a PhD should be able to teach English 99.'

'He doesn't have a PhD,' Hogan said.

'*What?*'

'They have a different system in England, Morris. The
PhD isn't so important.'

'You mean the jobs are hereditary?'

Recollecting all this reminded Morris that he had not been able to prise any information about his own teaching programme from Rummidge before leaving Euphoria.

The girl finally got the door open and he went in. He was pleasantly surprised: it was a large, comfortable room, well-furnished with desk, table, chairs and bookshelves of matching polished wood, an armchair and a rather handsome rug. Above all, it was warm. Morris Zapp was to experience the same sense of surprise and paradox many times in his first weeks at Rummidge. Public affluence and private squalor, was how he formulated it. The domestic standard of living of the Rummidge faculty was far below that of the Euphoric faculty, but even the most junior teacher here had a large office to himself, and the Staff House was built like a Hilton, putting Euphoric State's Faculty Club quite in the shade. Even the building in which Morris's office was situated had its own spacious and comfortable lounge, restricted to faculty, where you could get fresh coffee and tea served in real china cups and saucers by two motherly women, whereas Dealer Hall boasted only a small room littered with paper cups and cigarette ends where you fixed yourself instant coffee that tasted like hot disinfectant. 'Public affluence' was perhaps too flattering to Rummidge, and it couldn't be the socialism he'd heard so much about, either. It was more like a narrow band of privilege running through the general drabness and privation of life. If the British university teacher had nothing else, he had a room he could call his own, a decent place to sit and read his newspaper and the use of a john that was off-limits to students. That seemed to be the underlying principle. Such coherent thoughts were not yet forming in Morris Zapp's mind, however, as he first cast his eyes round Philip Swallow's room. He was still in a state of culture shock, and it gave him a giddy feeling when he looked out of the window and saw the familiar campanile of Euphoric State flushed an angry red and shrunk to half its normal size, like a detumescent penis.

'It's a bit stuffy in here, I'm afraid,' said the secretary, making a move to open a window. Morris, already basking in the radiator's warmth, lurched with clumsy haste to prevent her, and she shrank back, quivering, as if he had been about to put his hand up her skirt – which, given its dimensions, wouldn't have been difficult, it could easily happen accidentally just shaking hands with her. He tried to soothe her by making conversation.

'Don't seem to be many people on campus today.'

She looked at him as if he had just arrived from outer space. 'It's the vacation,' she said.

'Uhuh. Is Professor Masters around?'

'No, he's in Hungary. Won't be back till the beginning of term.'

'At a conference?'

'Shooting wild pigs, I'm told.'

Morris wondered if he had heard aright, but let it go. 'What about the other professors?'

'There's only the one.'

'I mean the other teachers.'

'It's the vacation,' she repeated, speaking with deliberation, as if to a slow-witted child. 'You do get them coming in from time to time, but I've not seen anybody this morning.'

'Who should I see about my teaching programme?'

'Dr Busby did say something about it the other day . . .'

'Yes?' Morris prompted, after a pause.

'I've forgotten, now,' said the girl dejectedly. 'I'm leaving in the summer to get married,' she added, as if she had decided on this course as the only way out of a hopeless situation.

'Congratulations. Would there be a file on me somewhere?'

'Well, there might be. I could have a look,' said the girl, obviously relieved to escape. She left Morris alone in his office.

He sat down at the desk and opened the drawers. In the top right-hand one was an envelope addressed to himself. It contained a long hand-written letter from Philip Swallow.

Dear Professor Zapp,

I gather you'll be using my room while you're here. I'm afraid
I've lost the key to the filing cabinet, so if you have anything really
confidential I should keep it under the carpet, at least I always do.
Do feel free to use my books, though I'd be grateful if you wouldn't
lend them to students, as they *will* write in them.

I gather from Busby that you'll probably be taking over my
tutorial groups. The second-year groups are rather hard going,
especially the Joint Honours, but the first-year group is quite
lively, and I think you'll find the two final-year groups very
interesting. There are a few points you might like to bear in mind.
Brenda Archer suffers badly from pre-menstrual tension so don't
be surprised if she bursts into tears every now and again. The other
third-year group is tricky because Robin Kenworth used to be
Alice Murphy's boy-friend but lately he's been going around with
Miranda Watkins, and as they're all in the same group you may
find the atmosphere rather tense . . .

The letter continued in this vein for several pages, des-
cribing the emotional, psychological and physiological
peculiarities of the students concerned in intimate detail.
Morris read through it in total bewilderment. What kind of
a man was this, that seemed to know more about his students than their own mothers? And to care more, by the
sound of it.

He opened the other drawers in the desk, hoping to find
further clues to this eccentric character, but they were
empty except for one containing a piece of chalk, an exhausted ball-point, two bent pipe-cleaners and a small,
empty can that had once contained an ounce of pipe tobacco, Three Nuns Empire Blend. Sherlock Holmes might
have made something of these clues . . . Morris moved on to
examine the cupboards and bookshelves. The books did no
more than confirm Swallow's confession that he had no particular scholarly field, being a miscellaneous collection of English literature, with a thin representation of modern criticism,
Morris's own not included. He established that the cupboards were empty, except for one at the top of the bookshelves which was too high for him to reach. Its inaccessi-
bility convinced Morris that it contained the revelation he

was looking for – a dozen empty gin bottles, for instance, or a collection of women's underwear – and he clambered on to a chair to reach the catch of the sliding door. It was stuck, and the whole bookshelf began to sway dangerously as he tugged. The catch suddenly gave, however, and a hundred and fifty-seven empty tobacco cans, Three Nuns Empire Blend, fell on his head.

'You've been allocated room number 426,' said Mabel Lee, the petite Asian secretary. 'That's Professor Zapp's office.'

'Yes,' said Philip. 'He'll be using my room at Rummidge.'

Mabel Lee gave him an amiable, but non-attending smile, like that of an air-hostess – whom, indeed, she resembled, in her crisp white blouse and scarlet pinafore dress. The Departmental Office was full of people just admitted to the building, loudly discussing the bomb which had exploded in the fourth-floor mensroom. Opinion seemed to be fairly evenly divided between those who blamed the Third World Students who were threatening to strike in the coming quarter, and those who suspected police provocateurs aiming to discredit the Third World Students and their strike. Though the conversation was excited, Philip missed the expected note of outrage and fear.

'Does, er, this sort of thing . . . happen often?' he asked.

'Hmm? Oh, yeah. Well, I guess it's the first *bomb* we've had in Dealer.' With this ambiguous reassurance Mabel Lee proceeded to hand over the keys to his room, together with a wad of forms and leaflets which she briskly explained to him, dealing them out on the counter that divided the room: 'Identity Card, don't forget to sign it, application for car parking, medical insurance brochures – choose any one plan, typewriter rental application – you can have electric or manual, course handbook, income tax immunity form, key to the elevator in this building, key to the Xerox room, just sign your name in the book each time you use the machine . . . I'll tell Professor Hogan you've arrived,' she

64

concluded. 'He's busy with the Fire Chief right now. I know he'll call you.'

Philip found his room on the fourth floor. A sallow youth with a mop of frizzy hair was squatting outside, smoking a cigarette. He was wearing some kind of army combat jacket with camouflage markings and he looked, Philip couldn't help thinking, just the sort of chap who might plant a bomb somewhere. As Philip fitted his key into the Yale lock, he scrambled to his feet. A fluorescent KEEP KROOP button glowed on his lapel.

'Professor Swallow?'

'Yes?'

'Could I see you?'

'What, now?'

'Now would be great.'

'Well, I've only just arrived . . .'

'You have to run that key twice.'

This was true. The door opened suddenly and Philip dropped some of his papers. The young man picked them up adroitly and made this an opportunity to follow him into the room. It was stuffy, and smelled of cigars. Philip threw up the window and observed with satisfaction that it opened on to a narrow balcony.

'Nice view,' said the youth, who had stolen up silently behind him. Philip started.

'What can I do for you, Mr, er . . . ?'

'Smith. Wily Smith.'

'Willy?'

'Wily.'

Wily perched himself on the only part of the desk that was not covered with books. Philip's first thought was that it was rather careless of the Zapp fellow to leave his room so untidy. Then he registered that many of the books were still in unwrapped postal packaging and addressed to himself. 'Good Lord,' he said.

'What's the problem, Professor Swallow?'

'These books . . . Where have they come from?'

'Publishers. They want you to assign them for courses.'

'And what if I don't?'

'You keep them anyway. Unless you want to sell them. I know a guy will give you fifty per cent of the list price . . .'

'No, no,' Philip protested, greedily tearing the wrappers from huge, heavy anthologies and sleek, seductive paperbacks. A free book was a rare treat in England, and the sight of all this unsolicited booty made him slightly delirious. He rather wished Wily Smith would leave him to gloat in solitude.

'What is it you want to see me about, Mr Smith?'

'You're teaching English 305 next quarter, right?'

'I really don't know what I'm teaching yet. What is English 305?'

'Novel-writing.'

Philip laughed. 'Well, it's certainly not me, then. I couldn't write a novel to save my life.'

Wily Smith frowned and, plunging his hand inside his combat jacket, produced what Philip feared might be a bomb but which turned out to be a catalogue of courses. 'English 305,' he read out, 'an advanced course in the writing of extended narrative. Selective enrolment. Winter Quarter: Professor Philip Swallow.'

Philip took the catalogue from his hands and read for himself. 'Good Lord,' he said weakly. 'I must stop this at once.'

With Wily Smith's assistance he telephoned the Chairman of the Department.

'Professor Hogan, I'm sorry to bother you so soon, but –'

'Mr Swallow!' Hogan's voice boomed out of the receiver. 'Mighty glad to hear you arrived. Have a good flight?'

'Not at all bad, thank you. I –'

'Fine! Where are you staying, Mr Swallow?'

'At the Faculty Club for the time being, while I look –'

'Fine, that's fine, Mr Swallow. You and I must have lunch together real soon.'

'Well, that would be very nice, but what I –'

'Fine. And while I think of it, Mrs Hogan and I are having some folks round for drinks on Sunday, 'bout five, could you make it?'

'Well, yes, thank you very much. About my courses –'

'Fine. That's just fine. And how are you settling in, Mr Swallow?'

'Oh, fine, thanks,' said Philip mechanically. 'I mean, no, that is –' But he was too late. With a last 'Fine', Hogan had rung off.

'So do I get into the course?' said Wily Smith.

'I would strongly advise you against it,' said Philip. 'Why are you so keen, anyway?'

'I have this novel I want to write. It's about this black kid growing up in the ghetto . . .'

'Isn't that going to be rather difficult?' said Philip. 'I mean, unless you actually *are* . . .'

Philip hesitated. He had been instructed by Charles Boon that 'black' was the correct usage these days, but he found himself unable to pronounce a word associated in Rummidge with the crudest kind of racial prejudice. 'Unless you've had the experience yourself,' he amended his sentence.

'Sure. Like the story is autobiographical. All I need is technique.'

'Autobiographical?' Philip scrutinized the young man, narrowing his eyes and cocking his head to one side. Wily Smith's complexion was about the shade of Philip's own a week after his summer holiday, when his tan would begin to fade and turn yellow. 'Are you sure?'

'Sure I'm sure.' Wily Smith looked hurt, not to say insulted.

Philip hastily changed the subject: 'Tell me, that badge you're wearing – what *is* Kroop?'

Kroop turned out to be the name of an Assistant Professor in the English Department who had recently been refused tenure. 'But there's a grass-roots movement to have him kept on here,' Wily explained. 'Like he's a real groovy teacher and his classes are very popular. The other professors make out he hasn't published enough, but really they're sick as hell because of the raves he gets in the *Course Bulletin*.'

And what was that? It was apparently a kind of consumers' guide to teachers and courses based on questionnaires handed out to students in previous quarters. Wily produced the current issue from one of his capacious pockets.

'You won't be in there, Professor Swallow. But you will next quarter.'

'Really?' Philip opened the book at random.

English 142. Augustan Pastoral Poetry. Asst. Professor Howard Ringbaum. Juniors and Seniors. Limited enrolment.

Ringbaum, according to most reports, does little to make his subject interesting to students. One commented: 'He seems to know his material very well, but resents questions and discussion as they interrupt his train of thought.' Another comment: 'Dull, dull, dull.' Ringbaum is a strict grader and, according to one report, 'likes to set insidious little quizzes.'

'Well,' said Philip with a nervous smile. 'They certainly don't mince their words, do they?' He leafed through other pages on English courses.

English 213. The Death of the Book? Communication and Crisis in Contemporary Culture. Asst. Professor Karl Kroop. Limited enrolment.

Rise early on Enrolment Day to sign on for this justly popular interdisciplinary multi-media head-trip. 'Makes McLuhan seem slow,' was one comment, and another raved: 'the most exciting course I have ever taken.' Heavy reading assignments, but flexible assessment system. Kroop takes an interest in his students, is always available.

'Who compiles these reports?' Philip inquired.

'I do,' said Wily Smith. 'Do I get into your course?'

'I'll think about it,' said Philip. He continued to browse.

English 350. Jane Austen and the Theory of Fiction. Professor Morris J. Zapp. Graduate Seminar. Limited enrolment.

Mostly good reports of this course. Zapp is described as vain, sarcastic and a mean grader, but brilliant and stimulating. 'He makes Austen swing,' was one comment. Only 'A' students need apply.

Miss Slade was just about to knock on Morris Zapp's door to inform him that there was nothing in the files about his teaching programme, when she heard the noise of the hundred and fifty-seven tobacco cans falling out of the cupboard. He listened to the sound of her high heels fleeing down the corridor. She did not return. Neither did anyone else violate his privacy.

Morris came into the University most days to work on his *Sense and Sensibility* commentary and at first he appreciated the peace and quiet; but after a while he began to find these amenities oppressively absolute. In Euphoria he was constantly being pursued by students, colleagues, administrators, secretaries. He didn't expect to be so busy at Rummidge, at least not initially; but he had vaguely supposed the faculty would introduce themselves, show him around, offer the usual hospitality and advice. In all modesty Morris imagined he must be the biggest fish ever to swim into this academic backwater, and he was prepared for a reception of almost exaggerated (if that were possible) interest and excitement. When nobody showed, he didn't know what to do. He had lost the art, cultivated in youth, of making his existence known to people. He was used, by now, to letting the action come to him. But there was no action.

As the beginning of term approached, the Departmental corridor lost its tomb-like silence, its air of human desertion. The faculty began to trickle back to their posts. From behind his desk he heard them passing in the corridor, greeting each other, laughing and opening and shutting their doors. But when he ventured into the corridor himself they seemed to avoid him, bolting into their offices just as he emerged from his own, or else they looked straight through him as if he were the man who serviced the central heating. Just when he had decided that he would have to take the initiative by ambushing his British colleagues as they passed his door at coffee-time and dragging them into his office, they began to acknowledge his presence in a way which suggested long but not deep familiarity, tossing him a perfunctory smile as they passed, or nodding their heads, without breaking step or their own conversations. This new behaviour implied that they all knew perfectly well who he was, thus making any attempt at self-introduction on his part superfluous, while at the same time it offered no purchase for extending acquaintance. Morris began to think that he was going to pass through the Rummidge English Department without anyone actually speaking to him. They would fend him off for six months with their little smiles and nods and then the waters would close over him and it would be as if he had never disturbed their surface.

Morris felt himself cracking under this treatment. His vocal organs began to deteriorate from disuse – on the rare occasions when he spoke, his own voice sounded strange and hoarse to his ears. He paced his office like a prisoner in his cell, wondering what he had done to provoke this treatment. Did he have halitosis? Was he suspected of working for the CIA?

In his lonely isolation, Morris turned instinctively for solace to the media. He was at the best of times a radio and TV addict: he kept a radio in his office at Euphoric State tuned permanently to his favourite FM station, specializing in rock-soul ballads; and he had a colour TV in his study at home as well as in the living-room because he found it easier to work while watching sports broadcasts at the same time. (Baseball was most conducive to a ready flow of words, but football, hockey and basketball would also serve.) He rented a colour TV soon after moving into his apartment in Rummidge, but the programmes were disappointing, consisting mainly of dramatizations of books he had already read and canned American series he had already seen. There was, naturally, no baseball, football, hockey or basketball. There was soccer, which he thought he might get interested in, given time – he sniffed, there, the mixture of spite and skill, gall and grace, which characterized an authentic spectator sport – but the amount of screen time devoted to it was meagre. There was a four-hour programme of sport on Saturday afternoons which he had settled down to watch expectantly, but it seemed to be some kind of conspiracy to drive the population out to the soccer stadiums or to the supermarkets or anywhere rather than watch ladies' archery, county swimming championships, a fishing contest and a table-tennis tournament all in breathtaking succession. He switched on to the other channel and that seemed to be a cross-country race for wheel-chairs, as far as you could tell through the sleet.

He had a brief honeymoon with Radio One that turned into a kind of sado-masochistic marriage. Waking early in the Rummidge hotel on that morning when his breath turned to steam, he had flicked on his transistor and listened to what he took, at the time, to be a very funny parody of the worst kind of American AM radio, based on the simple but effective formula of having non-commercial commercials. Instead of advertising products, the disc-jockey advertised *himself* – pouring out a torrent of drivel generally designed to convey what a jolly, amusing and lovable guy he was – and also advertised his listeners, every one of whose names and addresses he seemed determined to read out over the air, plus, on occasion, their birthdays and car registration numbers. Now and again he played musical jingles in praise of himself or reported, in tones of unremitting jollity, a multiple accident on the freeway. There was almost no time left for playing records. It was a riot. Morris thought it was a little early in the morning for satire, but listened entranced. When the programme finished and was followed by one of exactly the same kind, he began to get restive. The British, he thought, must be gluttons for satire: even the weather forecast seemed to be some kind of spoof, predicting every possible combination of weather for the next twenty-four hours without actually committing itself to anything specific, not even the existing temperature. It was only after four successive programmes of almost exactly the same formula – DJ's narcissistic gabble, lists of names and addresses, meaningless anti-jingles – that the awful truth dawned on him: *Radio One was like this all the time*.

Morris's only human contact these lonely days was Doctor O'Shea, who came in to watch Morris's colour TV and to drink his whisky, and perhaps to escape the joys of family life for an hour or so, because he knocked softly on the door and tiptoed into the room, winking heavily and raising a cautionary finger as if to restrain Morris from speaking until the door was shut against the wails of Mrs O'Shea and her babies rising up the staircase. O'Shea puzzled Morris. He didn't look like a doctor, not like the doctors Morris knew – sleek prosperous men who drove the biggest cars and owned the plushest houses in any neighbourhood he had ever lived in. O'Shea's suit was baggy and threadbare, his shirts were frayed, he drove a small car that had seen better days, he looked short of sleep, money, pleasures, everything except worries. By the same token Morris's possessions, few as they were, seemed to throw the doctor into fits of envious awe, as if his eyes had never beheld such opulence. He examined Morris's Japanese cassette recorder with the half-fearful, half-covetous curiosity of a nineteenth-century savage handling a missionary's tinder-box; he seemed astounded that a man might own so many shirts that he could send them to the laundry half-a-dozen at a time; and, invited to fix himself a drink, he was almost (but not quite) incapable of making a choice from three varieties of whisky, groaning and muttering under his breath as he handled the bottles and read the labels, 'Mother of God, what is it we have here, Old Grandad Genuine Kentucky Bourbon and here's th'old josser himself looking none the worse for it, would you believe it . . .'

The installation of the colour TV had made Dr O'Shea quite ill with excitement. He followed the delivery men up the stairs and skipped around the room getting in their way and sat enraptured before the tuning signal for hours after they left, getting up now and again to lay his hand reverently on the cabinet as if he expected to derive some special grace from the contact. 'Sure, if I hadn't seen it with me own eyes I shouldn't have believed it,' he said with a sigh. 'You're a fortunate man, Mr Zapp.'

'But I just rented it,' Morris protested in bewilderment. 'Anybody can rent one. It only costs a few dollars a week.'

'Well, now, that's easily said, Mr Zapp, for a man in your position, that's easily said, but easier said than done, Mr Zapp.'

'Well, if there's anything you want to see, just drop by . . .'

'That's very kind of you, Mr Zapp, very thoughtful. I'll take you up on that generous invitation.' And so he did. Unfortunately, O'Shea's tastes in TV ran to situation comedy and sentimental serials, to which he reacted with naïve, unqualified credulity, writhing and jumping up and down in his seat, pounding the arm of his chair and nudging Morris vigorously in the ribs, maintaining a stream of highly personal commentary on the action: 'Ahah! Caught you there, laddie, you weren't expecting that . . . Oh! What's this, what's this, you little hussy? Ah, now, that's better, that's better . . . NO, DON'T DO IT! DON'T DO IT! Mother of God, that boy will be the death of me . . .' and so on. Fortunately, Dr O'Shea usually fell asleep halfway through the programme, exhausted by the strains of audience participation and the rigours of the day's labours, and Morris would turn down the sound and get out a book. It wasn't exactly company.

To his considerable mortification, Philip Swallow's chief social asset at Euphoric State turned out to be his association with Charles Boon. He carelessly let this information slip in conversation with Wily Smith and, within hours it seemed, the news had been flashed to all points of the campus. His office began to fill up with people anxious to make his acquaintance for the sake of some anecdote of Charles Boon's early life, and before the end of the afternoon the Chairman's wife, Mrs Hogan, had phoned to plead for Philip's assistance in persuading Boon to attend their cocktail party. It was hard to believe, but the Charles Boon

Show was all the rage at Euphoric State. Philip listened to it at the first opportunity, and, by some kind of sado-masochistic compulsion, at most subsequent opportunities.

The basic formula of the programme – an open line on which listeners could call up to discuss various issues with the compère and with each other – was a familiar one. But the Charles Boon Show was different from the ordinary phone-in programme in several respects. To begin with, it was put out by the non-commercial network, QXYZ, which was supported by listeners' subscriptions and foundation grants, and was therefore free from business and political pressures. Where the compères of most American phone-in programmes were bland, evasive, middle-of-the-road men, giving a fair hearing to all sides of the question – endlessly patient, endlessly courteous, ultimately without convictions – Charles Boon was violently, wilfully opinionated. Where they provided the reassurance of a surrogate father or uncle, he offered the provocation of a delinquent-son-figure. He took an extreme radical position on all such issues as pot, sex, race, Viet Nam, and argued heatedly – often rudely – with callers who disagreed with him, sometimes abusing his control of the telephone line by cutting them off in mid-sentence. It was rumoured that he collected the phone numbers of likely-sounding girls and called them back after the programme to make dates. He would sometimes begin a programme by quoting a passage of Wittgenstein or Camus or by reading a poem of his own composition, and use this as a starting point for a dialogue with his listeners. And an extraordinary variety of listeners they were, those who faithfully tuned into QXYZ at midnight – students, professors, hippies, runaways, insomniacs, drug addicts and Hells Angels. Housewives sitting up for laggard husbands confided their marital problems to the Charles Boon Show; truck-drivers listening to the programme in their shuddering cabs, unable to suppress their rage at Boon, or Camus, any longer, swerved off the freeway to phone in their incoherent contributions from emergency call-boxes. Already a considerable folk-lore had accumulated about the Charles Boon

Show, and Philip was regaled with the highlights of certain past programmes so often that he came to believe that he had heard them himself: the time, for instance, Boon had talked a panic-stricken pregnant mother through her first labour-pains, or when he argued a homosexual clergyman out of suicide, or when he invited – and obtained – post-coital reflections on the Sexual Revolution from bedside telephones around the Bay. There were, of course, no commercials on the progamme, but just to annoy the rival networks Boon would sometimes give an unsolicited and unpaid testimonial to some local restaurant or movie or shirt-sale that had taken his fancy. To Philip it seemed obvious that beneath all the culture and the eccentricity and the human concern there beat a heart of pure show-business, but to the local community the programme evidently appeared irresistibly novel, daring and authentic.

'Isn't Mr Boon with you?' was his hostess's first question when he presented himself at the Hogans' palatial ranch-style house for their cocktail party. Her eyes raked him from head to foot as though she suspected that he had concealed Boon somewhere on his person. Philip assured her that he had passed on the invitation, as Hogan himself loomed up and crunched Philip's fingers in a huge, horny handclasp.

'Hi, there, Mr Swallow, mighty glad to see you.' He ushered Philip into the spacious living-room, where forty or more people were already assembled, and helped him to a gin and tonic of giant proportions. 'Now, who would you like to meet? Nearly all English Department folk here, I guess.'

Only one name would come into Philip's head. 'I haven't met Mr Kroop yet.'

Hogan went slightly green about the jowls. 'Kroop?'

'I've read so much about him, in buttonholes,' Philip quipped, to cover what was evidently a *faux pas*.

'Yeah? Oh yeah. Ha, ha. I'm afraid you won't see Karl at many cocktail parties – Howard!' Hogan's enormous paw fell heavily on the shoulder of a sallow, bespectacled young man cruising past with a tumbler of Scotch held to pursed lips. He staggered slightly, but skilfully avoided spilling the drink. Philip was introduced to Howard Ringbaum. 'I was telling Mr Swallow,' said Hogan, 'that you don't often see Karl Kroop at faculty social gatherings.'

'I hear,' said Ringbaum, 'that Karl has totally rethought his course on "The Death of the Book?" He's removing the query mark this quarter.'

Hogan guffawed and thumped Ringbaum between the shoulder blades before moving away. Ringbaum, swaying with the punch, kept his balance and his drink intact.

'What are you working on?' he asked Philip.

'Oh, I'm just trying to sort out my teaching at the moment.'

Ringbaum nodded impatiently. 'What's your field?'

'Yours is Augustan pastoral, I believe,' Philip returned evasively.

Ringbaum looked pleased. 'Right. How did you know? You've seen my article in *College English*?'

'I was looking through the Course Bulletin the other day . . .'

Ringbaum's countenance darkened. 'You don't want to believe everything you read in that.'

'Oh no, of course . . . What d'you think of this chap Kroop then?' Philip inquired.

'As little as possible. I'm coming up for tenure myself this quarter, and if I don't make it nobody around here is going to be wearing RETAIN RINGBAUM buttons.'

'This tenure business seems to create a lot of tension.'

'You must have the same thing in England?'

'Oh no. Probation is more or less a formality. In practice, once you're appointed they can never get rid of you – unless you seduce one of your students, or something equally scandalous.' Philip laughed.

'You can screw as many students as you like here,' said Ringbaum unsmilingly. 'But if your publications are unsatisfactory . . .' He drew a finger expressively across his throat.

'Hey, Howard!'

A young man dressed in a black grained-silk shirt with a

red kerchief knotted round his throat, accosted Philip's companion. He towed behind him a delectable blonde in pink party pyjamas. 'Hey, Howard, somebody just told me there's an English guy at this party who asked Hogan to introduce him to Karl Kroop. I'd love to have seen the old man's face.'

'Ask him,' said Ringbaum, nodding towards Philip.

Philip blushed and laughed uneasily.

'Oh my God, you aren't the English guy by any chance?'

'You goofed again, Sy, dear,' said the woman.

'I'm terribly sorry,' said the man. 'Sy Gootblatt is the name. This is Bella. You might think by the way she's dressed that she's just got out of bed, and you wouldn't be far wrong.'

'Take no notice of him, Mr Swallow,' said Bella. 'How are you liking Euphoria?'

Of the two questions he was asked at the cocktail party by everyone he met, this was the one he preferred. The other was, 'What are you working on?'

'What are you working on, Mr Swallow?' Luke Hogan asked him when they bumped into each other again.

'Luke,' said Mrs Hogan, saving Philip from having to think of a reply, 'I really think Charles Boon is here at last.'

There was a flurry of activity in the hall, and heads turned all across the room. Boon had indeed arrived, dressed offensively in singlet and jeans, and escorting a handsome, haughty Black Pantheress who was to appear on his programme later that night. They sat in a corner of the room drinking Bloody Marys and giving audience to a neck-craning circle of entranced faculty and their wives. The Pantheress did little except look coolly around at the Hogans' opulent furnishings as if calculating how well they would burn, but Boon more than compensated for her taciturnity. Philip, who had rather counted on being himself the evening's chief focus of attention, found himself standing neglected on the fringes of this little court. Disgruntled, he wandered out of the living-room on to the terrace. A solitary woman was leaning against the balustrade, staring moodily at the Bay, where a spectacular sunset was in progress, the orange globe of the sun just balanced, it seemed, on the suspension cables of the Silver Span bridge. Philip took up his stand some four yards away from the woman. 'Delightful evening,' he said.

She looked at him sharply, then returned to the contemplation of the sunset. 'Yeah,' she said, at length.

Philip sipped his drink nervously. The silent, brooding presence of the woman made him uncomfortable, spoiled his enjoyment of the view. He decided to return to the living-room.

'If you're going back inside . . .' said the woman.

'Yes?'

'You might freshen my drink for me.'

'Certainly,' said Philip, taking her glass. 'More ice?'

'More ice, more vodka. No more tonic. And look for the Smirnoff bottle under the bar. Ignore the gallon jar of cut-price stuff on the top.'

Philip duly found the concealed Smirnoff bottle and re-filled the woman's glass, rather underestimating the space required for ice, which (inexperienced in handling liquor) he added last. Boon was still talking away in the background, about his plans for a TV arts programme: 'Something entirely different . . . art in action . . . train a camera on a sculptor at work for a month or two, then run the film through at about fifty thousand frames per second, see the sculpture taking shape . . . put an object in front of two painters, let them get on with it, use two cameras and a split screen . . . contrast . . . auction the pictures at the end of the programme . . .' Philip topped up his own gin and tonic and carried the two glasses out on to the terrace.

'Thanks,' said the woman. 'Is that little shit still shooting off his mouth in there?'

'Yes, he is, actually.'

'You're not a fan?'

'Definitely not.'

'Let's drink to that.'

They drank to it.

'Wow,' said the woman. 'You mix a stiff drink.'

'I just followed your instructions.'

'To the brim,' said the woman. 'I don't think we've met, have we? Are you visiting here?'

'Yes, I'm Philip Swallow – exchanging with Professor Zapp.'

'Did you say Zapp?'

'You know him?'

'Very well. He's my husband.'

Philip choked on his drink. 'You're Mrs Zapp?'

'Is that so surprising? You think I look too old? Or too young?'

'Oh, no,' said Philip.

'Oh no which?' Her small green eyes glinted with mockery. She was a red-head, striking but by no means pretty, and not particularly well-groomed. He guessed she was in her mid-thirties.

'I was just surprised,' said Philip. 'I suppose I assumed you had gone to Rummidge with your husband.'

'Your wife with you?'

'No.' She responded with a gesture which implied clearly enough that his assumption was therefore demonstrably unwarranted. 'I would have liked to have brought her,' he said. 'But my visit was arranged at rather short notice. Also we have children, and there were problems about schooling and so on. And there was the house . . .' He heard himself going on like this for, it seemed, several hours, as if he were answering a formal accusation in court. He felt increasingly foolish, but Mrs Zapp somehow kept him talking, involving himself deeper and deeper in implied guilt, by her silence and her mocking regard. 'Do you have children yourself?' he concluded desperately.

'Two. Twins. Boy and girl. Aged nine.'

'Ah, then you understand the problems.'

'I doubt if we have the same problems, Mr Sparrow.'

'Swallow.'

'Mr Swallow. Sorry. A much nicer bird.' She turned back to contemplate the sun, now sinking into the sea behind the Silver Span, and took a reflective draught from her glass. 'Less promiscuous, for instance. How does your wife feel about it, Mr Swallow, I mean is she with you about the kids and the schools and the house and all? She doesn't mind being left behind?'

'Well, we discussed it very thoroughly, of course . . . It was a difficult decision. I left it to her ultimately . . .' (He felt himself slipping into the groove of compulsive self-justification again.) 'After all, she has the worst part of the bargain . . .'

'What bargain?' said the woman sharply.

'Just a figure of speech. I mean, for me, it's a great opportunity, a paid holiday if you like. But for her it's just life as usual, only lonelier. Well, you must know what it's like yourself.'

'You mean, Morris being in England? It's great, just great.'

Philip politely pretended not to have heard this remark.

'Just to be able to stretch out in my own bed' – she gestured appropriately, revealing a rusty stubble under her armpit – 'without finding another human body in my way, breathing whisky fumes all over my face and pawing at my crotch . . .'

'I think I'd better be going back inside,' said Philip.

'Do I embarrass you, Mr Sparrow – Swallow? I'm sorry. Let's talk about something else. The view. Don't you think this is a great view? We have a view, too, you know. The same view. Everybody in Plotinus has the same view, except for the blacks and the poor whites on the flats down there. You've got to have a view if you live in Plotinus. That's the first thing people ask when you buy a house. Has it got a view? The same view, of course. There's only one view. Every time you go out to dinner or to a party, it's a different house, and different drapes on the windows, but the same fucking view. I could scream sometimes.'

'I'm afraid I can't agree,' said Philip stiffly. 'I could never get tired of it.'

'But you haven't lived with it for ten years. Wait a while. You can't rush nausea, you know.'

'Well, I'm afraid that after Rummidge . . .'

'What's that?'

'Where I come from. Where your husband's gone.'

'Oh yeah . . . What's it called, Rubbish?'

'Rummidge.'

'I thought you said Rubbish.' She laughed immoderately, and spilled some vodka on her frock. 'Shit. What's it like, then, Rummidge? Morris tried to make out it was the greatest, but everybody else says it's the asshole of England.'

'Both would be exaggerations,' said Philip. 'It's a large industrial city, with the usual advantages and disadvantages.'

'What are the advantages?'

Philip racked his brains, but couldn't think of any. 'I really ought to go back inside,' he said. 'I've scarcely met anyone . . .'

'Relax, Mr Sparrow. You'll meet them all again. It's the same people at all the parties in this place. Tell me more about Rubbish. No, on second thoughts, tell me more about your family.'

Philip preferred to answer the first question. 'Well, it's not really as bad as people make out,' he said.

'Your family?'

'Rummidge. I mean it has a decent art gallery, and a symphony orchestra and a Rep and that sort of thing. And you can get out into the country quite easily.' Mrs Zapp had lapsed into silence, and he began to listen to himself again, registering his own insincerity. He hated concerts, rarely visited the art gallery and patronized the local repertory theatre perhaps once a year. As for 'getting out', what was that but the dire peregrinations of Sunday afternoons? And in any case, what kind of a recommendation for a place was it that you could get out of it easily? 'The schools are pretty good,' he said. 'Well, one or two –'

'Schools? You seem really hung up on schools.'

'Well, don't you think education is terribly important?'

'No. I think our culture's obsession with education is self-defeating.'

'Oh?'

'Each generation is educating itself to earn enough money to educate the next generation, and nobody is actually *doing* anything with this education. You're knocking yourself out to educate your children so they can knock themselves out educating their children. What's the point?'

'Well, you could say the same thing about the whole business of getting married and raising a family.'

'*Exactly!*' cried Mrs Zapp. 'I do, I do!' She looked at her watch suddenly, and said, 'My God, I must go,' somehow managing to imply that Philip had been detaining her.

Unwilling to make a Noël-Coward-type entrance through the French windows in the company of Mrs Zapp, Philip bade her good evening and lingered alone on the terrace. When he had allowed her enough time to get off the premises, he would plunge back into the throng and try to find some congenial people who would offer him a lift home and perhaps invite him to share a meal. At that moment he became aware that the throng had fallen eerily silent. Alarmed, he hurried through the French windows and found that the living-room was quite deserted, except for a coloured, or rather black, woman emptying ashtrays. They stared at each other for a few moments.

'Er, where is everybody?' Philip stammered.

'Everybody gone home,' said the woman.

'Oh dear. Is Professor Hogan somewhere? Or Mrs Hogan?'

'Everybody gone home.'

'But this *is* their home,' Philip protested. 'I just wanted to say good-bye.'

'They gone somewhere to eat, I guess,' said the woman with a shrug, and recommenced her leisurely tour of the ashtrays.

'Damn,' said Philip. He heard the sound of a car starting

outside the house, and hurried to the front door just in time to see Mrs Zapp driving away in a big white station wagon.

Morris Zapp was standing at the window of his office at Rummidge, smoking a cigar (one of the last of the stock he had brought with him into the country) and listening to the sound of footsteps hurrying past his door. The hour for tea had arrived, and Morris debated whether to fetch a cup back to his office rather than drink it in the Senior Common Room, where the rest of the faculty would gather to gossip in the opposite corner or peer at him over their newspapers from his flanks. He gazed moodily down at the central quadrangle of the campus, a grassed area now thinly covered with snow. For some days, now, the temperature had wavered between freezing and thawing and it was difficult to tell whether the sediment thickening the atmosphere was rain or sleet or smog. Through the murk the dull red eye of a sun that had scarcely been able to drag itself above roof level all day was sinking blearily beneath the horizon, spreading a rusty stain across the snow-covered surfaces. Real pathetic fallacy weather, Morris thought. At which moment there was a knock on his door.

He swung round startled. *A knock on his door!* There must be some mistake. Or his ears were playing him tricks. The darkness of the room – for he had not yet switched on the lights – made this seem more plausible. But no – the knock was repeated. 'Come in,' he said in a thin, cracked voice, and cleared his throat. 'Come in!' He moved eagerly towards the door to welcome his visitor, and to turn the lights on at the same time, but collided with a chair and dropped his cigar, which rolled under the table. He dived after it as the door opened. A segment of light from the corridor fell across the floor, but did not reveal the hiding-place of the cigar. A woman's voice said uncertainly, 'Professor Zapp?'

'Yeah, come in. Would you switch the light on, please?'

The lights came on and he heard the woman gasp. 'Where are you?'

'Under here.' He found himself staring at a pair of thick

fur-lined boots and the hemline of a shaggy fur coat. To these was added, a moment later, an inverted female face, scarved, red-nosed and apprehensive. 'I'll be right with you,' he said. 'I dropped my cigar somewhere under here.'

'Oh,' said the woman, staring.

'It's not the cigar I'm worried about,' Morris explained, crawling around under the table. 'It's the rug . . . CHRIST!'

A searing pain bored into his hand and shot up his arm. He scrambled out from under the table, cracking his head on the underside in his haste. He stumbled round the room, cursing breathlessly, squeezing his right hand under his left armpit and clasping his right temple with his left hand. With one eye he was vaguely aware of the fur-coated woman backing away from him and asking what was the matter. He collapsed into his archchair, moaning faintly.

'I'll come back another time,' said the woman.

'No, don't leave me,' said Morris urgently. 'I may need medical attention.'

The fur coat loomed over him, and his hand was firmly removed from his forehead. 'You'll have a bump there,' she said. 'But I can't see any skin broken. You should put some witch-hazel on it.'

'You know a good witch?'

The woman tittered. 'You can't be too bad,' she said. 'What's the matter with your hand?'

'I burned it on my cigar.' He withdrew his injured hand from his armpit and tenderly unclasped it.

'I can't see anything,' said the woman, peering.

'There!' He pointed to the fleshy cushion at the base of his thumb.

'Oh, well, I think those little burns are best left alone.'

Morris looked at her reproachfully and rose to his feet. He went over to the desk to find a fresh cigar. Lighting it with trembling fingers, he prepared a little quip about getting your nerve back after a smoking accident, but when he turned round to deliver it the woman had disappeared. He shrugged and went to close the door, tripping, as he did so, over a pair of boots protruding from under the table.

'What are you doing?' he said.

'Looking for your cigar.'

'Never mind the cigar.'

'That's all very well,' came the muffled reply. 'But it isn't your carpet.'

'Well, it isn't yours either, if it comes to that.'

'It's my husband's.'

'Your husband's?'

The woman, looking rather like a brown bear emerging from hibernation, backed slowly out from under the table and stood up. She held, between the thumb and forefinger of one gloved hand, a squashed and soggy cigar-end. 'I didn't get a chance to introduce myself,' she said. 'I'm Hilary Swallow. Philip's wife.'

'Oh! Morris Zapp.' He smiled and extended his hand. Mrs Swallow put the cigar butt into it.

'I don't think it did any damage,' she said. 'Only it's rather a good carpet. Indian. It belonged to Philip's grandmother. How do you do?' she added suddenly, stripping off a glove and holding out her hand. Morris disposed of the dead cigar just in time to grab it.

'Glad to meet you, Mrs Swallow. Won't you take off your coat?'

'Thanks, but I can't stop. I'm sorry to barge in on you like this, but my husband wrote asking for one of his books. I've got to send it on to him. He said it was probably in here somewhere. Would you mind if I . . .' She gestured towards the bookshelves.

'Go ahead. Let me help you. What's the name of the book?'

She coloured slightly. 'He said it's called *Let's Write a Novel*. I can't imagine what he wants it for.'

Morris grinned, then frowned. 'Perhaps he's going to write one,' he said, while he thought to himself, 'God help the students in English 305.'

Mrs Swallow, peering at the bookshelves, gave a sceptical grunt. Morris, drawing on his cigar, examined her with curiosity. It was difficult to tell what manner of woman was hidden beneath the woollen headscarf, the huge shapeless fur coat, the thick zippered boots. All that could be seen was a round, unremarkable face with rosy cheeks, a red-tipped nose and the hint of a double chin. The red nose was evidently the result of a cold, for she kept sniffing discreetly and dabbing at it with a Kleenex. He went over to the bookshelves. 'So you didn't go to Euphoria with your husband?'

'No.'

'Why was that?'

The look she gave him couldn't have been more hostile if he had inquired what brand of sanitary towels she used. 'There were a number of personal reasons,' she said.

'Yeah, and I bet you were one of them, honey,' said Zapp, but only to himself. Aloud he said: 'What's the name of the author?'

'He couldn't remember. It's a book he bought second-hand, years ago, off a sixpenny stall. He thinks it has a green cover.'

'A green cover . . .' Morris ran his index finger over the rows of books. 'Mrs Swallow, may I ask you a personal question about your husband?'

She looked at him in alarm. 'Well, I don't know. It depends . . .'

'You see that cupboard over your head? In that cupboard there are one hundred and fifty-seven tobacco cans. All the same brand. I know how many there are because I counted them. They fell on my head one day.'

'They fell on your head? How?'

'I just opened the cupboard and they fell on my head.'

A ghost of a smile hovered on Mrs Swallow's lips. 'I hope you weren't hurt?'

'No, they were empty. But I'm curious to know why your husband collects them.'

'Oh, I don't suppose he collects them. I expect he just can't bear to throw them away. He's like that with things. Is that all you wanted to know?'

'Yeah, that's about all.' He was puzzled why a man who

used so much tobacco bought it in little tiny cans instead of the huge one-pound canisters like the ones Luke Hogan kept on his desk, but he thought this would be too personal for Mrs Swallow.

'The book doesn't seem to be here,' she said with a sigh. 'And I must be going, anyway.'

'I'll look out for it.'

'Oh, please don't bother. I don't suppose it's all that important. I'm sorry to have been such a nuisance.'

'You're welcome. I don't have too many visitors, to tell you the truth.'

'Well, it's nice to have met you, Professor Zapp. I hope you'll enjoy your stay in Rummidge. If Philip were here I'd like to ask you round for dinner one evening, but as it is . . . You understand.' She smiled regretfully.

'But if your husband was here, I wouldn't be,' Morris pointed out.

Mrs Swallow looked nonplussed. She opened her mouth a number of times, but no words came out. At last she said, 'Well, I mustn't keep you any longer,' and abruptly departed, closing the door behind her.

'Uptight bitch,' Morris muttered. Little as he coveted her company, he hungered for a home-cooked meal. He was tiring rapidly of TV dinners and Asian restaurants, which was all Rummidge seemed to offer the single man.

He found *Let's Write a Novel* five minutes later. The cover had come away from the spine, which was why they hadn't spotted it earlier. It had been published in 1927, as part of a series that included *Let's Weave a Rug*, *Let's Go Fishing* and *Let's Have Fun With Photography*. 'Every novel must tell a story,' it began. 'Oh, dear, yes,' Morris commented sardonically.

And there are three types of story, the story that ends happily, the story that ends unhappily, and the story that ends neither happily nor unhappily, or, in other words, doesn't really end at all.

Aristotle lives! Morris was intrigued in spite of himself. He turned back to the title page to check out the author. 'A. J.

Beamish, author of *A Fair But Frozen Maid, Wild Mystery, Glynis of the Glen*, etc., etc.' He read on.

The best kind of story is the one with a happy ending; the next best is the one with an unhappy ending, and the worst kind is the story that has no ending at all. The novice is advised to begin with the first kind of story. Indeed, unless you have Genius, you should never attempt any other kind.

'You've got something there, Beamish,' Morris murmured. Maybe such straight talking wouldn't hurt the students in English 305 after all, lazy, pretentious bastards, most of them, who thought they could write the Great American Novel by just typing out their confessions and changing the names. He put the book aside for further reading. Then he would take it round to Mrs Swallow one suppertime and stand on her stoop, salivating ostentatiously. Morris had a hunch she was a good cook, and he prided himself he could pick out a good cook in a crowd as fast as he could spot an easy lay (they were seldom the same person). Good plain food, he would predict; nothing fancy, but the portions would be lavish.

There was a knock at his door. 'Come in,' he called, expectantly, hoping that Mrs Swallow had repented and returned to invite him to share a chicken dinner. But it was a man who bustled in, a small, energetic, elderly man with a heavy moustache and bright beady eyes. He wore a tweed jacket, curiously stained, and advanced into the room with both hands extended. 'Mmmmmmmmmner, mmmmmmmmm-mmmmmmner, mmmmmmmmmmmmmmmmmmner,' he bleated. 'Mmmmmmmmmmmmmmmner mmmmmmmmmm-mmmmmmmmmner Masters.' He pumped Morris's hands up and down in a double handshake. 'Mmmmmmmmmmner Zapp? Mmmmmmmmmmmmmmmmner all right? Mmmmm-mmmmmmmmmmmmmner cup of tea? Mmmmmmmmmmmner jolly good.' He stopped bleating, cocked his head to one side and closed one eye. Morris deducted that he was in the presence of the Head of the Rummidge English Department, home from his Hungarian pig-shoot, and was being invited to partake of refreshment in the Senior Common Room.

Evidently the return of Professor Masters was the signal for which the rest of the faculty had been waiting. It was as if some obscure taboo had restrained them from introducing themselves before their chief had formally received him into the tribe. Now, in the Senior Common Room, they hurried forward and clustered around Morris's chair, smiling and chattering, pressing upon him cups of tea and chocolate cookies, asking him about his journey, his health, his work in progress, offering him belated advice about accommodation and discreetly interpreting the strangled utterances of Gordon Masters for his benefit.

'How d'you know what the old guy is saying?' Morris asked Bob Busby, a brisk, bearded man in a double-breasted blazer with whom he found himself walking to the car park – or rather running, for Busby maintained a cracking pace that Morris's short legs could hardly match.

'I suppose we've got used to it.'

'Has he got a cleft palate or something? Or is it that moustache getting between his teeth when he talks?'

Busby stepped out faster. 'He's a great man, really, you know,' he said, with faint reproach.

'He is?' Morris panted.

'Well, he was. So I'm told. A brilliant young scholar before the war. Captured at Dunkirk, you know. One has to make allowances . . .'

'What has he published?'

'Nothing.'

'Nothing?'

'Nothing anybody's been able to discover. We had a student once, name of Boon, organized a bibliographical competition to find something Gordon had published. Had students crawling all over the Library, but they drew a complete blank. Boon kept the prize.' He gave a short, barking laugh. 'Terrific cheek he had, that chap Boon. I wonder what became of him.'

Morris was pooped, but curiosity kept him moving along

beside Busby. 'How come,' he gasped, 'Masters is Head of your Department?'

'That was before the war. Gordon was extraordinarily young, of course, to get the Chair. But the Vice-Chancellor in those days was a huntin', shootin', fishin' type. Took all the candidates down to his place in Yorkshire for a spot of grouse-shooting. Naturally Gordon made a great impression. Story goes the most highly qualified candidate had a fatal accident with a gun. Or that Gordon shot him. Don't believe it myself.'

Morris could keep up the pace no longer. 'You'll have to tell me more another time,' he called after the figure of Busby as it receded into the gloom of the ill-lit car park.

'Yes, good night, good night.' To judge by the sound of his feet on the gravel, Busby had broken into a trot. Morris was left alone in the darkness. The flame of sociability lit by Masters' return seemed to have gone out as abruptly as it had flared up.

But the excitements of the day were not over. The very same evening he made the acquaintance of a member of the O'Shea ménage hitherto concealed from his view. At the customary hour the doctor knocked on his door and pushed into the room a teenage girl of sluttish but not unsexy appearance, raven-haired and hollow of cheek, who stood meekly in the middle of the floor, twisting her hands and peeping at Morris through long dark eyelashes.

'This is Bernadette, Mr Zapp,' said O'Shea gloomily. 'You've no doubt seen her about the house.'

'No. Hi, Bernadette,' said Morris.

'Say good evening to the gentleman, Bernadette,' said O'Shea, giving the girl a nudge which sent her staggering across the room.

'Good evening, sir,' said Bernadette, making a clumsy little bob.

'Manners a little lacking in polish, Mr Zapp,' said O'Shea in a loud whisper. 'But we must make allowances. A month ago she was milking cows in Sligo. My wife's people, you know. They have a farm there.'

90

Morris gathered that Bernadette had come to live with the O'Sheas as domestic slave labour, or 'Oh pear' as O'Shea preferred to phrase it. As a special treat the doctor had brought her along this evening to watch the colour TV. 'If that's not inconveniencing you, Mr Zapp?'

'Sure. What is it you want to watch, Bernadette, "Top of the Pops"?'

'Er, no, not exactly, Mr Zapp,' said O'Shea. 'The BBC 2 has a documentary on the Little Sisters of Misery, and Bernadette has an aunt in the Order. We can't get BBC 2 on the set downstairs, you see.'

This was not Morris's idea of an evening's entertainment, so having switched on the TV he retired to his bedroom with a copy of *Playboy* that had caught up with him in the mail. Stretched out on the penultimate resting place of Mrs O'Shea Sr., he ran an expert eye over Miss January's boobs and settled down to read a photo-feature on the latest sports cars, including the Lotus Europa which he had just ordered. One of the few satisfactions Morris had promised himself from his visit to England was the purchase of a new sports car to replace the Chevrolet Corvair which he had bought in 1965 just three days before Ralph Nader published *Unsafe at Any Speed*, thus reducing its value by approximately fifteen hundred dollars overnight and depriving Morris of any further pleasure in owning it. He had left Désirée with instructions to sell the Corvair for what she could get for it: that wouldn't be much, but he would save a considerable amount on the Lotus by taking delivery in England and shipping it back to Euphoria himself. *Playboy*, he was glad to note, approved of the Lotus.

Returning to the living-room to fetch a cigar, he found O'Shea asleep and Bernadette looking sullenly bored. On the screen a lot of nuns, photographed from behind, were singing a hymn.

'Seen your aunt yet?' he inquired.

Bernadette shook her head. There was a knock on the door and one of the O'Shea children stuck his head round the door.

'Please sir, will you tell me Dad Mr Reilly phoned and Mrs Reilly is having one of her turns.'

Such summonses were a common occurrence in the life of Dr O'Shea, who seemed to spend a fantastic amount of time on the road – compared, anyway, to American doctors, who in Morris's experience would only visit you at home if you were actually dead. Roused from his slumbers, O'Shea departed, groaning and muttering under his breath. He offered to remove Bernadette, but Morris said she could stay to watch out the programme. He returned to his bedroom and after a few minutes heard the sound of plainsong change abruptly into the driving beat of a current hit by the Jackson Five. There was still hope for Ireland, then.

A few moments later he heard footsteps thundering up the stairs, and the sound of the TV reverted to sacred music. Morris went into the living-room just as O'Shea burst in through the opposite door. Bernadette cowered in her seat, looking between the two men as if calculating which one was going to beat her first.

'Mr Zapp,' O'Shea panted, 'the devil take me if I can get my car to start. Would you be so good as to give me a push down the road? Mrs O'Shea would do it, but she's feeding the baby at this minute.'

'You want to use my car?' said Morris, producing the keys.

O'Shea's jaw sagged. 'God bless you, Mr Zapp, you're a generous man, but I'd hate to take the responsibility.'

'Go ahead. It's only a rented car.'

'Aye, but what about the insurance?' O'Shea went into the matter of insurance at such length that Morris began to fear for the life of Mrs Reilly, so he cut the discussion short by offering to drive O'Shea himself. The doctor thanked him effusively and galloped down the stairs, shouting over his shoulder to Bernadette that she was to leave Morris's room. 'Take your time,' said Morris to the girl, and followed him out.

Between giving Morris directions through the badly-lit back streets, O'Shea complimented Morris extravagantly on his car, a perfectly ordinary, rather underpowered Austin that he had rented at London Airport. Morris tried with some difficulty to imagine the likely reaction of O'Shea when he drove up in the burnt-orange Lotus, with its black leather bucket seats, remote-control spot lamp, visored headlights, streamlined wing-mirrors and eight-track stereo. Mother of God, he'd have a coronary on the spot.

'Down there, down there to your left,' said Dr O'Shea. 'There's Mr Reilly at the door, looking out for us. God bless you, Mr Zapp. It's terribly good of you to turn out on a night like this.'

'You're welcome,' said Morris, drawing up in front of the house, and fending off the attempts of the distracted Mr Reilly, evidently under the impression that Morris was the doctor, to drag him from behind the wheel.

But it *was* good of him, uncharacteristically good of Morris Zapp. The truth of the sentiment struck him more and more forcibly as he sat in the cold and cheerless parlour of the Reilly house waiting for O'Shea to finish his ministrations, and as he drove him back through the shadowy streets, listening with half an ear to lurid descriptions of Mrs Reilly's symptoms. He cast his mind back over the day – helping Mrs Swallow look for her husband's book, letting the Irish kid watch his TV, driving O'Shea around to his patients – and wondered what had come over him. Some creeping English disease of being nice, was it? He would have to watch himself.

Philip decided it was not too far to walk home from the Hogans' party, but wished he had phoned for a cab when it began to rain. He would really have to set about getting himself a car, a business he had postponed from fear of tangling with American second-hand car dealers, no doubt even more intimidating, venal and treacherous than their British counterparts. When he arrived at the house on Pythagoras Drive he discovered that he had forgotten his latch-key – the final aggravation of an evening already thoroughly spoiled by Charles Boon and Mrs Zapp. Fortunately someone was in the house, because he could hear music playing faintly; but he had to ring the bell several times before the door, retained by a chain, opened a few inches and the face of Melanie Byrd peered apprehensively through the aperture. Her face brightened.

'Oh, hi! It's you.'

'Terribly sorry – forgot my key.'

She opened the door, calling over her shoulder, 'It's OK, only Professor Swallow.' She explained with a giggle: 'We thought you were the fuzz. We were smoking.'

'Smoking?' Then his nostrils registered a sweetish, acrid odour on the air and the penny dropped. 'Oh, yes, of course.' The 'of course' was an attempt to sound urbane, but succeeded only in sounding embarrassed, which indeed he was.

'Like to join us?'

'Thank you, but I don't smoke. Not, that is . . .'

Philip floundered. Melanie laughed. 'Have some coffee, then. Pot is optional.'

'Thanks awfully, but I'd better get myself something to eat.' Melanie, he couldn't help observing, looked remarkably fetching this evening in a white peasant-style dress that reached to her bare feet, her long brown hair loose about her shoulders, her eyes bright and dilated. 'First,' he added.

'There's some pizza left from dinner. If you like pizza.'

Oh, yes, he assured her, he loved pizza. He followed Melanie down the hall to the ground-floor living-room, luridly lit by a large orange paper globe suspended about two feet from the floor, and furnished with low tables, mattresses, cushions, an inflatable armchair, brick-and-plank bookshelves and an expensive-looking complex of stereo equipment emitting plaintive Indian music. The walls were covered with psychedelic posters and the floor was littered with ashtrays, plates, cups, glasses, magazines and record sleeves. There were three young men in the room and two young women. The latter, Melanie's flat-mates Carol and Deirdre, Philip had already met. Melanie introduced him casually to the three young men, whose names he promptly forgot, identifying them by the various kinds of fancy dress they wore – one in Confederate Civil War uniform, one in cowboy boots and a tattered ankle-length suede topcoat and the third in loose black judo garb – he was also black himself and wore sunglasses with black frames, just in case there was any doubt about where he stood on the racial issue.

Philip sat down on one of the mattresses, feeling the shoulders of his English suit ride up to nuzzle his ears as he did so. He took off the jacket and loosened his tie in a feeble effort to fit in with the general sartorial style of the company. Melanie brought him a plate of pizza and Carol poured him a glass of harsh red wine from a gallon bottle in a wicker basket. While he ate, the others passed from hand to hand what he knew must be a 'joint'. When he had finished the pizza he hastily lit his pipe, thus excusing himself from partaking of the drug. Puffing clouds of smoke into the air, he gave a humorous account, which went down quite well, of how he had found himself left alone in the Hogans' house.

'You were trying to make out with this woman?' asked the black wrestler.

'No, no, I got trapped. As a matter of fact, she's the wife of the man I'm replacing here. Professor Zapp.'

Melanie looked startled. 'I didn't know that.'

'D'you know him?' Philip asked.

'Slightly.'

'He's a fascist,' said the Confederate Soldier. 'He's a well-known campus fascist. Everybody knows Zapp.'

'I took a course with Zapp once,' said the Cowboy. 'Gave me a lousy "C" for a paper that got an "A" the last time I used it. I told him, too.'

'What did he say.'

'Told me to fuck off.'

'Man!' The black wrestler dissolved into giggles.

'How about Kroop?' said the Confederate Soldier. 'Kroop lets his students grade themselves.'

'You're putting us on,' said Deirdre.

'It's true, I swear.'

'Don't everybody give themselves "A"s?' asked the black wrestler.

'It's funny, but no. As a matter of fact there was a chick who flunked herself.'

'Come on!'

'No bullshit. Kroop tried to talk her out of it, said her paper was worth at least a "C", but no, she insisted on flunking.'

Philip asked Melanie if she was a student at Euphoric State.

'I was. I sort of dropped out.'

'Permanently?'

'No. I don't know. Maybe.'

All of them, it appeared, either were or had been students at the University, but like Melanie they were vague and evasive about their backgrounds and plans. They seemed to live entirely in the present tense. To Philip, who was always squinting anxiously into his putative future and casting worried glances over his shoulder at the past, they were scarcely comprehensible. But intriguing. And friendly.

He taught them a game he had invented as a postgraduate student, in which each person had to think of a well-known book he hadn't read, and scored a point for every person present who *had* read it. The Confederate Soldier and Carol were joint winners, scoring four points out of a possible five with *Steppenwolf* and *The Story of O* respectively, Philip in each case accounting for the odd point. His own nomination, *Oliver Twist* – usually a certain winner – was nowhere.

'What d'you call that game?' Melanie asked Philip.

'Humiliation.'

'That's a great name. *Humiliation* . . .'

'You have to humiliate yourself to win, you see. Or to stop others from winning. It's rather like Mr Kroop's grading system.'

Another joint was circulating, and this time Philip took a drag or two. Nothing special seemed to happen, but he had been drinking the red wine steadily enough to keep up with the developing and enveloping mood of the party – for a party was what it appeared to be, or perhaps encounter group. This was a term new to Philip, which the young people did their best to explain to him.

'It's like, to get rid of your inhibitions.'

'Overcome loneliness. Overcome the fear of loving.'

'Recover your own body.'

'Understand what's really bugging you.'

They exchanged anecdotes.

'The worst is the beginning,' said Carol. 'When you're feeling all cold and uptight and wishing you hadn't come.'

'And the one I went to,' said the Confederate Soldier, 'we didn't know who was the group leader, and he didn't identify himself, like deliberately, and we all sat there for an hour, a solid hour, in total silence.'

'Sounds like one of my seminars,' said Philip. But they were too engrossed in the subject to respond to his little jokes.

Carol said: 'Our leader had a neat idea to break the ice. Everybody had to empty their purses and wallets on to the table. The idea was total self-exposure, you know, turning yourself inside out, letting everybody see what you usually keep hidden. Like rubbers and tampax and old love letters and holy medals and dirty pictures and all. It was a revelation, you've no idea. Like one guy had this picture of this man on a beach, completely naked except for a gun in a holster. Turned out to be the guy's father. How about that?'

'Groovy,' said the Confederate Soldier.

'Let's do it now,' said Philip, tossing his wallet into the ring.

Carol spread the contents on the floor. 'This is no good,' she said. 'Just what you'd expect to find. All very boring and moral.'

'That's me,' sighed Philip. 'Who's next?' But no one else had a wallet or a purse to hand.

'That's a lot of crap anyway,' said the Cowboy. 'In *my* group we're trying to learn body-language . . .'

'Are these your children?' Melanie asked, going through his photographs. 'They're cute, but they look kind of sad.'

'That's because I'm so uptight with them,' said Philip.

'And is this your wife?'

'She's uptight, too,' he said. He found the new word expressive. 'We're a very uptight family.'

'She's lovely.'

'That was taken a long time ago,' said Philip. 'Even I was lovely then.'

'I think you're lovely now,' said Melanie. She leaned over and kissed him on the mouth.

Philip felt a physical sensation he hadn't felt for more than twenty years: a warm, melting sensation that began in some deep vital centre of his body and spread outwards, gently fading, till it reached his extremities. He recaptured, in that one kiss, all the helpless rapture of adolescent eroticism – and all its embarrassment too. He couldn't bring himself to look at Melanie, but stared sheepishly at his shoes, dumb, his ears burning. Fool! Coward!

'Look, I'll show you,' said the Cowboy, stripping off his suede coat. He stood up and shoved aside with his foot some of the dirty crockery littering the floor. Melanie stacked up the plates and carried them out to the kitchen. Philip trotted ahead of her, opening doors, happy at the prospect of a tête-à-tête at the sink. Washing up was more his scene than body language.

'Shall I wash or wipe?' he asked, and then, as she looked blank: 'Can I help you with the dishes?'

'Oh, I'll just leave them to soak.'

'I don't mind washing up, you know,' he wheedled. 'I quite like it, really.'

Melanie laughed, showing two rows of white teeth. One of the upper incisors was crooked: it was the only flaw he could detect in her at this moment. She was pretty as a poster in her long white dress gathered under the bosom and falling straight to her bare feet.

'Let's just leave them here.'

He followed her back to the living-room. The Cowboy was standing back to back with Carol in the middle of the room. 'What you have to do is communicate by rubbing against each other,' he explained, suiting actions to words. 'Through your spine, your shoulder-blades –'

'Your ass . . .'

'Right, your ass. Most people's backs are dead, just *dead*, from not being used for anything, you dig?' The Cowboy made way for the Confederate Soldier, and began to supervise Deirdre and the black wrestler.

'You want to try?' Melanie said.

'All right.'

Her back felt straight and supple against his scholar's stoop, her bottom was pressed firmly and blissfully against his thin shanks, her hair was thrown back and cascaded down his chest. He was transported. She was giggling.

'Hey, Philip, what are you trying to tell me with the shoulder-blades?'

Someone dimmed the lights and turned up the sitar music. They swayed and pressed and wriggled against each other in the twanging, orange, smoky twilight, it was a kind of dance, they were all dancing, he was dancing – at last: the free, improvised, Dionysian dancing he'd hankered after. He was doing it.

Melanie's eyes were fixed on his, but vacantly. Her body was listening to the music. Her eyelids listened, her nipples listened, her little toes listened. The music had gone very quiet, but they didn't lose it. She swayed, he swayed, they all swayed, swayed and nodded, very slightly, keeping time, responsive to the sudden accelerations and slowings of the plucking fingers, the light patter of the drum, the swerves and undulations of tone and timbre. Then the tempo became faster, the twanging notes louder, faster and louder, and they moved more violently in response to the music, they writhed and twitched, stamped and lifted their arms and snapped their fingers and clapped their hands. Melanie's hair swept the floor and soared towards the ceiling, catching the orange light in its million fine filaments, as she bent and straightened from the waist. Eyes rolled, sweat glistened,

breasts bounced, flesh smacked flesh; cries, shrill and ec-
static, pierced the smoke. Then abruptly the music stopped.
They collapsed on to cushions, panting, perspiring, grinning.

Next, the Cowboy had them do foot massage. Philip lay
face down on the floor while Melanie walked up and down
his back in her bare feet. The experience was an exquisite
mixture of pleasure and pain. Though his face was pressed
to the hard floor, his neck twisted, the breath squeezed out of
his lungs, his shoulder-blades pushed nearly through his
chest and his spine was creaking like a rusty hinge, he
could have had an orgasm without difficulty – hardly surprising when you thought about it, some men paid good
money in brothels for this kind of thing. He groaned softly as
Melanie balanced on his buttocks. She jumped off.

'Did I hurt you?'

'No, no, it's all right. Carry on.'

'It's my turn.'

No, he protested, he was too heavy, too clumsy, he would
break her back. But she insisted, prostrated herself before
him in her white dress like a virgin sacrifice. Talk about
brothels . . . Out of the corner of his eye he saw Carol
jumping up and down on the mountainous figure of the
black wrestler, 'Stomp me baby, stomp me,' he moaned;
and in a dark corner the Cowboy and the Confederate
soldier were doing something extraordinary and complicated with Deirdre that involved much grunting and deep
breathing.

'Come on, Philip,' Melanie urged.

He took off his shoes and socks and climbed gingerly on to
Melanie's back, balancing himself with outstretched arms as
the flesh and bone yielded under his weight. Oh God, there
was a terrible kind of pleasure in kneading the soft girl's body
under his calloused feet, treading grapes must be rather like
it. He felt a dark Lawrentian joy in his domination over the
supine girl even as he felt concern for her lovely bosom
crushed flat against the hard floor, unprotected, unless he
was much mistaken, by any undergarment.

'I'm hurting you?'

'No, no, it's great, it's doing my vertebrae a whole lot of good, I can feel it.'

He balanced himself on one foot planted firmly in the small of her back and with the other gently rotated the cheek of each buttock in turn. The foot, he decided, was a much underestimated erogenous zone. Then he overbalanced and stepped backwards on to a coffee cup and saucer, which broke into several pieces.

'Oh dear,' said Melanie, sitting up. 'You haven't cut your foot?'

'No, but I'd better get rid of these pieces.' He slipped on his shoes and shuffled out to the kitchen with the broken fragments. As he was disposing of these in the trashcan, the Cowboy rushed into the kitchen and began opening cupboards and drawers. He was wearing only jockey shorts.

'Seen the salad oil anywhere, Philip?'

'People getting hungry again?'

'No, no. We're all gonna strip and rub each other with oil. Ever tried it? It's terrific. Ah!' He pulled out of a cupboard a large can of corn-oil and tossed it triumphantly in the air.

'Do you need pepper and salt?' Philip jested weakly, but the Cowboy was already on his way out. 'C'mon!' he threw over his shoulder. 'The party's beginning to swing.'

Philip laced up his shoes slowly, deferring decision. Then he went into the hall. Laughter, exclamations and more sitar music were coming from the darkened living-room. The door was ajar. He hesitated at the threshold, then moved on, out of the apartment, up the staircase to his own empty rooms, one part of himself saying ruefully, 'You're too old for that sort of thing, Swallow, you'd only feel embarrassed and make a fool of yourself and what about Hilary?' and another part of himself saying, 'Shit!' (a word he was surprised to hear himself using, even mentally) 'Shit, Swallow, when were you ever *young* enough for that sort of thing? You're just scared, scared of yourself and scared of your wife and think of what you've missed, rubbing salad oil into Melanie Byrd, just think of that!' Thinking of it, he actually turned round outside his door, debating whether to go back, but was surprised to find Melanie herself rustling up the stairs behind him to whisper, 'Mind if I crash in your place tonight? I happen to know one of those guys had clap not too long ago.'

'Not at all,' he murmured faintly, and let her in to the apartment, suddenly sober, his heart thumping and his bowels melting, wondering, was this it? – after twelve years' monogamy, was he going to make love to another woman? Just like that? Without preliminaries, without *negotiations*? He switched on the light inside the apartment, and they both blinked in the sudden dazzle. Even Melanie looked a little shy.

'Where d'you suggest I sleep?' she said.

'I don't know, where would you like to sleep?' He led her down the hall, throwing open doors like a hotel porter. 'This is the main bedroom,' he said, switching on the light and exhibiting the king-size bed that felt as big as a playing field when he stretched out in it at night. 'Or there's this other room which I use as a study, but it has a bed in it.' He went into the study and swept some books and papers off the couch. 'It's really quite comfortable,' he said, pressing the mattress with splayed fingers. 'Take your choice.'

'Well, I guess it depends on whether you want to fuck or not.'

Philip winced. 'Well, how do you feel about it?'

'I'd just as soon not, to tell you the truth, Philip. Nothing personal, but I'm tired as hell.' She yawned like a cat.

'In that case, you take my bed, and I'll sleep in here.'

'Oh no, I'll take the couch.' She sat down on it emphatically. 'This is fine, really.'

'Well, if you insist . . . the bathroom is at the end of the hall.'

'Thanks. This is really kind of you . . .'

'Don't mention it,' Philip said, bowing himself out of the room. He didn't know whether to feel glad or sorry at his dismissal, and the indecision kept him awake, rolling fretfully about in his king-size bed. He turned the clock-radio on low, hoping it would send him to sleep. It was tuned where he had left it the previous night, to the Charles Boon Show. The Black Pantheress was explaining to a caller the application of Marxist–Leninist revolutionary theory to the situation of oppressed racial minorities in a late stage of industrial capitalism. Philip switched off. After a while he went to the bathroom to get an aspirin. The door of his study was ajar, and without premeditation he turned into it. Melanie was sleeping peacefully: he could hear her deep, regular breathing. He sat down at his desk and turned on the reading lamp. Its hooded light threw a faint radiance on the sleeping girl, her long hair spread romantically over the pillow, one bare arm hanging to the floor. He sat in his pyjamas and looked at her until one of his feet went to sleep. As he tried to rub life back into it, Melanie opened her eyes, staring at him blankly, then fearfully, then with drowsy recognition.

'I was looking for a book,' he said, still rubbing his foot. 'Can't seem to get to sleep.' He laughed nervously. 'Too excited . . . at the thought of you in here.'

Melanie raised the corner of the coverlet in a silent gesture of invitation.

'Very kind of you, you're sure you don't mind?' he murmured, like someone for whom room has been made in a crowded railway compartment. The bed was indeed crowded when he got into it, and he had to cling to Melanie to avoid falling out. She was warm and naked and lovely to cling to. 'Oh,' he said, and, 'Ah.' But it wasn't altogether satisfactory. She was still half-asleep and he was half-distracted by the novelty of the situation. He came too soon and gave her little pleasure. Afterwards, in her sleep, tightening her arms round his neck, she whimpered, 'Daddy.' He stealthily disengaged himself from her embrace and crept back to his king-size bed. He did not lie down on it: he knelt at it, as though it were a catafalque bearing the murdered body of Hilary, and buried his face in his hands. Oh God, the guilt, the guilt!

*

And Morris Zapp felt some pangs of guilt as he listened, cowering behind his door, to the wails of Bernadette and the imprecations of Dr O'Shea, as the latter chastised the former with the end of his belt, having caught her in the act of reading a filthy book, and not merely reading it but abusing herself at the same time – an indulgence that was (O'Shea thundered) not only a mortal sin which would whisk her soul straight to hell should she chance to expire before reaching the confessional (as seemed, from her screams, all too possible) but was also a certain cause of physical and mental degeneration, leading to blindness, sterility, cancer of the cervix, schizophrenia, nymphomania and general paralysis of the insane . . . Morris felt guilty because the filthy book in question was the copy of *Playboy* he had been perusing earlier that evening, and which he himself had given to Bernadette an hour before, having discovered her reading it by the flickering light of the TV on his return from ferrying O'Shea to and from Mrs Reilly, so engrossed that she was a microsecond too late in closing the magazine and pushing it under the chair. Blushing and cringing, she stammered some apology as she sidled towards the door.

'You like *Playboy*?' Morris said soothingly. She shook her head suspiciously. 'Here, borrow it,' he said, and tossed her the magazine. It fell on the floor at her feet, opening, as it happened, on the centrefold of Miss January, tilting her ass invitingly at the camera. Bernadette flashed him a disconcertingly gap-toothed grin.

'T'anks mister,' she said; and snatching up the magazine, she disappeared.

Now her screams had subsided to a muffled sobbing and, hearing the footsteps of the outraged *paterfamilias* approaching, Zapp scuttled back to his chair and turned on the TV.

'Mr Zapp!' said O'Shea, bursting into the room and taking up his stand between Morris and the TV.

'Come in,' said Morris.

'Mr Zapp, it's no business of mine what you choose to read –'

'Would you mind raising your right arm just a little?' said Morris. 'You're cutting out part of the screen.'

O'Shea obligingly lifted his arm, thus resembling a man taking the oath in court. A luridly coloured advertisement for Strawberry Whip swelled like an obscene blister under his armpit. 'But I must ask you not to bring pornography into the house.'

'Pornography? Me? I haven't even got a pornograph,' Morris quipped, confident that the gag would be new to O'Shea.

'I'm referring to a disgusting magazine which Bernadette took from your room. Without your knowledge, I trust.'

Morris evaded this probe, which indicated that plucky Bernadette hadn't squealed. 'You don't mean my copy of *Playboy*, by any chance? But that's ridiculous, *Playboy* isn't *pornography*, for heaven's sake! Why, clergymen read it. Clergymen *write* for it!'

'Protestant clergymen, perhaps,' O'Shea sniffed.

'Can I have it back, please,' said Morris. 'The magazine.'

'I have destroyed it, Mr Zapp,' O'Shea declared severely. Morris didn't believe him. Inside thirty minutes he would be holed up somewhere, jerking himself off and drooling over the *Playboy* pix. Not the girls, of course, but the full-colour ads for whisky and hi-fi equipment . . .

The commercials on the TV ended and the credits for one of O'Shea's favourite series appeared on the screen accompanied by its unmistakable theme tune. The doctor began to watch out of the corner of his eye, while his body maintained a stiff pose of umbrage.

'Why don't you siddown and watch?' said Morris.

O'Shea subsided slowly into his customary chair.

'It's nothing personal you understand, Mr Zapp,' he muttered sheepishly. 'But Mrs O'Shea would never let me hear the last of it if she found the girl reading that sort of stuff. Bernadette being her niece, she feels responsible for the girl's moral welfare.'

'That's natural,' Morris said soothingly. 'Scotch or Bourbon?'

'A little drop of Scotch would be very welcome, Mr Zapp. I apologize for my outburst just now.'

'Forget it.'

'We're men of the world, of course. But a young girl straight from Sligo . . . I think it would put our minds at rest if you would keep any inflammatory reading matter under lock and key.'

'You think she may break in here?'

'Well she does come in to clean the rooms, in the day-time . . .'

'You don't say?'

Morris paid an extra thirty shillings a week for this service, and doubted whether much, if any, of the money found its way to Bernadette. Passing her on the stairs the next morning, Morris slipped her a pound note. 'I understand you've been cleaning my rooms,' he said. 'You've done a real nice job.' She flashed him her toothless grin and looked yearningly into his eyes.

'Shall I come to ye tonight?'

'No, no.' He shook his head in alarm. 'You misunderstand me.' But she had heard the heavy tread of Mrs O'Shea on the landing, and passed on. There was a time when Morris would have snapped up a chance like this, teeth or no teeth, but now – whether it was his age, or the climate, he didn't know – but he didn't feel up to it, he couldn't make the effort, or face the possible complications. He could picture all too easily the consequences of being found by the O'Sheas in bed with Bernadette, or even behind a door at which she was suing for admittance. Nothing was worth the price of looking for new accommodation in Rummidge in mid-winter. To avoid any accidents, and to give himself a well-deserved break, Morris decided to take a trip to London and stay overnight.

Philip woke sweating from a dream in which he was washing up in the kitchen at home. Plate after plate dropped from his nerveless fingers and smashed on the tiles underneath the sink. Melanie, who seemed to be helping him, was staring with dismay at the growing pile of shards. He groaned and rubbed his eyes. At first he was conscious only of physical discomfort: indigestion, headache and a sulphurous taste in his mouth. On his way to the bathroom his bleary gaze was drawn, through the open door of his study, to the tousled sheets on the couch, and he remembered. He croaked her name: 'Melanie?' There was no answer. The bathroom was empty. So was the kitchen. He drew the curtains in the living-room and cringed as daylight flooded the room. Empty. She had gone.

Now what?

His soul, like his stomach, was in turmoil. Melanie's casual compliance with his tired, clumsy lust seemed, in retrospect, shocking, moving, exciting, baffling. He couldn't guess what significance she might attach to the event; and didn't know, therefore, how to behave when they next met. But, he reminded himself, holding his throbbing head in both hands, problems of etiquette were secondary to problems of ethics. The basic question was: did he want to do it again? Or rather (since that was a silly question, who wouldn't want to do it again) *was* he going to do it again, if the opportunity presented itself? Not for nothing had he taken up residence in a Slide Area, he thought sombrely, gazing out of the window at the view.

He did a lot of looking out of the window that day, unwilling to venture out of his apartment until he had decided what to do about Melanie – whether to cultivate the connection, or pretend that nothing had happened. He thought of putting through a long-distance call to Hilary to see whether the sound of her voice would act like some kind of electro-shock therapy on his muddled mind, but at the last minute his courage failed him and he asked the operator for Interflora instead. The sun set on his indecision. He retired early and woke in the middle of the night after a wet dream. Clearly he was reverting rapidly to adolescence. He turned on the radio and the first word he heard was 'pollution'. Charles Boon was talking about the end of the world. Apparently the US Army had buried some canisters of nerve gas, enough to kill the entire population of the globe, deep in underground caves and encased in solid concrete, but unfortunately the US Army had overlooked the fact that the caves were on the line of the same geological fault that ran through the state of Euphoria.

The thing to do, Philip decided, was to see Melanie and have a heart-to-heart talk with her. If he explained his feelings, perhaps she could sort them out for him. What he had vaguely in mind was a mature, relaxed, friendly relationship which wouldn't entail their sleeping together again, but wouldn't entirely rule out such a possibility either. Yes, tomorrow he would see Melanie. He fell asleep again and dreamed, this time, that he was the last man out of Esseph at the time of its second and final earthquake. He was alone in an airplane taking off from Esseph airport, and as it hurtled down the runway he looked out of the window and saw cracks spreading like crazy paving in the tarmac. The plane lifted off just as the ground seemed to open to swallow it. It climbed steeply, and banked, and he stared out of the window at the unbelievable sight of the city of Esseph, its palaces and domes, its cloud-capped skyscrapers, burning and collapsing and sliding into the sea.

Next morning the Bay and the city were still there, smiling in the sunshine, awaiting the rabbit punch of the earthquake; but Melanie was not to be found – not that day, nor the next day, nor the day after that. Philip went in and out of the house at all hours, found pretexts for lingering in the hall and whistled loudly on the stairs, all to no avail. He saw Carol and Deirdre often enough and eventually summoned up the courage to ask them if Melanie was around. No, they said, she had gone away for a few days. Was there anything they could do for him? He thanked them: no.

That afternoon he fell over a pair of boots in a corridor of Dealer Hall which proved to belong to the Cowboy, squatting on the floor outside Howard Ringbaum's door, waiting for a consultation.

'Hi!' said the Cowboy, with a leer. 'How's Melanie?'

'I don't know,' said Philip. 'I haven't seen her lately. Have you?'

The Cowboy shook his head.

Ringbaum's thin, nasal voice floated out into the corridor: 'You seem to confuse the words *satire* and *satyr* in your paper, Miss Lennox. A satire is a species of poem; a satyr is a lecherous creature, half man, half goat, who spends his time chasing nymphs.'

'I have to be going,' said Philip.

'Ciao,' said the Cowboy. 'Hang loose.'

That was easier said than done. He felt himself sliding into obsession. That night he was sure it was Melanie's voice that he heard talking to Charles Boon on the radio. Tantalizingly, it was only the tail-end of the conversation that he caught when he switched on. 'Don't you think,' Melanie was saying, 'that we have to aim towards a whole new concept of interpersonal relationships based on sharing rather than owning? I mean, like a socialism of the emotions . . .'

'Right on!'

'And a socialism of sensations, and . . .'

'Yeah?'

'Well, that's all, I guess.'

'Well, thanks anyway, that was great.'

'Well, that's what I think, Charles. Good night.'

'Good night, and call again. Anytime,' Boon added meaningfully. The girl – was it Melanie? – laughed and rang off.

'Queue Ex Why Zee Underground Radio,' Charles Boon intoned. 'This is the Charles Boon Show, the one Governor Duck tried to get banned. Call 024-9898 and let's hear what's on your mind.'

Philip jumped out of bed, pulled on his dressing gown, and ran downstairs to the ground-floor apartment. He rang the bell. After a longish pause, Deirdre came to the door and called through it.

'Who are you?'

'It's me, Philip Swallow. I want to speak to Melanie.'

Deirdre opened the door. 'She's not here.'

'I just heard her speaking on the radio. She phoned in to the Charles Boon show.'

'Well, she didn't call from here.'

'Are you sure?'

Deirdre opened the door wide. 'You want to search the apartment?' she inquired ironically.

'I'm terribly sorry,' said Philip.

I must snap out of this, he said to himself as he climbed the stairs. I need a break, some distraction. On his next free day he took a bus across the long, double-decker bridge into downtown Esseph. He alighted at exactly the same moment (though seven hours earlier by the clock) that Morris Zapp, seated in the grill-room of the London Hilton, sank his teeth luxuriously into the first respectable-looking steak he had seen since arriving in England.

The Hilton was a damned expensive hotel, but Morris reckoned that he owed himself some indulgence after three weeks in Rummidge and in any case he was making sure that he got full value out of his occupation of the warm, sound-proofed and sleekly furnished room on the sixteenth floor. He had already showered twice since checking in, and walked about naked on the fitted carpet, bathed in fluent waves of heated air, had climbed back into bed to watch TV and ordered his lunch from Room Service – a club sandwich with french fries on the side preceded by a large Manhattan and followed by apple pie *à la mode*. All simple everyday amenities of the American way of life – but what rare pleasures they seemed in exile.

However, perhaps it was time he put his nose outside the revolving doors and took a look at Swinging London, he conceded, as he waddled from the dining-room with a comfortably full belly and selected an expensive Panatella from the cigar store in the lobby. He donned overcoat and gloves and a Khrushchev hat in black nylon fur he had bought from a Rummidge chain store, and sallied out into the raw London night. He walked along Piccadilly to the Circus, and then, via Shaftesbury Avenue, he found himself in Soho. Touts shivering in the doorways of strip-clubs accosted him every few yards.

Now Morris Zapp, who had lived for years on the doorstep of one of the world's great centres of the strip industry, namely South Strand in Esseph, had never actually sampled this form of entertainment. Blue movies, yes. Dirty books, of course. Pornography was an accepted diversion of the Euphoric intelligentsia. But strip-tease, and all the specialized variations on it indigenous to Esseph . . .

Which at this very moment Philip Swallow is observing for the first time: having walked to the South Strand district to look up old haunts he now stands gawping incredulously at the strip-joints that jostle each other all along Cortez Avenue – topless and bottomless ping-pong, roulette, shoe-shine, barbecue, all-in wrestling and go-go dancing – where once stood sober saloons and cafés and handicraft shops and art galleries and satirical nightclubs and poetry cellars, now GIRLS! GIRLS! GIRLS! and STRIP-STRIP-STRIP-STRIP in giant neon letters strain against the sun (for it is still only afternoon in Euphoria) and seek to lure the idle male into the smoky-coloured darkness behind the velvet curtains where rock music twangs and thuds and the girls pictured outside with huge polished breasts like the nose-cones of missiles 'DANCE BEFORE YOU ENTIRELY NAKED THEY HIDE ABSOLUTELY NOTHING . . .'

. . . that was strictly for hicks, tourists and businessmen. Morris Zapp's reputation as a sophisticate would have been destroyed the moment he was seen by a colleague or student patronizing one of the South Strand strip-bars. 'What, Morris Zapp? going to *topless* shows? Morris Zapp *paying* to see bare tits? What is this, Morris, not getting enough of it these days?' And so on and thus would have been the badinage. So Morris had never crossed the threshold of any strip-club on South Strand, though he had often felt a stab of low curiosity, passing on his way to a restaurant or movie-house; and now, standing amid the alien porn of Soho, six thousand miles from home, only strangers around to observe him, and not many of those (for it is a cold, raw night) he thinks, 'Why not?' and ducks into the very next strip-joint he comes to, under the nose of a disconsolate-looking Indian at the door.

And 'Why not?' thought Philip Swallow. 'It's something I've never seen and always wanted to and what's the harm and who's to know and anyway it's a phenomenon of cultural and sociological interest. I wonder how much it would cost.' He walked up and down the length of the Avenue assessing the establishments that were open this early in the day and eventually selected a small bar calling itself the Pussycat Go-go, which promised topless and bottomless dancers with no cover charge or other extras. He took a deep breath and plunged into the darkness.

'Good evening, sir,' said the Indian, smiling brilliantly. 'One pound, please sir. The performance is about to begin, sir.'

Morris paid his pound and pushed through a baize curtain and a swing door. He found himself in a small, dimly-lit room, with three rows of bentwood chairs drawn up before a small, low stage. A spotlight threw a pool of violet light on to the stage, and an ancient amplifier wheezed laboured pop music. The room was very cold and, except for Morris, entirely empty. He sat down in the middle of the front row of chairs and waited. After a few minutes, he went back to the entrance.

'Hey,' he said to the Indian.

'You like a drink, sir? Beer, sir?'

'I'd like to see some strip-tease.'

'Certainly, sir. One moment sir. If you would be a little patient. The girl arrives very soon, sir.'

'Is there only one?'

'One at a time, sir.'

'And it's cold as hell in there.'

'I bring heat, sir.'

Morris returned to his place and the Indian followed, trailing a small electric heater on a long cord – but not quite long enough to reach Morris. The heater glowed feebly in the violet murk some yards from his seat. Morris put on his hat and gloves, buttoned up his topcoat, and grimly lit a fresh cigar, determined to stick it out. He had made a terrible mistake, but he wasn't going to admit it. So he sat and smoked and stared at the empty stage, chafing his chilled limbs from time to time to keep the circulation going.

While Philip Swallow, having been prepared to be disappointed, cheated, frustrated and finally bored (for was that not the conventional wisdom concerning commercialized sex, that it was a fake and a bore?) found that on the contrary he was not at all bored, but quite entranced and delighted, sitting over a gin and tonic (dear at $1.50, but it was true there was no cover charge) while one of three beautiful young girls danced quite naked not three yards from his nose. And not only were they beautiful, but also unexpectedly wholesome and intelligent-looking, not at all the blowsy, blasé hoydens he had anticipated, so that one might almost suppose that they did it for love rather than money – as though liking, in any case, to shuffle their feet and wiggle their hips to the sound of pop music they thought they might as well take off their clothes while they were about it and give a little harmless pleasure to others at the same time. Three of them there were, and while one danced, another served drinks and the third rested. They wore briefs and little shifts like children's vests and they slipped in and out of these simple garments modestly but quite unselfconsciously in full view of the bar's clientele, for there was no changing-room in the cramped premises, striptease was quite the wrong term, there was no tease about it at all, and they gave each other little friendly pats on the shoulder as they changed over, with all the considerate camaraderie of a convent school relay team. Nothing could have been less sordid.

*

Morris's cigar was about half smoked when he heard the voice of a girl raised – apologetically or protestingly, he couldn't be sure, for she was suffering from a head cold – on the other side of the baize curtain. At length the Indian escorted her behind a rough-and-ready screen in one corner of the room. As she scuffed past in boots like Mrs Swallow's, wearing a headscarf and carrying a little plastic zipper-bag, she looked about as sexy as a Siberian Miss Five Year Plan. The Indian, however, plainly thought his reputation was saved. He was all smiles. Picking up a hand mike and fixing his gaze on Morris, who was still the only customer, he boomed out:

'GOOD EVENING LADIES AND GENTLEMEN! Our first performer this evening is Fifi the French Maid. Thank you.'

The music swelled as the Indian manipulated the knobs on his tape recorder, and a blonde wearing a minuscule lace apron over black underwear and stockings stepped into the spotlight and posed with a feather duster.

'Well I'm damned,' said Morris aloud.

Mary Makepeace (for that was who it was) took a step forward, shielding her eyes against the light. 'Who's that? I know that voice.'

'How was Stratford-upon-Avon?'

'Hey, Professor Zapp! What are you doing here?'

'I was going to ask you the same question.'

The Indian hurried forward. 'Please! please! Customers are not permitted to converse with the artistes. Kindly continue the performance, Fifi.'

'Yeah, continue, Fifi,' said Morris.

'Listen, this is no customer, this is someone I know,' said Mary Makepeace. 'I'm darned if I'm going to strip for *him*. With nobody else in the audience, too. It's indecent.'

'It's supposed to be indecent. That's what strip-tease is for,' said Morris.

'Please Fifi!' the Indian pleaded. 'If you begin, maybe other customers will come.'

'No,' said Mary.

'You're fired,' said the Indian.

'OK,' said Mary.

'Come and have a drink,' said Morris.

'Where?'

'At the Hilton?'

'You talked me into it,' said Mary. 'I'll fetch my coat.'

Morris hurried off eagerly to get a cab. The evening had been suddenly redeemed. He looked forward to getting better acquainted with Mary Makepeace in his cosy room at the Hilton. As the cab drew away from the kerb, he put his arm round her shoulders.

'What's a nice girl like you doing in a joint like that?' he said. 'To coin a phrase.'

'I hope it's understood I'm just having a drink with you, Professor Zapp?'

'Of course,' he said blandly. 'What else?'

'For one thing, I'm still pregnant. I didn't go through with the abortion.'

'I'm very glad to hear it,' Morris said flatly, removing his arm.

'I thought you would be. But there was nothing ethical about my decision, you understand? I still believe in a woman's right to determine her own biological destiny.'

'You do?'

'But I chickened out at the last moment. It was the nursing home. Girls wandering about in bedsocks with tears streaming down their cheeks. Toilet bowls full of blood . . .'

Morris shuddered. 'Spare me the details,' he begged. 'But what about the stripping bit? Isn't that exploitation?'

'Sure, but I desperately need the bread. This is one job you can do without a work permit.'

'What d'you want to stay in this lousy country for?'

'To have the baby here. I want him to have dual nationality, so he can avoid the draft when he grows up.'

'How d'you know it's going to be a boy?'

'Either way, I can't lose. Having babies is free in this country.'

'But how much longer can you do this type of work? Or are you changing your act to Fifi the pregnant maid?'

'I see your sense of humour hasn't changed, Professor Zapp.'

'I do my best,' he said.

While Philip, now nursing his fourth gin and tonic, and having studied the anatomies of the three Pussycat Go-go girls for some two hours, had reached, he felt, a profound insight into the nature of the generation gap: it was a difference of age. The young were younger. Hence more beautiful. Their skin had a bloom, they still had their back teeth, their bellies were flat, their breasts (ah!) were firm, their thighs (ah! ah!) were not veined like Danish Blue cheese. And how was the gap to be bridged? By love, of course. By girls like Melanie generously giving their firm young flesh to withered old sticks like himself, restoring the circulation of the sap. Melanie! How simple and good her gesture seemed in the clear light of his new understanding. How needlessly he had complicated it with emotions and ethics.

He stood up to leave at last. His foot had gone to sleep again, but his heart was full of goodwill to all men. It seemed entirely natural that, coming out of the Pussycat Go-go, dazzled by the sunbeams slanting low over Cortez Avenue, and a trifle unsteady on his feet because of the liquor and the pins and needles, he should collide with Melanie Byrd herself, as if she had materialized on the pavement in obedience to his wishes.

'Why, Professor Swallow!'

'Melanie! My dear girl!' He grasped her fondly with both hands. 'Where have you been? Why did you run away from me?'

'I didn't run away from anybody, Professor Swallow.'

'"Philip", please.'

'I've just been staying here in the city, with a friend.'

'A boy friend?' he asked anxiously.

'A girl friend. Her husband's in jail – he's one of the

Euphoria Ninety-Nine, you know? She gets kind of lonely . . .'

'I'm lonely too. Come back to Plotinus with me, Melanie,' he said, the words sounding thrillingly passionate and poetic to his own ears.

'Well, I'm kind of tied up right now, Philip.'

'Come live with me and be my love. And we will all the pleasures prove.' He leered at her.

'Take it easy, Philip.' Melanie smiled apprehensively, and attempted to disengage her arms from his grip. 'Those go-go girls have gotten you all excited. Tell me, I've always wondered, are they really quite naked?'

'Quite. But not as beautiful as you, Melanie.'

'That's very sweet of you, Philip.' She managed to free herself. 'I guess I must be going now. See you.' She began walking briskly towards the junction of Cortez Avenue and Main Street. Philip limped along beside her. The Avenue was getting busy. Cars honked and hummed in the road, pedestrians jostled them on the pavement.

'Melanie! You can't disappear again. Have you forgotten what happened the other night?'

'Do you have to tell everybody in the street?'

Philip lowered his voice: 'It was the first time it ever happened to me.'

She stopped and stared 'You mean — you were a *virgin*?'

'I mean apart from my wife, of course.'

She put her hand sympathetically on his arm. 'I'm sorry Philip. If I'd realized what a big deal it was for you, I wouldn't have gotten involved.'

'I suppose it meant absolutely nothing to you?' he said bitterly, hanging his head. The sun had dropped behind the rooftops and he shivered in a sudden gust of chill wind off the Bay. The glory had gone from the afternoon.

'It was one of those things that happen when you get a little high. It was nice, but . . . you know.' She shrugged.

'I know it wasn't very successful,' he mumbled. 'But give me another chance.'

'Philip, please.'

'At least have dinner with me here. I must talk . . .'

She shook her head. 'Sorry, Philip. I just can't. I have a date.'

'A date? Who with?'

'Just a guy. I don't know him all that well, actually, so I don't want to keep him waiting.'

'What are you going to do with him?'

Melanie sighed. 'If you must know, I'm going to help him look for an apartment. Seems his roommate freaked out on LSD and burned their place down last night. See you, Philip.'

'He can sleep in my spare room, if you like,' Philip bid desperately, clutching at her arm.

Melanie frowned, hesitated. 'Your spare room?'

'Just for a few days, while he's looking round. Phone him up and tell him. Then come and have dinner with me.'

'You can tell him yourself,' said Melanie. 'He's over there outside Modern Times.'

Philip stared across the gleaming, throbbing river of cars to the Modern Times Bookshop, once famous as the head-quarters of the Beat Generation. Outside, hunched slightly against the wind, hands thrust deep into the pockets of his jeans, making a bulge like a codpiece, was Charles Boon.

3. Corresponding

Hilary to Philip

Dearest,

Many thanks for your airletter. We were all glad to hear
that you had arrived safely, especially Matthew, who saw
pictures of an air-crash in America on television and was
convinced that it was your plane. Now he's worried by your
joke about living in a house that's going to slide into the sea
at any moment, so will you please put that right in your
next letter.

I expect the girls underneath you will take pity on your
wifeless state and offer to wash your shirts and sew buttons
etc. I can't see you coping with that washing-machine in the
basement. Incidentally I'm afraid our own washing-
machine is making a terrible grinding noise and the service
man says the main bearing is going and it will cost £21 to
repair. Is it worth it, or shall I trade it in for a new one
while it's still working?

Yes, the view, I do remember it so well, though from the
other side of the Bay of course – you remember that funny
little attic apartment we had in Esseph. When we were
young and foolish . . . Ah well, no point in getting sentimental, with you 6000 miles away, and me with the washing
up still to do.

Oh – before I forget – I've not been able to find *Let's Write
a Novel*, either here or at the University. Though I couldn't
make a really thorough search at the University because Mr
Zapp is already occupying your room. I can't say I took to
him. I asked Bob Busby how he was settling in, and he said
that very few people had seen much of him – he seems to be a

rather silent and standoffish person, who spends most of his time in his room.

Fancy your meeting that rogue Charles Boon on the plane, and his being such a success out there. Americans *are* rather gullible, aren't they?

Love from all of us here,
Hilary

Désirée to Morris

Dear Morris,

Thank you for your letter. Really. I enjoyed it. Especially the bits about Dr O'Shea and about the four different kinds of electric sockets in your rooms and the Department notice-board. The kids enjoyed those bits too.

I guess it's the first real letter I've ever received from you – I mean apart from scrawls on hotel notepaper about meeting you at the airport or sending on your lecture notes. Reading it made you seem almost human, somehow. Of course, I could see you were trying like hell to be witty and charming, but that's all right, as long as I'm not taken in. And I'm not. Are you receiving me, Morris? I AM NOT TAKEN IN.

I'm not going to change my mind about the divorce, so please don't waste typewriter ribbon trying to make me. And for that matter, don't abstain from sexual intercourse on my account, either. There was a hint to that effect in your letter, and I'd hate you to feel, when you return, that you'd thrown away six months' good screwing for nothing.

A propos of that, isn't the Lotus Europa you've ordered a somewhat *young* car for you? I saw one in downtown Esseph yesterday and, well, frankly it's just a penis on wheels, isn't it? As regards the Corvair, I didn't forget to put a card in the Co-op last week, but there's been only one inquiry so far and unfortunately I was out. Darcy took the call and God knows what he told the guy.

The Winter quarter begins this week and, surprise,

surprise, there are signs of trouble on campus. A bomb exploded in the men's john on the fourth floor of Dealer last week, presumably intended to go off while one of your colleagues was taking a crap, but the building was evacuated as the result of a tip-off. The Hogans invited me to a lousy cocktail party, but I didn't talk to anyone much, it was the usual crowd of schmucks plus a new one, Charles Boon of the ditto radio show. Oh yes, I nearly forgot, and I met your opposite number, Philip Swallow. I was somewhat slewed by this time and kept calling him Sparrow, but he took it straight on the stiff upper lip. Jesus, if all the British are like him I don't know how you're going to survive. He hadn't even

Coincidence: just as I was writing that last sentence, I looked out of the window and who should be walking up the drive but Mr Swallow himself. Not so much walking, actually, as crawling up on his hands and knees. He'd climbed all the way up here on foot from the campus – said it didn't look so far on the street map and he hadn't realized that the road was practically vertical. Turned out he was the guy who had called about the Corvair and he'd come to look at it. So it was too bad I'd met him at the Hogans because of course I had to tell him all about Nader etc. And naturally enough he decided against it. Actually, I felt kind of sorry for him. Apparently he's already been conned into renting a house built on a slide area so if he'd bought the Corvair he'd have been a pretty lousy actuarial risk whether he went out or stayed at home.

It is very quiet and pleasant here without you, Morris. I have turned the TV to the wall, and spend a lot of time reading and listening to classical music on the hi-fi – Tchaikovsky and Rimsky-Korsakov and Sibelius, all that Slav romanticism you made me feel ashamed of liking when we first met.

The twins are fine. They spend a lot of time holed up together somewhere and I expect they are experimenting sexually but figure there's nothing I can do about it. Biology is their great passion at the moment. They have even developed an interest in gardening, which I have encouraged, naturally, by donating a sunny corner of our precipitous yard. They send you their love. It would be hypocritical of me to do the same.

Désirée

PS. No, I haven't seen Melanie around. Why don't you write to her yourself?

Hilary to Philip

Dearest,

A man from Johnson's came round this morning with a huge bunch of red roses which he said you had sent by Interflora. I said there must be some mistake because it wasn't my birthday or anything, but he wouldn't take them back to the shop. I phoned Johnson's and they said, yes, you had ordered them. Philip, is anything the matter? It's not like you. Roses in January must have cost the earth. They were hothouse, naturally, and are dying already.

Did you get my last letter about not being able to find *Let's Write a Novel*? It seems a long time since we heard from you. Have you started teaching yet?

I met Janet Dempsey at the supermarket and she said that Robin was determined to move if he doesn't get promotion this session. But surely they can't give him a senior lectureship before you, can they? He's so much younger.

Write soon, love from
Hilary

PS. The noise from the washing-machine is getting worse.

Philip to Hilary

Darling,

I was stricken with guilt as soon as I saw your second airletter this morning. *Mea culpa*, but it has been a rather hectic week, with the term, or quarter as they call it, beginning;

and I'd hoped that the roses would have been some assurance that I was alive and kicking and thinking of you. Instead of which they seem to have had the opposite effect. I confess I'd put back a fair amount of gin the night before, and perhaps the roses were a morning-after act of atonement. The cocktail party was given by Luke Hogan, the Chairman of the Department, whose wife enlisted my help in coaxing Charles Boon to come and be lionized, an irony I could have done without. Among the other guests was Mrs Zapp, extremely tight, and in a highly aggressive mood. I didn't take to her at all, but since then, through an odd coincidence, I've had to revise my estimate somewhat in her favour. I followed up an advertisement for a second-hand Chevrolet Corvair, which turned out to be the Zapps' second car. But when Mrs Zapp recognized me she told me that the Corvair is considered an unsafe model, and very honestly advised me not to buy it.

The Zapps live in a luxurious house, in some disarray when I called, at the top of an incredibly steep hill. There are two young Zapps, twins, called rather preposterously Elizabeth and Darcy (Zapp is a Jane Austen man, of course – indeed *the* Jane Austen man in the opinion of many). The gossip here is that their marriage is breaking up, and Mrs Zapp intimated as much to me, so I suppose that might account for her rather off-putting manner, and his too, by the sound of it. The divorce rate is fantastically high here. It's rather disturbing when one is used to a more stable social environment. So is the way everybody, including Mrs Zapp, uses four-letter words all the time, even in front of their own children. It's a bit of a shock at first, hearing faculty wives and nice young girls saying 'shit' and 'fuck', as one might say 'Gee whizz', or 'darn it'. Rather like one's first week in the army.

I confess I had something of the raw-recruit feeling when I went to meet my classes for the first time this week. The system is so different, and the students are so much more heterogeneous than they are at home. They've read the most outlandish things and not read the most obvious ones.

I had a student in my room the other day, obviously very bright, who appeared to have read only two authors, Gurdjieff (is that how you spell him?) and somebody called Asimov, and had never even heard of E. M. Forster.

I'm teaching two courses, which means I meet two groups of students three times a week for ninety minutes, or would do if it weren't for the Third World Students' strike. There's a student called Wily (*sic*) Smith, who claims he's black, though in fact he looks scarcely darker than me, and he pestered me from the day I arrived to let him enrol in my creative writing course. Well, I finally agreed, and then on the first occasion the class met, what d'you think happened? Wily Smith harangued his fellow students and persuaded them that they must support the strike by boycotting my class. There's nothing personal in it, of course, as he was kind enough to explain, but it did seem rather a nerve.

Well, darling, I hope the length of this letter will make up for my remissness of late. Please assure Matthew that my house is not about to slide into the sea. As to Robin Dempsey, I think it's unlikely that he'll get a senior lectureship this year, promotion prospects being what they are at Rummidge, but not through any competition with me, I'm afraid. He has published quite a lot of articles.

All my love,
Philip

Morris to Désirée

All right, so you're determined to divorce me, Désirée. OK, so you hate my guts, but don't break my heart. I mean, punish me if you must, but there's no need to be downright sadistic about it. Unless you're joking. You're joking, yes? You didn't really throw away the chance to sell the Corvair to Swallow? You didn't actually *advise* him NOT to buy it? Swallow – very probably the only prospective purchaser of a used Corvair in the State of Euphoria. If by any chance Mr Swallow is still thinking it over, get on the phone at once, please, and offer to come down a couple of hundred dollars. Offer green stamps and a tankful of gas, too, if that will help.

Désirée, your letter did nothing to lighten a heavy week. It isn't true after all that there are no students at British universities: this week they returned from their prolonged Christmas vacation. Too bad, I was just beginning to get the hang of things. Now the teaching has thrown me back to square one. I swear the system here will be the death of me. Did I say system? A slip of the tongue. There is no system. They have something called tutorials, instead. Three students and me, for an hour at a time. We're supposed to discuss some text I've assigned. This, apparently, can be anything that comes into my head, except that the campus bookshop doesn't have anything that comes into my head. But supposing we manage to agree, me and the students, on some book of which four copies can be scratched together, one of them writes a paper and reads it out to the rest of us. After about three minutes the eyes of the other two glaze over and they begin to sag in their chairs. It's clear they have stopped listening. I'm listening like hell but can't understand a word because of the guy's limey accent. All too soon, he stops. 'Thank you,' I say, flashing him an appreciative smile. He looks at me reproachfully as he blows his nose, then carries on from where he paused, in mid-sentence. The other two students wake up briefly, exchange glances and snigger. That's the most animation they ever show. When the guy reading the paper finally winds it up, I ask for comments. Silence. They avoid my eye. I volunteer a comment myself. Silence falls again. It's so quiet you can hear the guy's beard growing. Desperately I ask one of them a direct question. 'And what did *you* think of the text, Miss Archer?' Miss Archer falls off her chair in a swoon.

Well, to be fair, it only happened once, and it had something to do with the kid's period that she fainted, but somehow it seemed symbolic.

Believe it or not, I'm feeling quite homesick for Euphoric State politics. What this place needs is a few bomb outrages. They could begin by blowing up the Chairman of the

English Department, one Gordon Masters, whose main interest is murdering wildlife and hanging the corpses on the walls of his office. He was captured at Dunkirk and spent the war in a POW camp. I can't imagine how the Germans stood him. He runs the Department very much in the spirit of Dunkirk, as a strategic withdrawal against overwhelming odds, the odds being students, administrators, the Government, long hair on boys, short skirts on girls, promiscuity, Casebooks, ball-point pens – just about the whole modern world, in short. I knew he was mad the first time I saw him, or half-mad, because it only shows in one eye and he's cunning enough to keep it closed most of the time, while he hypnotizes the faculty with the other one. They don't seem to mind. The tolerance of people here is enough to turn your stomach.

If you notice a certain acidity in my prose today, and hypothesize some wound inflicted on that tender plant, my pride, you wouldn't be far wrong, Désirée, my dear. I was in the Library today, looking through the files of *The Times Literary Supplement* for something, when quite by chance I turned up a long review of that Festschrift for Jackson Milestone that I contributed to in '64, remember? No, of course, you make a point of forgetting anything I have written. Anyway, take my word for it, I wrote a dashing piece on 'Apollonian-Dionysian Dialectic in the novels of Jane Austen' for this collection, but for some reason I had never seen this particular review before. Naturally I skimmed through the columns to see whether there was any comment on my contribution, and sure enough there it is: 'Turning to Professor Zapp's essay . . .' and I can see at a glance that my piece is honoured with extensive discussion.

Imagine receiving a poison-pen letter, or an obscene telephone call, or discovering that a hired assassin has been following you about the streets all day with a gun aimed at the middle of your back. I mean, the shock of finding some source of anonymous malice in the world directed specifically at you, without being able to identify it or account for it. Because this guy really wanted to hurt. I mean, he wasn't content merely to pour scorn on my arguments and my evidence and my accuracy and my style, to make my article out to be some kind of monument to imbecility and perversity in scholarship, no, he wanted my blood and my balls too, he wanted to beat my ego to a pulp.

Of course I need hardly say that the author was completely out of his mind, that his account of my essay was a travesty, and his own arguments riddled with false assumptions and errors of fact that a child could have seen through. But, but – this is the turn of the screw – there's nothing I can do about it. I mean I can't write to the *TLS* saying, in the usual style, 'My attention has been drawn to a review published in your journal four years ago . . .' I should just look ridiculous. That's what bugs me about the whole business – the time-slip. It's only just happened to *me*, but to everybody else it's history. All these years I've been walking around with a wound I never knew had been inflicted. All my friends must have known – they must have seen the knife sticking out between my shoulder-blades – but not one sonofabitch had the decency to tell me. Afraid I'd bite their fucking heads off, I suppose, and so I would have done, but what are friends for anyway? And my enemy, who is he? Some PhD student I flunked? Some limey scholar whose book I chewed up in a footnote? Some guy whose mother I ran over in my car without noticing? Do you remember, Désirée, any exceptionally heavy bump in the road, driving somewhere four or five years ago?

Désirée, your concern that I should have a full sex-life while I am over here is touching, but you should think twice before you put such generous thoughts in writing: it could louse up your divorce petition, though I continue to hope that our marital problem is not terminal. In any case, I haven't felt inclined to avail myself of your kind dispensation. They have winter here, you see, Désirée – the old seasonal bit, and the sap is sunk low at the moment.

Tell me more about the twins. Or, better, ask them to write a line to their old Dad, if the Euphoric public school system is still teaching such outdated skills as writing. But that is great about the gardening. O'Shea is what you might call an avant-gardener. He believes in randomness. His yard is a wilderness of weeds and heaps of coal and broken play equipment and wheelless prams and cabbages, silted-up bird baths and great gloomy trees slowly dying of some unspecified disease. I know how they must feel.

Love,
Morris

PS. I did write to M. but it was sent back marked Not Known Here. Try to get me her new address, will you, from the Dean of Students' Office?

Hilary to Philip

Dearest,

Many thanks for your long and interesting letter. What a pity, though, that you had to write those words in it. Because I couldn't of course let Amanda read it, though she pestered me for days. Rather thoughtless of you, dear, wasn't it, because naturally the children are interested in your letters. And I must say it seemed to me quite uncalled for.

You didn't tell me, by the way, that there was a bomb explosion in your building shortly after you arrived, but I suppose you didn't want to worry us. Were you in any danger? If things get any worse you'll just have to come home, and bother the money.

By the way, as you didn't answer my question about the washing-machine I have bought a new one. Fully automatic and rather expensive, but it's super.

I heard about the bomb from Mr Zapp. A very curious encounter, which I must tell you about. He came round the other evening with *Let's Write a Novel*, which he'd found in your room after all. It was the most awkward time, about 6, just as I was about to serve up the dinner, but I felt I had to invite him in since he'd taken the trouble to bring your book round and he looked rather pathetic standing in the

slush outside the front door wearing galoshes and an absurd
kind of cossack's hat. He didn't need any persuading –
practically knocked me over in his eagerness to get in the
house. I took him into the front room for a quick sherry, but
it was like an iceberg – I don't bother to light a fire in there
now you're away – so I had to take him into the dining-
room, where the children were just beginning a fight because they were hungry for their dinner. I asked him if he
would mind finishing his drink while I served the children
their meal, hoping this would be a hint to him to leave
promptly, but he said no, he didn't mind and I should eat
too, and he took off his hat and coat and sat down to watch
us. And I mean watch us. His eyes followed every movement
from dish to plate to mouth. It was acutely embarrassing.
The children fell eerily silent, and I could see that Amanda
and Robert were looking at each other and going red in the
face with suppressed giggles. In the end I had to ask him if he
wouldn't like to join us at the table.

I don't think I've ever seen anyone so heavily built move
quite so fast. It was lucky that I'd cooked a biggish joint
because there wasn't much left on the bone by the time Mr
Zapp had had his third helping. Though his table manners
left something to be desired, I didn't really begrudge him the
food, since he was obviously starved of decent home cooking.
He also did his best to entertain the children, and made quite
a hit with Amanda because he seemed to know all about her
favourite pop songs – the names of the singers and the titles of
the records and how high they had got in the Top Twenty
and so on, which seemed to me quite extraordinary in a man
of his age and profession, but impressed the children hugely,
especially Amanda as I say. But I presumed he'd have the
tact to scoot off fairly soon after dinner, and served coffee
straight away to give him the hint. No such luck. He sat on
and on, telling stories – admittedly rather funny ones – about
the extraordinary household he is living in (a doctor called
O'Shea – have you heard of him?) until eventually I just
had to send Matthew off to bed and Robert and Amanda to
do their homework. When I started ostentatiously clearing

the table he insisted on helping me wash up. He obviously had no idea how to do it and broke two plates and a glass before I could stop him. By this time I was beginning to panic a bit, wondering if I was ever going to get him out of the house.

Then suddenly he completely changed. He asked me where the lavatory was and when he came back he was fully dressed in his outdoor clothes and scowling all over his face. He growled out a good-bye and a curt thank you and rushed out of the house into a whirling snowstorm. He started his car and let out the clutch far too quickly and as a result got stuck in the gutter. I listened to his wheels spinning and his engine howling until I couldn't stand it any longer. So I put on my fur coat and boots and went out to give him a push. I got him out all right, but overbalanced in the process and fell sprawling.

As I picked myself off the ground I saw him disappear round the corner, skidding wildly, for he didn't stop or even call out thank you. If Mrs Zapp wants to divorce him she has my sympathy.

I saw Janet Dempsey again this morning (we seem to have fixed on the same day for supermarket shopping) and she said Robin knows that he's definitely on Gordon's list of nominations for senior lectureships. Are you on it? I think what gets me is the way Janet implies that I'm naturally going to be as fascinated by her husband's career as she is. Also the pointed way she never refers to or asks about yours, as if it were a dead issue. Professor Zapp says you have to push yourself to get on in the academic world, that nobody ever gets anything unless they ask for it, and I'm inclined to think he's right.

Do you still want me to send on *Let's Write a Novel*? What a funny little book it is. There's a whole chapter on how to write an epistolary novel, but surely nobody's done that since the eighteenth century?

Love from all of us here,
Hilary

Philip to Hilary

Darling,

Many thanks for your letter. What an extraordinary fellow Zapp seems to be. I hope he won't bother you any more. Frankly, the more I hear about him, the less I like him. In particular, I shouldn't like Amanda to see more of him than is absolutely unavoidable. The fact is that the man is entirely unprincipled where women are concerned, and while he's not, as far as I know, another Humbert Humbert, I feel he might have an insidiously corrupting influence on an impressionable girl of Amanda's age. So, at least, I infer from Mrs Zapp, who recited a catalogue of her husband's sins to me in the course of an extremely drunken and disorderly party to which we were both invited last Saturday. Our hosts were Sy and Bella Gootblatt. He's a young associate professor here – very brilliant, I believe, has written the definitive study of Hooker. The Hogans were there, and three other couples all from the English Department, which may sound rather inbred, but you must remember that the English Department here is nearly as big as the entire Arts Faculty at Rummidge.

The tempo of a Plotinus dinner party takes some getting used to. To begin with, the invitation for eight really means eight-thirty to nine, as I realized from the consternation on my host's face when I appeared on his doorstep one minute after the appointed hour; and even when all the guests are assembled there are several hours' hard drinking to be got through before you actually sit down to eat. During this time the hostess (Bella Gootblatt in see-through blouse and flared crushed velvet trousers) brings from the kitchen delicious snacks – sausages rolled in crisp bacon, cheese fondue, sour-cream dips, tender hearts of artichokes, smoked fish and suchlike tangy delicacies, thus increasing one's thirst for the lavish whisky-sours and daiquiris being prepared by the host. The consequence is that when you finally sit down to dine, at about eleven pm, everyone is totally sloshed and not very hungry. The food is half-spoiled anyway by being kept warm so long. Everybody drinks a great deal of wine to try and wash down a respectable amount of food and so they all get drunker than ever. Everybody is shouting at the tops of their voices and cracking jokes frenziedly and screaming with laughter and then someone will say something just a bit too outrageous and suddenly there's murder in the air.

Mrs Zapp was seated next to me at dinner. As we were sitting over the coffee and the ruins of some intolerably sweet chocolate gateau, I tried to stem her flow of intimate reminiscence by teaching the company how to play 'Humil-iation'. Do you remember that old game? You've no idea how difficult it was to get across the basic idea. On the first round they kept naming books they *had* read and thought everyone else hadn't. But when they finally got the hang of it, they began to play with almost frightening intensity, especially a young chap called Ringbaum who ended up having a tremendous row with our host and left the house in a huff. The rest of us stayed on for an hour or so, mainly (as far as I was concerned anyway, for I was quite exhausted) to smooth over the awkwardness of this contretemps with Ring-baum.

The bomb, yes, I didn't think there was any point in worrying you by mentioning it. There's been no repetition of the incident, though there's still a good deal of disruption on campus due to the strike. As I write this, sitting in my 'office' as they call it, I can hear the chanting of the pickets rising up from Mather gate just below my window, 'ON STRIKE, SHUT IT DOWN, ON STRIKE, SHUT IT DOWN!' A very strange sound in an academic environment. Every now and then there is a confrontation at the Gate between the pickets and people trying to get through and then the cam-pus police intervene and occasionally the Plotinus police force too and there's usually a scuffle and a few arrests. Yesterday the police made a sweep through the campus and students were running in all directions. I was sitting at my desk reading *Lycidas* when Wily Smith burst into my room and shut the door behind him, leaning against it with closed eyes, just like a film. He was wearing a motor-cycle helmet as protection against the police truncheons (nightsticks as they rather sinisterly call them) and his face was glistening with Vaseline which is supposed to protect your skin against MACE. I asked him what he wanted and he said he wanted a consultation. I had my doubts but dutifully plied him with questions about his ghetto novel. He answered distractedly, his ears cocked for sounds of police activity in the building. Then he asked me if he could use my window. I said, certainly. He threw his leg over the sash and climbed out on to the balcony. After a few minutes I put my head out, but he had disappeared. I suppose he must have found a window open further along the balcony and left that way. The noise gradually faded. I went on reading *Lycidas* . . .

I've no idea whether I've been nominated for a Senior Lectureship and I'd rather keep it that way, since I shan't then have the mortification of knowing that I was definitely turned down. If Dempsey wants to poke his nose into such matters, let him. I think myself that there's a lot to be said for the English system of clandestine patronage. Here, for instance, it's a jungle in which the weakest go to the wall. There's been the most tremendous row going on all this week about a question of tenure – involving the Ringbaum chap, as it happens – and I'm glad to be well out of it.

You'll be surprised to learn that Charles Boon is living with me at the moment! He had to leave his previous quarters at short notice due to a fire and I offered to put him up temporarily at the request of his girl friend, who lives downstairs. I can't say he's applied himself very energetically to looking for a new apartment, but he's not much trouble to me as he sleeps most of the day and is out most of the night.

All my love,
Philip

What does he look like, Désirée, for Christ's sake? What manner of man is he? Swallow, I mean. Do his canines hang out over his lower lip? Is his handshake cold and clammy? Do his eyes have a murderous glint?

He wrote it, Désirée, he wrote that review, out of pure impersonal spite, one sunny day five years ago he dipped his pen in gall and plunged it into the heart of my lovely article.

I can't prove it – yet. But the circumstantial evidence is overwhelming.

When I think that you dissuaded him from buying the Corvair . . . the perfect revenge! Désirée, how could you?

I found a copy of that Festschrift, you see, in his house. In the john, to be exact. A very strange john it is, too, a large room obviously designed originally for some other purpose, perhaps ballroom dancing, in which the WC has been placed on a plinth in one corner. A tiled floor and a small oil lamp burning to prevent the water pipes from freezing give the whole place a slightly spooky ecclesiastical atmosphere. There are books there too, not specially selected reading for the can, but overspill from the rest of the house, which is practically lined with crappy old books stinking of wet-rot and bookworm droppings. The Milestone book has been festering in my subconscious ever since I read that review in the *TLS*, so I identified its binding and gilt lettering right away. A curious coincidence, I thought to myself, picking the volume off the shelf – for after all it wasn't exactly a world best-seller – and leafed through it as I sat on the can. Imagine my feelings when I turned to my article and found that *the passages which had been marked exactly corresponded to those cited by the TLS reviewer*. Imagine the effect on my bowels.

Why don't you write to me any more, Désirée? I am lonely here these long English nights. Just to give you an idea how lonely I am, this evening I'm going to the English Department's Staff Seminar to listen to a paper on linguistics and literary criticism.

Love,
Morris

Dear Morris,

If you really want to know, Philip Swallow is about six feet tall and weighs I should say about 140 pound – that is, he's tall and skinny and stooped. He holds his head forward as if he's hit it too often on low doorways. His hair is the texture of Brillo pads before they've been used and is deeply receding at the temples. He has dandruff, but who hasn't? He has nice eyes. I couldn't say anything positively in favour of his teeth, but they don't protrude like fangs. His handshake is normal in temperature, if a little on the limp side. He smokes one of those patent air-cooled pipes which leaks tobacco juice all over his fingers.

I had an opportunity to observe all this because I was seated next to him at dinner last Saturday. The Gootblatts invited me. There seems to be a general conspiracy here to pretend that I am lonely in your absence and must be invited out. It turned out to be a fairly sensational evening, with our friend Swallow right in the centre of the action.

Doing his British best to redeem what was looking to be a draggy dinner, he taught us a game he claims to have invented, called 'Humiliation'. I assured him I was married to the World Champion, but no, he said, this was a game you won by humiliating *yourself*. The essence of the matter is that each person names a book which he hasn't read but assumes the others have read, and scores a point for every person who has read it. Get it? Well, Howard Ringbaum didn't. You know Howard, he has a pathological urge to succeed and a pathological fear of being thought uncultured, and this game set his two obsessions at war with each other, because he could succeed in the game only by exposing a gap in his culture. At first his psyche just couldn't absorb the paradox and he named some eighteenth-century book so obscure I can't even remember the name of it. Of course, he came last in the final score, and sulked. It was a stupid game, he said, and refused to play the next round. 'I pass, I pass,' he said sneeringly, like Mrs Elton on Box Hill (I may not read your

135

books, Zapp, but I remember my Jane Austen pretty good). But I could see he was following the play attentively, knitting his brows and twisting his napkin in his fingers as the point of the game began to dawn on him. It's quite a groovy game, actually, a kind of intellectual strip poker. For instance, it came out that Luke Hogan has never read *Paradise Regained*. I mean, I know it isn't his field, but to think you can get to be Chairman of the English Department at Euphoric State without ever having read *Paradise Regained* makes you think, right? I could see Howard taking this in, going a bit pale when he realized that Luke was telling the truth. Well, on the third round, Sy was leading the field with *Hiawatha*, Mr Swallow being the only other person who hadn't read it, when suddenly Howard slammed his fist on the table, jutted his jaw about six feet over the table and said:

'*Hamlet!*'

Well, of course, we all laughed, not very much because it didn't seem much of a joke. In fact it wasn't a joke at all. Howard admitted to having seen the Lawrence Olivier movie, but insisted that he had never read the text of *Hamlet*. Nobody believed him of course, and this made him sore as hell. He said did we think he was lying and Sy more or less implied that we did. Upon which Howard flew into a great rage and insisted on swearing a solemn oath that he had never read the play. Sy apologized through tight lips for having doubted his word. By this time, of course, we were all cold sober with embarrassment. Howard left, and the rest of us stood around for a while trying to pretend nothing had happened.

A piquant incident, you must admit – but wait till I tell you the sequel. Howard Ringbaum unexpectedly flunked his review three days later and it's generally supposed that this was because the English Department dared not give tenure to a man who publicly admitted to not having read *Hamlet*. The story had been buzzed all round the campus, of course, and there was even a paragraph alluding to it in the *Euphoric State Daily*. Furthermore, as this created an unexpected vacancy in the Department, they've reconsidered the case of Kroop and offered him tenure after all. I don't suppose he's read *Hamlet* either, but nobody was asking. The students are wild with joy. Ringbaum is convinced Swallow conspired to discredit him in front of Hogan. Mr Swallow himself is blissfully ignorant of his responsibility for the whole drama.

I'm sorry to have to report that the twins' sudden craze for gardening turned out to be an attempt to cultivate marijuana. I had to root up all the plants and burn them before the cops got wise.

I'm told Melanie hasn't enrolled this term, so I couldn't get her address from the University.

Désirée

Hilary to Philip

Dearest,

I had the most frightful shock this morning. Bob Busby rang me up to ask how you were. I said you were fine as far as I knew, and he said, 'Jolly good, so he's out of hospital, then?' and poured out a horrifying story he'd got from some student about how you had been taken hostage by a gang of desperate Black Panthers and held out of a fourth-floor window by your ankles and finally shot in the arm when the police burst into the building blazing away with their guns. It was only about halfway through this lurid tale that I recognized it as a wildly distorted and embroidered version of an anecdote in your last letter which I presumably put into circulation in the first place. I think I must have mentioned it to Janet Dempsey.

Incidentally, Bob told me that Robin took rather a pasting from Morris Zapp at the last Staff Seminar. It seems that Mr Zapp, despite his somewhat Neanderthal appearance and loutish manners, is really quite clever and knows all about these fashionable people like Chomsky and Saussure and Lévi-Strauss that Robin has been browbeating the rest of you with, or at least enough about them to make Robin look fairly silly. I gather all present derived a certain quiet satisfaction from the proceedings. Anyway, I began to think more kindly of Mr Zapp, which was rather fortunate for him, as he turned up again yesterday evening to beg a rather odd favour.

It took him some time to get to the point. He kept looking round the room, and asking me about the house and how many bedrooms it had, and wasn't I lonely living on my own, until I began to fear that he wanted to move in with me. But no, it appeared he was looking for accommodation for a friend, a young lady, and he wondered whether I would consider, as a special favour, letting her rent a room. I told him that we'd had students living in the house once and found it such hell that we'd vowed never to have lodgers again. He looked rather crestfallen at that, so I asked him if he'd looked in the Rummidge papers. He shook his head dolefully and said it was no good, they'd already tried several addresses and nobody would have the girl. People were prejudiced against her, he said. Was she coloured, I asked compassionately. No, he said, she was pregnant.

Well, after what you'd said in your last letter about Mr Zapp's reputation, I drew my own conclusions, which must have been pretty clearly written on my face, for he hastily assured me that he was not responsible. He'd met her on the plane coming over, he said, and he was the only person she knew in England, so she'd turned to him for help. She's an American girl who came to England to get an abortion, but decided at the last moment that she didn't want to go through with it. She wants to have the baby in England because it would then have dual nationality and if it was a boy he would be able to avoid the draft, should the Viet Nam War still be going on in twenty years' time. She'd worked illegally for a while in Soho as a waitress, but had to give it up because her pregnancy was beginning to show. And then she had some money stolen.

Well, this story sounded so implausible that I wondered whether he could possibly have invented it. I didn't know what to think. Where was this girl now, I asked? Outside in his car, he replied, to my astonishment. Well, it was a freezing night, so I told him to bring her inside at once. He was off like a shot and I followed him to the front door. It was like some scene from a Victorian novel, the snow, the fallen woman, etc., but in reverse, because she was coming in instead of going out, if you see what I mean. And I admit to feeling a mite sentimental as she crossed the threshold, with snowflakes melting in her long blonde hair. She was turning blue with cold, poor thing, and practically speechless either from that or shyness. Mary Makepeace is her name. There didn't seem to be anything else to do but ask her to stay the night, so I made some soup (Professor Zapp wolfed three bowls) and packed her off to bed with a hot water bottle. I told Mr Zapp I would have her to stay for a few days while they worked out something but that I couldn't commit myself to having her indefinitely. However, I'm seriously thinking of letting her stay on. She seems to be a very nice girl, and would be company in the evenings. You know I still get frightened in the night sometimes – silly, I know, but there it is. I'll have to see how we get on on closer acquaintance, of course, and I haven't made any promises. But if I should be inclined to let Mary stay, I presume you wouldn't have any objections? She'd pay for her board and lodging, of course – apparently she didn't lose all her money, and Mr Zapp was very insistent that he would help financially. I imagine he can afford it. He was driving some incredibly low-slung and expensive-looking orange sports car yesterday, which is to replace the one you didn't buy.

I hope, by the way, that Charles Boon is making a contribution to *your* rent. A hint to that effect might be one way of getting rid of him.

All love,
Hilary

ps. Mr Zapp asked particularly that if I wrote to you about Mary you should regard all information about her as confidential.

Darling,

Just a note in haste to say that I should think very carefully before you take this girl of Zapp's into the house. And she surely *is* Zapp's girl. Whether he's the father of her child, or not, is another question, but doesn't affect the likely nature of their relationship. I can understand how you would naturally feel sorry for the girl and want to help, but I think you've got to consider yourself in this, and the children, especially Amanda. She's at a very sensitive and impressionable age now – have you thought of the consequences of having an unmarried mother on the premises? The same goes for Robert, for that matter. I can't believe that it would be a good thing for the children. Then Zapp would no doubt be in and out of the house all day – and possibly all night too. Have you thought of *that*? I'm a reasonably tolerant person but I draw the line at providing a room in my house for Mr Zapp to have it off with his pregnant girl-friend, and I wonder whether you would be able to cope with such a situation, should it arise. Then one has to face the fact, whether one likes it or not, that 'people will talk' – and I don't mean just the neighbours, but the people at the University, too.

All in all, I'm not in favour. But of course you must do what you think best.

The situation is getting uglier here. Some windows have been smashed, and catalogue cards in one of the small specialist libraries scattered over the floor. Every lunch hour there is a ritual confrontation which I watch from the balcony outside my room. A large crowd of students, hostile to the police if not positively sympathetic to the strikers, gathers to watch the pickets parading. Eventually someone is jostled, the police intervene, the crowd howls and screams, rocks are thrown, and out of the scrimmage the police come running, dragging some unfortunate student behind them and take him to a temporary lockup under the Administration building, pursued by the hooting mob. Perched up on my safe balcony I feel rather despicable, like those ancient kings who used to watch their set battles from specially built towers. Afterwards one goes home and watches it all over again on the local TV news. And the next morning there are reports and photos in the *Euphoric State Daily* – that's the campus paper, produced with incredible speed and professionalism by the students; makes our own once-a-week *Rumble* seem a rather amateurish effort.

All my love,
Philip

PS. I hope you realize that Mary Makepeace is almost certainly an *illegal immigrant* in the eyes of the law, and that you could get into trouble for harbouring her?

Hilary to Philip

Dear Philip,

I may as well come straight to the point. I've had what I believe is called a poison-pen letter from Euphoria, an anonymous letter. It says you are having an affair with Morris Zapp's daughter. I know it's not true but please write at once and tell me that it isn't. I keep bursting into tears and can't tell anybody why.

Love,
Hilary

XY42 Ab 151 INTL PLOTINUS EUPH 60 9
WESTERN UNION

MRS HILARY SWALLOW
49 ST JOHNS RD
RUMMIDGE
ENGLAND

POTTY UPPERCOCK COCK COCK COCK
UTTER POPPYCOCK OF COURSE STOP ZAPPS

DAUGHTER ONLY NINE YEARS OLD STOP
LETTER FOLLOWS LOVE PHILIP

PHILIP SWALLOW
1037 PYTHAGORAS DR
PLOTINUS EUPH

Morris to Désirée

Will you do me a favour, Désirée, and move your ass over to
1037 Pythagoras Drive and find out what the hell is going on
there? I had a letter this morning, no signature, saying that
Philip Swallow is shacked up with Melanie at that address.
You may laugh, but just check it out for me, will you?
There is a kind of outrageous logic in the notion that makes
me think it may just be true. It would fit my idea of Swallow
and the role he seems destined to play in my life. Having
assassinated my academic character in the *TLS*, he pro-
ceeds to screw my daughter. That figures. I tremble,
Désirée, I tremble.

                                                    Morris

PS. The envelope is franked by the University, so it must be
someone on the faculty or a secretary who sent the letter.
Who?

Philip to Hilary

Darling Hilary,
    This is the most difficult letter I have ever had to write.
    Morris Zapp *has* got a daughter – apart from the nine-
year-old. Her name is Melanie and I *did* sleep with her once.
Just once. So the wire I sent you was not quite true. But it
wasn't a lie, either. I have only just discovered that Zapp is
Melanie's father and it's been as much of a shock to me as it
will have been to you. Let me try and explain.

142

Melanie is Zapp's daughter by his first marriage. She calls herself Melanie Byrd, which is her mother's maiden name, because she doesn't want to be associated with her father at Euphoric State, for several good reasons. She came here as a student because as the child of a tenured faculty member she is entitled to free tuition, but she has stayed away from Zapp as much as possible and kept their relationship strictly secret. I got all this information from Mrs Zapp and Melanie this afternoon. They were in the house together when I got home. I should explain that Melanie is one of the girls on the ground floor. Early on in my time here I quite by chance got drawn into a kind of impromptu party downstairs. I'd just come from cocktails at the Hogans' and was a bit squiffy already. What with one thing and another I suppose I got quite 'high', but when they started making preparations for an orgy, I retired gracefully. So, however, did Melanie. She took it for granted that we should sleep together. So I'm afraid we did.

I'm not going to try and justify or excuse myself. I was wretched afterwards, thinking what I'd done to you. It wasn't even particularly enjoyable at the time, because I was fuddled with drink and Melanie was half-asleep. I'm quite sure it meant absolutely nothing to her, and you must believe that it only happened on that one occasion. In fact since then – this would be funny in a less anguished context – she's become Charles Boon's steady girl friend. In the circumstances, there seemed to be no point in upsetting you by saying anything about the episode, and it began to sink into oblivion. When I got your letter it revived my guilty conscience, though I didn't connect Melanie with Morris Zapp for a moment. I presumed someone was playing a rather sick joke – who and for what reason I couldn't, and still can't – imagine. But it put me in a difficult moral dilemma.

Well, as you know, I took the easier way out, one which I persuaded myself would also be easier on you. But when I discovered the true state of affairs, I immediately sat down to put the record straight. It's now about midnight, so you'll realize how difficult I've found it. I'm sorry, very sorry, Hilary. Please forgive me.

All my love,
Philip

Désirée to Morris

Dear Morris,

Much as I hate to do you a favour, my curiosity got the better of me, so I hied me over to 1037 Pythagoras in accordance with your brusque instructions. I had to take a detour through the downtown area as the traffic was snarled up due to riots on the Campus at the Cable Street entrance. I could hear gas grenades popping and a lot of yelling and a police helicopter circling overhead all the time: I tell you, it gets more like Viet Nam here every day.

1037 Pythagoras is a house that has been converted into two apartments. Nobody answered the bell on the first floor so I went upstairs and tried the second-floor apartment. Eventually Melanie answered the door, looking flushed and rumpled. Before you start grinding your teeth and fingering your horsewhip, let me finish. We were both surprised, Melanie more so, naturally. 'Désirée! What are you doing here?' she exclaimed. 'I might ask you the same question,' I snapped back in my best Perry Mason manner. 'I thought Philip Swallow lived here.' 'He does but he's out.' 'Who is it, Mel, the Gestapo?' said a voice from within. I looked over Melanie's shoulder and there was Charles Boon, propped up against the wall dressed in a towelling bath-robe and smoking a cigarette. 'Somebody for Philip,' she called back. 'Philip's out,' he said. 'He's at the University.' 'Do you mind if I wait?' I asked. Melanie shrugged: 'Please yourself.'

I eased myself over the threshold and penetrated into the apartment. Melanie closed the door and followed me. 'This is Désirée, my father's second wife,' she said to the gaping

Boon. 'And this is –' 'I recognize Mr Boon, dear,' I interrupted. 'We were at the same party a few weeks ago. I didn't have the opportunity, Mr Boon,' I prattled on, 'to tell you how much I hate your show.' He smiled and blew smoke through his teeth while he thought up a riposte; one of his eyes was levelled on me while the other one was shooting about the room as if in search of inspiration. 'If someone your age liked the show,' he said at last, 'I'd know I'd failed.' We fenced like this for a while, weighing each other up. It was apparent that Boon was living in Swallow's apartment, which I must say surprised me because I always understood from Swallow that he couldn't stand the guy. However, it certainly looked as though Boon and Melanie had been in the sack together that afternoon, and as neither of them showed any sign of panic when Swallow's latchkey turned in the hall door I assumed that this was not a possibility they were anxious to conceal from him. He was startled of course to see me there, fussed around getting us all tea, but didn't seem particularly defensive. I had just decided that his relationship to Melanie was purely avuncular when it came out that you were her father. He went white, Morris. I mean, if he'd just discovered that he'd screwed his *own* daughter, he couldn't have looked more shocked. I suppose, on reflection, there is something kind of incestuous about sleeping with the daughter of the guy you've exchanged jobs with. Though if he's having sex with Melanie presently, it must be something very kinky because Charles Boon is right in there too, for sure.

As to the author of the poison-pen letter, I will hazard a guess that the author is Howard Ringbaum, who has a motive and is cheap enough to use university mail facilities for the purpose – he's the kind of guy who would make a heavy-breathing call collect if he could get away with it.

                                                            Désirée

Morris to Désirée

Many thanks for your quick reply, but why didn't you ask Swallow straight out for Chrissake? I enclose a Xerox of the anonymous letter so that you can confront him with it. What a louse. Mrs Swallow has been looking so miserable lately that I have a shrewd suspicion she's had one of those letters too. She's a kind-hearted person, I've found, and I feel sorry for her. She told me, by the way, that Boon was once a student of Swallow's. Yes, they're old buddies, so it's all too probable they've got some very corrupt scene going there with Melanie. Poor little Melanie. I feel really bad about her. I mean I didn't suppose she was still a virgin or anything, but that is no life for a young girl, being passed from one guy to another. Maybe if you and I could make a fresh start, Désirée, she would come and live with us.

Morris

Désirée to Morris

Dear Morris,

Will you stop putting on this concerned parent act before I die laughing? It's a little late in the day to start talking about giving a stable home life to 'little Melanie'. You should have thought about that before you walked out on her and her mother. Little Melanie, in case you've forgotten, hasn't forgiven you for that; and since it was me you walked out on her for (leaving her a five-dollar bill to buy candy, if I remember rightly, the most sordid transaction in the history of conscience-money) she isn't exactly spilling over with love for me either.

I've no intention of confronting Philip Swallow with your dirty little piece of paper. Neither he nor Melanie owe *me* any explanation. Write and ask them yourself if you must. But before you work up too much righteous indignation, and as long as explanations are the order of the day, you might come clean about that blonde cookie you've parked on big-hearted Mrs Swallow. Rumour has it that she's pregnant. Don't tell me that you're going to pollute the planet with another little Zapp, Zapp? I've heard about the hypocrisy of the English, but I didn't know it was contagious.

Désirée

Philip to Hilary

Darling Hilary,

It's two weeks now since I wrote to you, and I am finding it a strain waiting for your reply. If you haven't already written, please don't keep me waiting any longer. I had hoped that by making a clean breast of everything I should make it possible for you to forgive and forget, and that we could put the whole thing behind us.

I hope you aren't thinking of divorce, or anything silly like that?

It's very difficult to discuss these things by letter. How can you make up a misunderstanding when you're 6000 miles apart? We need to see each other, talk, kiss and make up. I've been thinking, why don't you come out here at Easter on a 17-day excursion? I know the fare is expensive, but what the hell. I expect your mother would take the children in the holiday, wouldn't she? Or perhaps you could even leave them with this Mary Makepeace girl. It would be a real holiday for both of us, away from the kids and everything. What is called a 'second honeymoon', I believe – a rather horribly coy phrase but not such a bad idea. D'you remember what fun we had in that scruffy little apartment in Esseph?

Do think about it seriously, darling, and don't be put off by the student troubles. The signs are that with the end of the winter quarter things will quieten down and some kind of compromise will be worked out between the students and the Administration. Today there were no arrests for the first time in weeks. Perhaps the weather has something to do with it. Spring has really arrived, the hills are green, the sky is blue, and it's eighty degrees in the shade. The bay is winking in the sun, and the cables of the Silver Span are shimmering like harpstrings on the horizon. I walked through the campus today at lunchtime and you could sense the change of mood. Girls in summer dresses and people playing guitars. You would enjoy it.

All my love,
Philip

Morris to Désirée

Désirée,

You're not going to believe this, I know, but Mary Makepeace and I are just good friends. I have never made love to her. I admit the thought has crossed my mind, but she was pregnant when I first met her and I'm squeamish about laying girls who are already pregnant by other guys. Something not quite kosher about it, if you know what I mean. Especially in this case, since the father is a Catholic priest. Did I tell you the plane I flew over in was full of women going to England for abortions? Mary was one of them – she was sitting next to me and we got talking. A few weeks ago I came back from the University one afternoon to be ambushed by O'Shea in the lobby. He leaped out at me from behind the grandfather clock and dragged me into the front parlour, which at this time of year is like the North Pole, huge upholstered armchairs looming out of the fog like icebergs. O'Shea was very agitated. He said that a young woman who was obviously in 'a certain condition', but not wearing a ring, had called asking for me and had insisted on waiting in my rooms. It was Mary, of course – she'd decided to stay in England and have the baby, but she'd just lost her job and had some money stolen and turned for help to the only person in the country she knew – me. I tried to calm O'Shea down, but he had the fear of God and Mrs O'Shea in him. It was obvious that nothing was going to persuade him I wasn't responsible for Mary's 'condition'.

He gave me an ultimatum: either Mary had to leave or me. I couldn't very well abandon the girl, so I tried to find her a place to stay. But there was nothing doing in Rummidge that night. The landladies we talked to obviously regarded Mary as a whore and me as a small-time gangster. I couldn't even find a hotel that admitted to having a vacant room. Then we happened to pass Mrs Swallow's house, and I thought, why not try her? Which we did, successfully. In fact the two of them have become great buddies and it looks like Mary is going to stay there until she has the baby. I didn't see the point of boring you with all this, and I didn't think Swallow would be so cheap as to run to you with the story.

Morris

Hilary to Philip

Dear Philip,

Many thanks for your last letter. I'm sorry I didn't reply immediately to the previous one, but as it took you six or seven weeks to get round to telling me about Melanie Zapp (or Byrd) it seemed to me that I was entitled to take as many days thinking about my reply.

That doesn't mean to say that I'm considering a divorce – a remarkably panicky reaction on your part, I thought. I take it that you've been quite candid with me, and that you're no longer involved with the girl. I must say it was unfortunate that of all the girls in Euphoria, you had to pick on Mr Zapp's daughter. Also somewhat ironic, not to say hypocritical, that you should have been so exercised about *his* bad influence on *your* daughter. I showed Mary your letters and she says your obsessive concern to protect Amanda's innocence indicates that you are really in love with her yourself, and that your affair with Melanie was a substitute gratification for the incestuous desire. An interesting theory, you must admit. Does Melanie look anything like Amanda?

As to your suggestion that I fly out to Euphoria for a holiday, it's not on, I'm afraid. First of all I wouldn't dream of asking either Mary or my mother to take on the responsibility of the children, and I don't think we could afford to fly them out to Euphoria – or me on my own for that matter. You see, Philip, I decided not to wait any longer for the central heating, but to have it put in immediately on the HP. It was the first thing I did after receiving your letter about Melanie: I got out the telephone book and began ringing round to heating contractors for estimates. I suppose that sounds funny, but it was quite logical. I thought to myself, here I am, slaving away, running a house and family single-handed for the sake of my husband's career and my children's education, and I'm not even warm while I'm doing it. If he can't wait for sex till he gets home, why should I wait for central heating? I suppose a more sensual woman would have taken a lover in revenge.

Mr Zapp kindly helped me with the estimates, and managed to knock £100 off the lowest – wasn't that clever of him? But of course the repayments are pretty heavy and the deposit has put our current account in the red, so please send some more money home soon.

But quite apart from the expense and the problem of the children, Philip, I don't think I would want to fly out anyway. I've read through your letter very carefully and I'm afraid I can't avoid the conclusion that you desire my presence mainly for the purpose of lawful sexual intercourse. I suppose you've been frightened off attempting any more extra-marital adventures, but the Euphoric spring has heated your blood to the extent that you're prepared to fly me six thousand miles to obtain relief. I'm afraid I'd find it a strain coming over in that kind of context, Philip. Even the 17-day excursion fare costs £165–15–6, and nothing I can do in bed could possibly be worth that money.

Does this sound cutting? It's not meant to be. Mary says that men always try to end a dispute with a woman by raping her, either literally or symbolically, so you're only conforming to type. Mary is full of fascinating theories about

men and women. She says there is a movement for the liberation of women starting in America. Have you come across
any signs of it?

I was glad to hear that things are quietening down on the
Euphoric campus at last. Believe it or not, we may be in for
some student trouble here. There is talk of a sit-in next term.
Apparently it's thrown the older members of staff into a flat
spin. According to Morris, Gordon Masters is quite un-
hinged – has taken to coming into the Department wearing
his old Territorial Army uniform.

Love,
Hilary

Désirée to Morris

Dear Morris,
Oddly enough I do believe you about this Mary Makepeace, though the kosher reference was despicable as only
you know how to be. But don't blame Philip Swallow for
the leak. It was your Irish colleen, the toothless Bernadette,
if orthography is any clue, who betrayed you and your
'yaller-hared whoor' in a smudged, greasy and tear-stained
epistle which I received the other day, unsigned.

Have you ever heard of Women's Liberation, Morris? I've
just discovered it. I mean I read about the way they busted
up the Miss America competition last November, but I
thought they were just a bunch of screwballs. Not at all.
They've just started up a discussion group in Plotinus, and
I went along the other night. I was fascinated. Boy, have
they got *your* number!

Désirée

4. Reading

COUPLE, mid-thirties, fat wife, would like to meet discreet couple.

NESTLING earth couple would like to find water brothers to grock with in peace.

NATURE is where it's at. Big Sur Dylan Hesse Bach baby racoons grass seashores sensitivity creativity sex and love. I want to groove with girl who likes same.

LOOKING for two or more bi girls for joyous 3 or more-somes with attractive man in early thirties. Shapely wife may also join in. Also, if desired, wife's young very feminine attractive transvestite cousin. Inquiries welcomed from gals in pairs or even singly. Especially urge novice inquiries from young singles or jaded housewives who'd like to try on the joys of group sex. Discretion assured. Photo optional but appreciated. If not sure, write anyway.

– small ads., *Euphoric Times*

PLOTINUS WOMEN ON MARCH

The Plotinus Women's Liberation Movement hit the streets Saturday in its first public appearance, to celebrate International Women's Day. Among the banners they carried: 'Is it smart to play Dumb?' 'You Earn More as a *Real* Whore' and 'Free Child Care Centers 24 Hours a Day'. The last of these slogans moved a Puerto Rican housewife to hold up the procession: where, please, could she find one of the Centers? The marchers explained regretfully that they didn't exist yet.

– *Plotinus Gazette*

153

Students and street people moved on to a vacant lot on Poplar Ave, between Clifton and King Streets, at the weekend, to construct what they declared a People's Garden. The land was acquired by the University two years ago, but has been used as an unofficial parking lot since then.

A spokesman for the gardeners said: 'This land does not belong to the University. If it belongs to anyone, it's the Costanoan Indians, from whom it was stolen by force two hundred years ago. If any Costanoans show, we'll gladly move out. Meanwhile, we're providing an open space for the people of Plotinus. The University has shown itself indifferent to the needs of the community.'

The gardeners worked through the weekend, digging and leveling the ground and laying turf. 'I never thought to see a hippie working,' said an elderly resident of nearby Pole St.
                                                            – *Plotinus Gazette*

EXTRAORDINARY MEETING OF
RUMMIDGE STUDENTS UNION COUNCIL

The following resolutions will be moved under Agendum 4 (*b*): That Union Council:

1. *Urges* the Union Executive to initiate direct action if the University Court of Governors, at its meeting of next Wednesday, does not agree to the following demands:

(*a*) acceptance *in toto* of the document *Student Participation* submitted by the Union to the Senate and Court last November.

(*b*) immediate action to set up a Commission to investigate the structure and function of the University.

(*c*) suspension of classes in all Departments for a two-day teach-in on the constitution and scope of the proposed commission.

HOUSE SLIDE

A small landslip on Pythagoras Avenue has made a house unsafe for habitation, public health officials decided today. Occupants of 1037 Pythagoras were woken at 1.30 am last Saturday night when their house slewed through a 45° turn due to subsidence after a freak rainstorm. No one was hurt.

– Plotinus Gazette

CONCERNING THE SITE ON POPLAR AVENUE
BETWEEN CLIFTON AND KING STREETS

This property was purchased and cleared by the University approximately 18 months ago. The University was unable to proceed promptly with the construction of a playing field on the site because of financial difficulties. Funds are now available, and plans for the playing field are moving ahead.

In fairness to those who have worked on the land in recent weeks – many of them motivated by a genuine spirit – the disutility of any additional labour there should be pointed out. The area will be cleared soon in preparation for work on the recreational field.

– Information Office, State University of Euphoria

PARADISE REGAINED

A new Eden is being created in the People's Garden in Plotinus – the most spontaneous and encouraging event so far in the continuing struggle between the University-Industrial-Military complex and the Alternative Society of Love and Peace. Not just street people and students are working and playing together in the Garden, but ordinary men and women, housewives and children – even professors!

– Euphoric Times

RUMMIDGE GRAND PRIX PROPOSED

A newly formed consortium of Rummidge businessmen and motor-racing enthusiasts put forward plans yesterday to hold Formula 1 motor races on the city's new Inner Ringway system. 'The new Ringway is just perfect for motor racing,' said the group's spokesman, Jack 'Gasket' Scott. 'You might have thought this was what the designers had in mind all along.'

Rummidge Evening Mail

EUPHORIC PROF AND STUDENTS
ARRESTED FOR BRICK THEFT

Sixteen persons, including a visiting professor from England and several students, were arrested on Saturday for stealing used bricks from the demolition site of the Lutheran Church on Buchanan Street. The bricks, valued at $7.50, were apparently destined for the People's Garden, where a People's Fishpond is under construction.

– Plotinus Gazette

MILITANT STUDENTS OCCUPY
RUMMIDGE UNIVERSITY ASSEMBLY HALL

Members of Rummidge University's Court of Governors had to push their way through student pickets to attend their meeting yesterday afternoon. The students were demanding that the meeting – called to discuss their Union's document *Student Participation* – should be open to all-comers. Eventually the President of the Union and two other students were allowed to address the Court, but the governors declined to give an immediate answer to the students' demands.

As soon as this was known, about 150 students, already prepared with sleeping bags and blankets, moved into the

Assembly Hall of the University. After a discussion on the ideal structure of a reorganized University, an improvised discotheque was set up. About 85 students were still in the hall at 2 am. Later this morning an Extraordinary General Meeting of the Union will debate a proposal that the occupation of University buildings be endorsed and extended.

– Rummidge Morning Post

VISITING PROF AND STUDENTS DISCHARGED

Professor Philip Swallow, British visitor to the English Department, was among sixteen people arrested on Saturday for allegedly stealing bricks from the demolition site on Buchanan St. Charges against the sixteen, mostly Euphoric students, were dismissed at Plotinus Municipal Court yesterday because the owner of the bricks, Mr Joe Mattiessen, refused to sign the complaint. Some of Professor Swallow's students gathered outside the Court and cheered as he emerged, smiling.

'I've never been busted before,' he said. 'It was a memorable experience, but I shouldn't care to repeat it.'

– Euphoric State Daily

STATEMENT BY CHANCELLOR BINDE

We have been presented with a Garden we hadn't planned or even asked for, and no one is entirely happy about it. The people who have been working on the Garden are anxious about the future of their gift. The residents of the area are unhappy about the crowds, the noise and the behaviour of some users of the Garden. The city officers are worried about the crime and control problems presented by the Garden. Many taxpayers are indignant at what they regard as an illegal seizure of university – and therefore State – property. The organizers of intramural sport are unhappy about the prospective loss of playing fields. Most people are worried about the possibility of a confrontation, although others are afraid there might not be one. As for me, I feel the burden of these worries and several I haven't mentioned.

So what happens next? First, we shall have to put up a fence to re-establish the conveniently forgotten fact that the field is indeed the University's property and to exclude un-authorized persons from the site. That's a hard way to make the point, but that's the way it has to be.

– Release from the Chancellor's Office,
State University of Euphoria

DEFEND THE GARDEN!

We have taken a solemn oath to defend the Garden, and wage a war of retaliation against the University if it moves against the Garden. If we fight the same way as we have worked together on the Garden – together in teams, with determination, in brotherhood – we shall win.

NO FENCES AGAINST THE PEOPLE
NO BULLDOZERS
BE MASTERS OF SILENCE, MASTERS OF THE
NIGHT WITH SHOVELS AND GUNS
POWER TO THE PEOPLE AND THEIR GUNS

The Gardeners
– Manifesto distributed on the streets of Plotinus

SUPPORT THE OCCUPATION

Students of Rummidge! Support the Occupation at today's Meeting, then join us in the Assembly Hall. Show the Administration that this is *your* University, not theirs.

– Flysheet issued by the Occupation Steering Committee

POLICE HOLD GARDEN, SHOOT 35. MARCH
TRIGGERS CABLE AV. GASSING. BYSTANDERS,
STUDENTS WOUNDED. EMERGENCY, CURFEW
ENFORCED.

A noon rally and march yesterday to protest the University's
seizure of the People's Garden erupted into a brutal battle
between police and demonstrators lasting all afternoon.
Sixty people were hospitalized and by dusk tear gas had
spread through the south campus and adjoining residential
districts. Police, openly wielding shotguns, fired birdshot into
surging crowds of demonstrators, many of whom fled with
blood streaming down their faces. One policeman was
stabbed and three others received minor injuries from rocks
and shattered glass. The National Guard has been called out
by Governor Duck, and a curfew has been enforced between the hours of 10 pm and 6 am.

At 6 am yesterday, after police had evicted students and
others sleeping out in the People's Garden, the Esseph
Fence Company arrived to erect a 10-foot high steel-link

(*Contd. back page*)

– *Euphoric State Daily*

RUMMIDGE SIT-IN CONTINUES

An extraordinary meeting of the Rummidge University
Students' Union, attended by over 1000 students, voted
today to endorse and continue the 'sit-in' already initiated
by 150 left-wing extremists yesterday evening. At the end of
their meeting the students went in a body to the Assembly
Hall and a number of them forced their way into the office
of the Vice-Chancellor's secretary and demanded that the
Vice-Chancellor Mr Stewart Stroud appear to hear their
grievances.

'It was a waste of time,' one of the students present commented afterwards. 'He showed no understanding of the

legitimate demands of students for democratic participation in university decision-making.'

The students occupied several offices in the Administration Block, causing 'considerable alarm' among the secretarial staff, according to a senior official.

– Rummidge Evening Mail

GARDENERS AND COPS,
GUARDSMEN CLASH IN DOWNTOWN PLOTINUS

Supporters of the fenced-off People's Garden played cat-and-mouse with police and National Guardsmen over the weekend. On Saturday they invaded the shopping area of downtown Plotinus. Milling over a three block area on Shamrock Ave, they were confronted by a line of guardsmen who herded them back at bayonet point.

At approximately 1 pm, Miranda County Sheriff's Deputies jumped and clubbed a young man spraying WELCOME TO PRAGUE on a window of Cooper's Department Store with an aerosol paint container. He was dragged off to the police station bleeding profusely, and was later identified as Wily Smith, 21, a black student at Euphoric State.

On Sunday a huge procession of Garden supporters coiled its way through the streets of Plotinus, planting miniature 'People's Gardens' on every vacant lot they passed. Asked why he had instructed his men to remove the grass and flowers, Sheriff O'Keene said, 'They're a violation of property.'

– Esseph Chronicle

UNIVERSITY AT WAR,
RUMMIDGE PROFESSOR WARNS

Gordon Masters, Professor of English Literature at the University of Rummidge, has condemned the present sit-in by students in strong terms.

'The situation closely resembles that of Europe in 1940,' he said yesterday. 'The unacceptable ultimatum, followed by a *Blitzkrieg* and occupation of neighbouring territory, was Hitler's basic strategy. But we did not yield then and we shall not yield now.'

On the wall of his office, Professor Masters has a large map showing the plan of the University's central heating system. 'The heating pipes are conveyed through a maze of tunnels,' he explained, 'which would make an excellent base for resistance activity should Senate and the Administration have to go underground. I don't doubt that the Vice-Chancellor has a secret bunker to which he can retreat at short notice.'

The Vice-Chancellor's Office declined to comment.

– *Rummidge Morning Post*

RIOT VICTIM ROBERTS DIES
STUDENT REFERENDUM TO BE HELD
ACADEMIC SENATE SETS MEETING ON GARDEN

– *Headlines, Euphoric State Daily*

WE ACCUSE! WE SHALL OVERCOME!

The People of Plotinus know who was responsible for the death of John Roberts.

Chancellor Binde, who declared war on the people over a piece of land.

Sheriff O'Keene, who armed his blue meanies with shotguns and let them loose on the streets.

The nameless pig who pumped two rounds of buckshot

into the back of a defenceless young man at pointblank range.

Our land is desecrated, but the spirit of the Garden is alive on Shamrock Avenue and Howle Plaza. The people of Plotinus are united against the pigs and tyrants. The bullshit barriers are coming down, the barricades of love are going up against the pigs. Street freaks, politicos, frat rats, sallys and jocks and mommas for peace are pulling off their masks of isolation and touching each other's hearts.

– Euphoric Times

PROFESSOR RESIGNS

Professor Gordon H. Masters, Professor of English at Rummidge University, yesterday tendered his resignation to the Vice-Chancellor, who has accepted it 'with regret'.

It is well known that Professor Masters, who was due to retire in a few years' time, has not enjoyed good health lately, and friends close to him say that the current student troubles at the University have been a source of severe strain for him.

Professor Masters' resignation takes effect from next October, but he has already left Rummidge for a period of rest and recuperation.

– Rummidge Morning Post

CHOPPER SPRAYS DEMONSTRATORS –
TEAR GAS BLANKETS CAMPUS

A National Guard helicopter clattered over the Euphoric State campus yesterday, spraying white tear gas over some 700 students and faculty trapped in Howle Plaza by a tight ring of guardsmen.

The gas attack was authorized by Miranda County Sheriff Hank O'Keene, to disperse the remnants of a procession of 3000 mourners marching in memory of John Roberts. Wind blew the gas and carried it hundreds of yards away. It blanketed residential houses, entered university classrooms and offices, seeped into the wards of the University Hospital. Faculty wives and children in the Blueberry Creek swimming pool ¾ mile away were affected by the gas. A group of faculty have lodged a strong protest with Chancellor Binde against the indiscriminate use of gas by the law enforcement agencies.

– *Esseph Chronicle*

AN EIGHT-YEAR-OLD'S VIEW OF THE CRISIS

I didn't get to see the People's Garden really, but I could feel that it was beautiful. In the Garden it was made of people's feelings, not just their hands, they made it with their heart, who knew if they made it to stay, there are hundreds of people that built that garden, and so we'll never know if they meant it to stay.

The police are just ruining their lives by being police, they're also keeping themselves from being a person. They act like they are some kind of nervous creatures.

– Submitted by Plotinus schoolteacher
to *Euphoric State Daily*

ASSEMBLY HALL TEACH-IN

This weekend the organizers of the sit-in have arranged a teach-in on the subject of THE UNIVERSITY AND THE COMMUNITY.

What is the role of the University in modern society?

What is the social justification of University Education?

What do ordinary people really think about Universities and Students?

These are some of the questions we shall be discussing.

– Handout, Rummidge University

most students don,t like the way colleges and universitys are run tats why they have protested and sit-in. When students are older they will find it was ran in a good way. Students waste people and police-mens time, i think just for a laff. Most of them are hippeys and act like big fools and waste thier brain when someone else would be proud to be brainy.

I think students are stupid they throw stink bombs at people on purpose ony because they want to be noticed. They are a load of old tramps with their long dirty hair. They look like they haven't had a wash. Their clothes are disgraceful and they don,t have any money. They go on the television and smoke drugs in front of the viewers. They cause riots in the streets fighting and destroying everything that comes their way. Some students are sensable they wear nice clothes and got nice hair, they have a nice home and are not stupid.

if a student came to me and said something i would walk on. Lets say you are a cat and the students pick you up and you think he is kind. but they cut you up and experiment on you. Some students are all right but they are stuck up noses.

I don,t like students cos they all follow each other in what they do they all wear the same clothes and they all talk like americans, and they smoke drugs and have injections to make themselves happy and they talk about love and peace when their unhappy.

if i was the police i would hang them.

– submitted to Rumble by Education student

RUMMIDGE DONS PROPOSE MEDIATOR

The non-professorial staff association at Rummidge University has proposed that a mediator be nominated to chair negotiations between the University Administration and the Students' Union Executive, to try and bring the sit-in to an end. Earlier today, the students voted to continue the sit-in.

Professor Morris J. Zapp, a visiting professor from the State University of Euphoria, USA, has been suggested as a possible candidate for the job of mediator.

– Rummidge Evening Mail

EARTHQUAKE CURE

Earthquakes, said a speaker at yesterday's Euphoric State teach-in on Ecology and Politics, were nature's way of protesting all the concrete that had been laid on top of the good earth. By planting things, one was liberating the ground, and therefore preventing earthquakes.

– Plotinus Gazette

CHANCELLOR PROPOSES LEASE OF GARDEN. MAYOR HAS DOUBTS. GIANT MARCH PLANNED FOR MEMORIAL DAY

Chancellor Harold Binde told a press conference yesterday that he thought the vexed problem of the People's Garden could be solved if the University leased part of the land to the City of Plotinus for development as a park, incorporating the present arrangements as far as possible.

Plotinus City Council will probably consider the proposal at its next meeting, but Mayor Holmes is known not to favour it. There is doubt, too, whether Governor Duck, an *ex officio* member of the University Council, would allow the lease to be approved, as he is bitterly opposed to any concession to the Gardeners.

Meanwhile the latter are making plans for an enormous march through the streets of Plotinus on Memorial Day. It is to be a peaceful, non-violent protest, organizers insist; but local citizens, hearing estimates that 50,000 may converge on Plotinus for the occasion, from places as far away as Madison and New York, are apprehensive.

'A permit for a march has been applied for,' a spokesman confirmed at the City Hall today, 'and is being studied by the appropriate officials.'

– Esseph Chronicle

ICE CUBE DAMAGES ROOF

A block of green ice one cubic foot in size fell through the roof of a house in south Rummidge last night, damaging a room on the top floor. The room was unoccupied and no one was hurt.

Scientists called in to examine the ice, at first thought to be a freak hailstone, quickly established that it was frozen urine. It is thought to have been illegally discharged from an airliner flying at high altitude.

The owner of the house, Dr Brendan O'Shea, said this morning, 'I'm flabbergasted. I don't even know if I'm insured against this kind of thing. Some people might say it was an act of God.'

– Rummidge Evening Mail

5. Changing

'You don't think it's on the small side?'

'It looks fine to me.'

'I've been thinking lately it was rather small.'

'A recent survey showed that ninety per cent of American men think their penises are less than average size.'

'I suppose it's only natural to want to be in the top ten per cent . . .'

'They aren't the *top* ten per cent, stupid, they're the ten per cent who aren't worried about it. The point is you can't have ninety per cent who are less than average.'

'Ah. I never was any good at statistics.'

'I'm disappointed in you, Philip, really I am. I thought you didn't have a virility hangup. That's what I like about you.'

'My small penis?'

'Your not demanding applause for your potency all the time. Like with Morris it had to be a four-star fuck every time. If I didn't groan and roll my eyes and foam at the mouth at climax he would accuse me of going frigid on him.'

'Was he one of the ninety per cent too?'

'Well, no.'

'Ah.'

'Anyway, it looks smaller to you, because you're always looking down on it. It gets foreshortened.'

'That's a thought.'

'Go take a look in the mirror.'

'No, I'll take your word for it.'

But the next morning, drying off after his shower, Philip stood on a chair to examine his torso in the mirror above the handbasin. It was true that one's normal angle of vision entailed a certain foreshortening effect, though not as much as one might have wished. Forty was admittedly a rather advanced age at which to begin worrying on this score, but it was only recently that he had acquired any standards of comparison. Not since he was at school, probably, had he taken a good look at another male organ until he came to Euphoria. Since then penises had been flaunted at him from all sides. First there was Charles Boon, who scorned pyjamas and was often to be encountered walking about the apartment on Pythagoras Drive in a state of nature. Then the record stores along Cable Avenue began displaying the John Lennon/Yoko Ono album with the full-frontal nude photo of the famous couple on the sleeve. There was the hero of *I am Curious Yellow*, which they had gone to see in Esseph, queuing two hours with what Désirée had described as a couple of hundred other middle-aged voyeurs hoping it would turn them on (which, one had to admit, it did); and the young man in the audience of an *avant-garde* theatre group who upstaged the actors by taking off his clothes before they did. These displays had impressed Philip with a sense of his own inferiority. Désirée was unsympathetic. 'Now you know what it was like growing up flat-chested in a big-tit culture,' she said.

'I think your chest is very nice.'

'What about your wife?'

'Hilary?'

'Is she well-stacked?'

'A good figure, yes. Mind you . . .'

'What?'

'She couldn't do without a bra, like you.'

'Why not?'

'Well, you know, it would be flopping about all over the place.'

'It? Don't you mean them?'

'Well, all right, them.'

'Who says they shouldn't flop? Who says they have to stick out like cantilevered terraces? I'll tell you who, the brassiere industry.'

'I expect you're right.'

'How would you like it if you had to wear a codpiece all the time?'

'I'd hate it, but I bet you could sell them if you advertised in *Euphoric Times*.'

'Morris was always a big-tit man. I don't know why he married me. I don't know why I married him. Why do people marry people? Why did you marry Hilary?'

'I don't know. I was lonely at the time.'

'Yes. That's about it. If you ask me, loneliness has a lot to answer for.'

Philip climbed down from the chair and finished drying off. He rubbed talcum into his skin, feeling with a certain narcissistic pleasure the new cushions of tissue that had appeared on his hips and chest. Since giving up smoking he had begun to put on weight, and he thought it rather suited him. His rib-cage was now covered by a smooth sheath of flesh, and his collar-bone no longer stood out with a frightening starkness that suggested he had swallowed a coat-hanger.

He shrugged on the cotton happi-coat that Désirée had loaned him. His own bathrobe had been left behind at Pythagoras Drive and Charles Boon had borrowed it so often that Philip no longer cared to recover it. If Boon wasn't walking about the apartment ostentatiously naked, he was forever pinching your clothes. How much nicer life was on Socrates Avenue. How providential, in retrospect, the landslip that had pitched him out of one address and into the other. The happi-coat was patterned in marine shades of blue and green, lined with white towelling and was immensely comfortable. It made him look, and even feel, vaguely athletic and masterful, like an oriental wrestler. He frowned at his reflection in the mirror, narrowing his eyes and dilating his nostrils. He did a lot of looking into mirrors lately. Hoping to surprise himself, perhaps, in some revealing, explanatory attitude or expression.

He padded into his bedroom, pulled back the covers on his bed and dented the pillow a little. It was his one, vestigial gesture towards the conventions: when he slept with Désirée, to rise early and come into his room to rumple the bed-clothes. Whom he was supposed to be fooling, he couldn't imagine. Not the twins, surely, because Désirée, in the terrifying way of progressive American parents, believed in treating children like adults and had undoubtedly explained to them the precise nature of her relationship with himself. I wish she would explain it to me, he thought wryly, gazing into another mirror, I'm damned if I can make head or tail of it.

Though not one of Nature's early risers, Philip found it no hardship to be up betimes these sunny mornings in 3462 Socrates. He liked showering in jets of hot water sharp as laser beams, walking about the quiet carpeted house in his bare feet, taking possession of the kitchen that was like the flight deck of some computer-guided spaceship, all gleaming white and stainless steel, with its dials, gadget sand immense humming fridge. Philip laid breakfast places for himself and the twins, mixed a jug of frozen orange juice, put bacon rashers in the electric Grillerette, turned it on low, and poured boiling water on to a teabag. Shuffling into a pair of abandoned mules, he took his tea through the patio into the garden and squatted against a sunny wall to absorb the unfailing view. It was a very still, clear morning. The waters of the Bay were stretched taut and you could almost count the cables on the Silver Span. Down on the ever-moving Shoreline Freeway, the cars and trucks raced along like Dinky toys, but their noise and fumes did not carry this far. Here the air was cool and sweet, perfumed with the sub-tropical vegetation that grew luxuriantly in the gardens of affluent Plotinus.

A silver jet, with engines cut back, planed in from the north almost at his eye level, and he followed its lazy progress across the cinemascope of the sky. This was a good hour to arrive in Euphoria. It was almost possible to imagine what it must have been like for the first mariners who sailed, probably quite by chance, through the narrow strait now bridged by the Silver Span, and found this stupendous bay in the state God left it at the creation. What was that passage in *The Great Gatsby*? 'A fresh, green breast of the new world . . . for a transitory enchanted moment man must have held his breath in the presence of this continent . . .' As Philip hunted the quotation through his mind the tranquillity of the morning was shattered by a hideous noise as of a gigantic lawn-mower passing overhead, and a dark spidery shadow flashed across the gardens on the hillside. The first helicopter of the day swooped down upon the Euphoric State campus.

Philip returned to the house. Elizabeth and Darcy were up. They came into the kitchen in their pyjamas, yawning and rubbing their eyes and pushing back their long matted hair. Not only were they identical twins, but to make things more difficult Darcy had the more feminine good looks, so that it was on Elizabeth's dental brace that Philip relied to tell them apart. They were an enigmatic pair. Communicating telepathically with each other, they were uncommonly sparing in their own use of ordinary language. Philip found this restful after his own precociously articulate and tirelessly inquisitive children, but disconcerting too. He often wondered what the twins thought of him, but they gave nothing away.

'Good morning!' he greeted them brightly. 'I think it's going to be hot.'

'Hi,' they murmured politely. 'Hi, Philip.' They sat down at the breakfast bar and began to munch large quantities of some patent sugar-coated cereal.

'Would you like some bacon?'

They shook their heads, mouths full of cereal. He extracted the crisp, uniform strips of bacon from the Grillerette and made himself a bacon sandwich and another cup of tea. 'What d'you want for your lunch today?' he inquired. The twins looked at each other.

'Peanut butter and jelly,' Darcy said.

'All right. What about you, Elizabeth?' As if he needed to ask.

'The same, please.'

He made the sandwiches with the ready-sliced, vitamin-enriched, totally tasteless white bread they seemed to like, and packed them with an apple each in their lunch-boxes. The twins took second helpings of cereal. *Euphoric Times* had recently reported an experiment in which rats fed on cornflake packets had proved healthier than rats fed on the cornflakes. He told them about it. They smiled politely.

'Have you washed?' he inquired.

While they were washing, he put the kettle on to boil for Désirée's coffee and picked up yesterday's *Chronicle*. 'It is to be a peaceful, non-violent protest, the organizers insist,' he read. 'But local citizens, hearing estimates that 50,000 may converge on Plotinus for the occasion, from places as far away as Madison and New York, are apprehensive.' He looked out of the window, down to where the helicopter darted and hovered like a dragonfly over downtown Plotinus. Over two thousand troops were in the city, some bivouacked in the Garden itself. It was said that they were secretly watering the flowers. Certainly the soldiers often looked as if they would like to throw down their arms and join the protesting students, especially when the girl supporters of the Garden taunted them by stripping to the waist and opposing bare breasts to their bayonets, a juxtaposition of hardware and software that the photographers of *Euphoric Times* found irresistible. Most of the troopers were young men who had only joined the National Guard to get out of the Viet Nam War anyway, and they looked now just like the GIs that one saw in Viet Nam on the television newsreels, bewildered and unhappy and, if they were bold enough, making peace signs to the cameras. In fact the whole episode of the Garden was much like the Viet Nam War in miniature, with the University as the Thieu regime, the National Guard as the US Army, the students and hippies as Viet Cong . . . escalation, overkill, helicopters, defoliation, guerilla warfare: it all fitted together perfectly. It would be something to say on the Charles Boon Show. He couldn't imagine what else he was going to say.

The twins reappeared in the kitchen to collect their lunch-boxes, looking marginally cleaner and tidier in blue jeans, sneakers and faded T-shirts.

'Have you said good-bye to your mother?'

They called perfunctorily, ''Bye, Désirée,' as they left the house, and received a muffled shout in reply. Philip put coffee, orange-juice, toasted muffins and honey on a tray and took it into Désirée's bedroom.

'Hi!' she said. 'Your timing is terrific.'

'It's a beautiful day,' he said, setting down the tray and going to the window. He adjusted the louvres of the Venetian blinds so that the sunshine fell across the room in long strips. Désirée's red plaits flamed against the saffron pillows of the huge bed.

'Was that a helicopter nearly took the roof off the house?' she asked, tucking zestfully into her breakfast.

'Yes, I was in the garden.'

'The sonofabitch. Kids get off to school OK?'

'Yes, I made them peanut butter sandwiches. I used up the last of the jar.'

'Yeah, I must go marketing today. You got anything planned?'

'I've got to go into the University this morning. The English faculty are holding a vigil on the steps of Dealer.'

'A what?'

'I'm sure it's the wrong word, but that's what they're calling it. A vigil is an all-night thing, isn't it? I think we're just going to stand on the steps for an hour or two. In silent protest.'

'You think Duck is gonna call off the National Guard just because the English faculty quit talking for a couple of hours? I admit it would be quite an achievement, but –'

'I gather the protest is aimed at Binde. He's got to be pressured into standing up to Duck and O'Keene.'

'Binde?' Désirée snorted derisively. 'Chancellor Facing-both-ways.'

'Well, you must admit he's in a difficult position. What would you do in his position?'

173

'I couldn't be in his position. The State University of Euphoria has never had a woman chancellor in its history. Are you going to be in tonight, by the way, because we'll need a baby-sitter if you're not. It's my Karate class.'

'I shall be out late. I've got to do this wretched broadcast with Charles Boon.'

'Oh, yeah. What are you talking about?'

'I think I'm supposed to give my impressions of the Euphoric scene, from a British point of view.'

'Sounds like a pushover.'

'But I don't feel British any more. Not as much as I used to, anyway. Nor American, for that matter. "Wandering between two worlds, one lost, the other powerless to be born."'

'You'll have plenty of questions about the Garden, anyway. As one of its most celebrated supporters.'

'That was a complete accident, as you very well know.'

'Nothing is completely accidental.'

'I never felt more than mildly sympathetic to the Garden. I've never even set foot in the place. Now people, complete strangers, come up to me and shake my hand, congratulate me on my commitment. It's most embarrassing.'

'There is a tide in the affairs of men, Philip. You've gotten caught up in the historical process.'

'I feel a complete fraud.'

'Why are you going on this vigil, then?'

'If I don't, it will look as if I've joined the other side, and that certainly isn't true. Anyway, I do feel strongly about getting the troops off campus.'

'Well, take care not to get arrested. It may not be so easy to bail you out next time.'

Désirée finished her muffin, licked her fingers and settled back into the pillows with a cup of coffee held to her lips. 'You know,' she said, 'you look really good in that happi-coat.'

'Where can I get one like it?'

'Keep it. Morris never wore the damn thing. I bought it for a Christmas present two years ago. Have you written to

Hilary, by the way? Or are you hoping another poison-pen letter will do the job for you?'

'I don't know what to say.' He paced the room, trying, for no reason at all, to avoid treading on the strips of sunlight. Three images of himself converged in the triptych of mirrors over Désirée's dressing-table, and cold-shouldered him as he turned to retrace his steps.

'Tell her what's happened and what you plan to do about it.'

'But I don't know what I'm going to do about it. I haven't got any plans.'

'Isn't your time running out?'

'I know, I know,' he said despairingly, running fingers through his hair. 'But I'm not used to this sort of thing. I've no experience in adultery. I don't know what would be best for Hilary, the children, for me, for you –'

'Don't worry about me,' said Désirée. 'Forget about me.'

'How can I?'

'I'll just say one thing. I've no intention of marrying again. Just in case it had crossed your mind.'

'You're going to get a divorce, aren't you?'

'Sure. But from now on I'm a free woman. I stand on my own two feet and without a pair of balls round my neck.' Perhaps he looked hurt, for she continued: 'Nothing personal, Philip, you know I like you a lot. We get on fine together. The kids like you too.'

'Do they? I often wonder.'

'Sure, you take them out to the park and suchlike. Morris never did that.'

'Funny, that's one of the things I thought I was getting away from when I came out here. It must be compulsive.'

'You're welcome to stay here as long as you like. Or go. Feel entirely free to do what you think best.'

'I have felt very free these last few weeks,' he said. 'Freer than I've ever felt in my life.'

Désirée flashed him one of her rare smiles. 'That's nice.' She got out of bed and scratched herself through her cotton nightdress.

'I just wish we could go on like this indefinitely. You and me and the twins here. And Hilary and the children quite happy and not knowing.'

'How much longer d'you have?'

'Well, the exchange ends officially in a month's time.'

'Could you stay on at Euphoric State if you wanted to? I mean, would they give you a job?'

'Not a hope.'

'Somebody told me you got a terrific write-up in the last *Course Bulletin*.'

'That was just Wily Smith.'

'You're too modest, Philip.' Pulling the nightdress over her head, Désirée walked into the adjoining bathroom. Philip followed her appreciatively, and sat on the toilet cover while she showered.

'Couldn't you get a job in one of the smaller colleges around here?' she called through the hiss of hot water.

'Perhaps. But there would be problems about visas. Of course, if I married an American citizen, there'd be no problem.'

'That sounds like blackmail.'

'It wasn't meant to be.' He stood up, and his reflection rose to face him in the mirror over the handbasin. 'I must shave. This conversation is getting more and more unreal. I'll go back in a month's time, of course. Back to Hilary and the children. Back to Rummidge. Back to England.'

'Do you want to?'

'Not in the least.'

'You could work for me if you like.'

'For you?'

'As a housekeeper. You do it very well. Much better than me. I want to go back to work.'

He laughed. 'How much would you pay me?'

'Not much. But there'd be no visa problems. Would you get me a towel from the closet, honey?'

He held the towel open as she stepped glistening from the shower, and began rubbing her down briskly.

'Mmm, that's nice.' After a while she said: 'You really ought to write home, you know.'

'Have you told Morris?'

'I don't owe Morris any explanations. Besides, he'd be round to your wife like a shot.'

'I hadn't thought of that. Of course, they both know I've been staying here . . .'

'But they think Melanie is here too, as chaperone. Or is it me who's supposed to be keeping an eye on you and Melanie? I've lost track.'

'I lost track weeks ago,' said Philip, rubbing less briskly. He was on his knees now, drying her legs. 'You know this is rather exciting.'

'Cool it, baby,' said Désirée. 'You have a vigil to keep, remember?'

Darling,
    Many thanks for your last letter. I'm glad to hear you have got over your cold. I haven't started my hay fever yet and am hoping that I won't be allergic to Euphoric pollen. By the way, I'm having an affair with Mrs Zapp. I should have mentioned it before but it slipped my . . .

Dear Hilary,
    Not 'Darling' because I've forfeited the right to that term of endearment. Only a few months after the Melanie affair . . .

Dearest Hilary,
    You were very perceptive when you said I seemed more relaxed and cheerful in my last few letters. Not to put too fine a point on it, I have been getting laid by Désirée Zapp three or four times a week lately, and it's done me the world of good . . .

He composed letters to Hilary in his head all the way to the campus, tearing them up, mentally, almost as soon as he had started them. His thoughts seemed to spin out of control, into absurdity, sentimentality, obscenity, as soon as he tried to bring into a single frame of reference images of home, Rummidge, Hilary and the children, and the image of his present existence. It was difficult to believe that by boarding an aeroplane he could be back, within hours, in that grey, damp, sedate environment from which he had come. As easy to believe that he could step through Désirée's dressing-table mirror and find himself back in his own bedroom. If only he could send home, when the time came, some zombie replica of himself, a robot Swallow programmed to wash dishes, take tutorials, make mortgage repayments on the 3rd of every month, while he himself lay low in Euphoria, let his hair grow and grooved quietly with Désirée . . . No one would notice in Rummidge. Whereas if he went back in person, in his present state of mind, they would say he was an impostor. *Will the real Philip Swallow please stand up?* I should be interested to meet him myself, Philip thought, steering the Corvair round the tight bends of Socrates Avenue, tyres squealing softly on the smooth tarmac, houses and gardens rotating dizzily in the rear-view mirror. He had ended up driving Morris Zapp's car after all. 'You might as well keep the battery charged,' Désirée had said, a few days after he moved into the house. 'I can't watch you going off to catch the bus every morning with that car idle in the garage.'

It all started, you see, on the night of the landslide. Mrs Zapp and I had been invited to the same party again, and she offered me a lift home, because there was a kind of tropical storm . . . Pythagoras Drive was like a river in flood. The rain swept in great folds across the beam of the headlights, drummed on the roof and almost overpowered the windscreen wipers. The streetlamps were out, shorted probably. It was like driving on the bottom of the sea. 'Jesus Christ,' Désirée muttered, peering through the flooded windshield. 'I think I'll sit this out, when I've dropped you.'

For politeness' sake he invited her in for a cup of coffee, and to his surprise she accepted. 'You're going to get awfully wet, I'm afraid,' he said.

'I've got an umbrella. We can run for it.'

They ran for it – straight into the side of the house.

'I can't understand it,' he said. 'The front door should be here.'

'You must be drunk,' said Désirée unsympathetically. Despite her umbrella, she was getting very wet. Philip was totally saturated. Furthermore they appeared to be standing in several inches of mud, instead of the garden path.

'I'm perfectly sober,' he said, groping in the dark for the porch steps.

'Somebody must have moved the house,' she said sarcastically.

Which, in a manner of speaking, was quite true. Rounding a corner of the building in search of the front door, they came upon three terrified girls in mud-stained nightwear – Melanie, Carol and Deirdre – who had just been jolted out of their beds as the house slewed round in a great arc (lucky Charles Boon was warm and dry in his snug studio). 'We thought it was the earthquake,' they said. 'We thought it was the end of the world.'

'You'd better all come home with me,' Désirée said.

It was, you see, purely an act of charity, and meant to be a very temporary arrangement. Just to give us a roof over our heads until we could return to Pythagoras Drive, or make other arrangements . . . Carol and Deirdre soon moved on. Melanie set up with Charles Boon in the South Campus area – they had thrown themselves wholeheartedly into the cause of the Garden, and wanted to be near the scene of the action. Eventually, of the refugees from the landslip, only Philip was left in the Zapps' house. He hung on, waiting to see if the house on Pythagoras Drive would be made safe: Désirée told him not to worry. He began to look desultorily for another apartment: Désirée told him to take his time. He didn't feel too bad about imposing on her because she was often out in the evenings at meetings and he saved her the trouble of getting baby-sitters. Also she was a slow riser and appreciated his willingness to make breakfast for the twins and see them off to school. Imperceptibly they settled into a routine. It was almost like being married. On Sundays he would drive the twins into the State Park on the other side of the Plotinus hills and take them for rambles through the pine-woods. He felt himself reverting to a more comfortable, loose-fitting version of his

179

life in England. The interregnum of Pythagoras Drive seemed like a drugged dream as it receded into the past. There had been something unnatural, unhealthy about it, after all, something ignoble and ridiculous about the role he had played there, a middle-aged parasite on the alternative society, hanging around the young folk with a doggy, ingratiating look, anxious to please, anxious not to offend, hoping for a game that never materialized: the game he had seen developing that first evening in the girls' downstairs apartment, with the Cowboy and the Confederate Soldier and the black wrestler. They never seemed to play it again, or else they took care to play it when he was out. He never sniffed the hint of an orgy from that night onwards, though he kept his senses alert for a sign. The nearest he got to group sex was reading the swingers' small ads in *Euphoric Times*. Perhaps he should have put one in himself. *British Professor, not especially well hung, likes Jane Austen, Top of the Pops, gin and tonic, seeks orgy, suitable beginner.* Or a personal message. *Melanie. Give me a second chance. I need you but can't speak. I am awake in my room and waiting for you.* Awake and sweating into the darkness, listening to the muffled sounds of her and Charles Boon making love in the next room. It had been sick, really. The landslip had swept away a whole Sodom and Gomorrah of private fantasies and unacted desires. He felt a new man in the calm, initially sexless atmosphere of Désirée Zapp's luxurious eyrie high up on the peak of Socrates Avenue. He began to eat better, sleep better. Together he and Désirée gave up smoking. 'If you'll throw away that stinking pipe, I'll throw away my stinking cigarettes, is that a deal?' It was the karate that determined her to quit, she said, she felt humiliated gasping for breath after ten minutes' exercise. Philip found it surprisingly easy and decided that he'd never really liked the pipe anyway. He was glad to be free of the paraphernalia of smoking. Now the days were warm and he could wear lightweight trousers and slimline shirts without displaying unsightly bulges like cysts all over his torso. Admittedly he drank more these days: usually a couple of gin and tonics before dinner, and wine or beer with the meal, and perhaps a Scotch afterwards as they watched the day's rioting on television. One evening when they were doing this he said, 'I found quite a nice apartment today. On Pole Street.'

'Why don't you stay on here?' Désirée said, without taking her eyes from the screen. 'There's plenty of room.'

'I can't go on imposing on you.'

'You can pay me rent if you like.'

'All right,' he said. 'How much?'

'How about fifteen dollars a week for the room plus twenty dollars a week for food and liquor plus three dollars heating and lighting that makes thirty-eight dollars a week or one hundred and sixty dollars per calendar month?'

'Goodness me,' said Philip. 'You're very quick off the mark.'

'I've been thinking about it. It seems like a very convenient arrangement to me. Are you in tomorrow night, by the way? I have a consciousness-raising workshop.'

Philip stopped at a red light and wound down his window. The buzz of a helicopter told him he was now in the militarized zone, though you wouldn't otherwise have guessed that there was any trouble at the University on this side of the campus, he thought, as he steered the car through the broad entrance on the West perimeter, past lawns and shrubberies where the spume of rotating water sprinklers rainbowed in the sun and a solitary security man in his shelter lifted a lazy hand in salute. But as he approached Dealer, the signs of conflict became more evident: windows smashed and boarded up, leaflets and gas canisters littering the paths, Guardsmen and campus police watchfully patrolling the paths, guarding buildings, muttering into walkie-talkies.

He found a vacant space in the car park behind Dealer, driving in beside Luke Hogan, just arrived in his big green Thunderbird.

'Nice car you've got there, Phil,' said the Chairman. 'Morris Zapp used to have one just like it.'

Philip shifted the subject of conversation slightly. 'One

thing to be said for the troubles on campus,' he observed, 'it makes parking easier.'

Hogan nodded dolefully. The crisis was no fun at all for him, sandwiched between his radical and conservative colleagues. 'I'm real sorry, Phil, that you had to visit us at a time like this.'

'Oh, it's quite interesting really. Perhaps more interesting than it ought to be.'

'You'll have to come back another year.'

'Supposing I asked you for a permanent job?' Philip asked, half-seriously, recalling his conversation with Désirée.

Hogan's response was entirely serious. An expression of great pain passed over his big, brown face, parched and eroded like a Western landscape. 'Gee, Phil, I wish I could . . .'

'I was only joking.'

'Well, that was a mighty fine review you had in the *Course Bulletin* . . . And these days, teaching counts, really counts.'

'I haven't got the publications behind me, I know that.'

'Well, I have to admit Phil . . .' Luke Hogan sighed. 'To make you an offer appropriate to your age and experience, we should expect a book or two. Now if you were *black*, of course, it would be different. Or better still, Indian. What I wouldn't give for an indigenous Indian with a PhD,' he murmured wistfully, like a man on a desert island dreaming of steak and chips. Part of the settlement of the previous quarter's strike had been an undertaking by the University to employ more Third World faculty, but most other universities in the country were pursuing the same quarry, so the supply was running short.

'That's another thing, I haven't got a PhD,' Philip observed.

This was a fact known to Hogan but he evidently considered it bad taste on Philip's part to draw attention to it, for he made no reply. They entered Dealer, and waited for the lift, in silence. A roughly painted notice on the wall said, 'ENGLISH FACULTY VIGIL, DEALER STEPS 11 A.M.' As the lift door slid open and they entered, Karl Kroop hurried in beside them. He was a short, bespectacled man with thinning hair – a disappointingly unheroic figure, Philip had thought when he first identified him. He still wore a KEEP KROOP button in his lapel, as a veteran might wear a combat medal. Or perhaps he wore it merely to embarrass Hogan, who had presided over his firing and re-hiring.

'Hi, Luke, hi, Philip,' he greeted them jauntily. 'See you guys on the steps later?'

Hogan responded with a sickly smile. ' 'Fraid I'm going to be tied up in a committee this morning, Karl.' He leapt out of the lift as soon as it opened, and disappeared into his office.

'Motherfucking liberal,' Kroop muttered.

'Well, I'm a liberal,' Philip demurred.

'Then I wish,' said Kroop, patting Philip on the back, 'that there were more liberals like you, Philip, prepared to lay their liberalism on the line, to go to jail for their liberalism. You're coming to the vigil?'

'Oh yes,' said Philip, blushing.

As he entered the Department Office to check his mailbox, Mabel Lee greeted him. 'Oh, Professor Swallow, Mr Boon left a note in your mailbox.' She simpered. 'Hear you're going to be on his show tonight. I'll be sure to listen.'

'Oh dear, I wouldn't recommend it.'

He took a copy of the *Euphoric State Daily* from the pile on the counter and scanned the front page: RESTRAINING ORDER ISSUED AGAINST SHERIFF O'KEENE . . . OTHER CAMPUSES PLEDGE SUPPORT . . . PHYSICIANS, SCIENTISTS PROBE ALLEGED BLISTER GAS . . . WOMEN AND CHILDREN IN PROTEST MARCH TO GARDEN. There was a photograph of the Garden, now rapidly reverting to a dusty waste lot, with a few pieces of play equipment and some withered shrubs in one corner, surrounded by the familiar wire fence. A few stolid soldiers inside, a crowd of women and children outside, like some surrealistic inversion of a concentration camp. Something for the Charles Boon Show? 'Who, one wonders, are the real prisoners here? Who is inside, and who is outside the fence?' Etc., etc. He lifted the flap on what he still called, to the immense amusement of his American colleagues, his pigeonhole. A small, queerly shaped package addressed in Hilary's handwriting gave him a moment of queasiness until he saw that it had come by surface mail and had been posted months ago. Mail from outside Euphoria disturbed him these days, reminding him of his connections and responsibilities beyond its borders; especially did he shrink from Hilary's airletters, pale blue, wafer-thin missives, the very profile of the Queen in the right-hand corner transmitting, to his guilty eye, a pained disapproval of his conduct. Not that the actual text of Hilary's recent letters had expressed any sense of grievance or suspicion. She chatted amiably enough about the chilren, Mary Makepeace, and Morris Zapp, who seemed to be taking quite a leading part in affairs at Rummidge these days, having successfully sorted out a spot of student bother they seemed to be having there . . . really, he had scarcely taken in her news, skimming the lines of neat, round script as quickly as he could to reassure himself that no rumour of his infidelity had been wafted to Rummidge to rebound in a cry of outrage and anger. It was no secret around Plotinus that he was living in the Zapps' house, but people seemed too preoccupied with the Garden troubles to inquire further. Either that or, as Désirée maintained, they thought Philip was gay because he had taken Charles Boon into his apartment and that she was a lesbian because of the Women's Liberation bit, so didn't imagine that the two of them might be having an affair. Also, Howard Ringbaum, prime suspect as author of the poison-pen letter about Melanie (the Cowboy, being one of his students, could have been his source of information) had left Euphoria, having been offered a job in Canada and released at short notice by a relieved Hogan.

Philip read Charles Boon's note reminding him of the time and place of the broadcast. He recalled their meeting on the plane, it seemed years ago. 'Hey, you must come on the programme one night . . .' Many things had changed since then, including his attitude to Charles Boon, which had swung through a whole spectrum of feelings – amusement, annoyance, envy, anger, raging sexual jealousy and now, all that passion spent, a kind of grudging respect. You saw Boon everywhere these days, on the streets and on television, wherever there was a march, or a demonstration, conspicuous by a white plaster cast on one arm, as though he were daring the police to break the other. His nerve, his cheek, his self-confidence, knew no bounds; it turned into a kind of courage. Melanie's infatuation, which showed no signs of slackening, had become a little more explicable.

He crumpled the note and tossed it into the wastepaper basket. The package from England he would open in the privacy of his office. On his way there he visited the men's room on the fourth floor that had been bombed on his first day – now repaired and repainted. It was said that the view through the open window above the urinal, straight across the Bay to the Silver Span, was the finest obtainable from such a position anywhere in the world, but today Philip kept his eyes down. Foreshortened, yes, definitely.

You must believe me, Hilary, that there was absolutely nothing sexual in the arrangement at all. On the few occasions we'd met up to that time we hadn't particularly taken to each other, and in any case Désirée was in the first flush of her conversion to this Women's Liberation business and extremely hostile to men in general. In fact, that was what appealed to her about our arrangement . . .

'Oh, dear!' Désirée sighed after they made love for the first time.

'What's the matter?'

'It was nice while it lasted.'

'It was tremendous,' he said. 'Did I come too soon?'

'I don't mean that, stupid. I mean our chastity was nice while it lasted.'

'Chastity?'

'I've always wanted to be chaste. It's been so nice these last few weeks, don't you think, living like brother and sister? Now we're having an affair, like everybody else. How banal.'

'You don't have to go on with it if you don't want to,' he said.

'You can't go back, once you've started. You can only go forwards.'

'Good,' he said, and to make quite sure of the principle, woke her up early the next morning to make love again. It took a long time to rouse her, but she came in the end in a series of backarching undulations that lifted him clean off the bed.

'If I didn't know the vaginal orgasm was a myth,' she said afterwards, 'you could have fooled me. It was never so good with Morris.'

'I find that hard to believe,' he said. 'But nice of you to say so.'

'It's true. His technique was terrific, in the old days anyway, but I always felt like an engine on a test-bed. Being, what do they call it, tested to destruction?'

He went into his office, opened the window and sat down at the desk. The package from Hilary evidently contained a book, and was marked 'DAMAGED BY SEA WATER' which explained its strange, almost sinister shape. He peeled the wrapping paper off to reveal a warped, faded, wrinkled volume which he could not immediately identify. The spine was missing and the pages were stuck together. He managed to prise it open in the middle, however, and read: 'Flash-backs should be used sparingly, if at all. They slow down the progress of the story and confuse the reader. Life, after all, goes forwards, not backwards.'

They assembled self-consciously on the steps of Dealer Hall, the professors, instructors and teaching assistants of the English Department. Karl Kroop bustled round handing out black armbands. There were a few home-made placards in evidence, which declared TROOPS OFF CAMPUS and END THE OCCUPATION NOW. Philip nodded and smiled to friends and acquaintances in the shirtsleeved, summer-frocked throng. It was a nice day for a demonstration. Indeed, the atmosphere was more like a picnic than a vigil. Karl Kroop seemed to think so, too, for he called the company to order with a clap of his hands.

'This is supposed to be a *silent* demonstration, folks,' he said. 'And I think it would add dignity to our protest if you didn't smoke during the vigil.'

'Or drink or have sex,' a wag in the back row added. Sy Gootblatt, standing beside Philip, groaned and threw down his cigarette. 'It's all right for you,' he said, 'you've quit. How d'ya do it?'

'I compensate with more drink and sex,' Philip replied, smiling. Telling the truth with a jesting air was, he had discovered, the safest way of protecting your secrets in Euphoria.

'Yeah, but what about the post-coital cigarette? Doncha miss it?'

'I smoked a pipe myself.'

'And remember,' said Karl Kroop gravely, 'if the cops, or the troopers try to break this up, just go limp, but don't resist. Any pig roughs you up, make sure you get his number, not that the motherfuckers wear their numbers these days. Any questions?'

'Suppose they use gas?' someone asked.

'Then we're screwed. Just retreat with as much dignity as you can. Walk, don't run.'

Sobriety at last settled on the group. The English Faculty contained very few genuine radicals, and no would-be martyrs. Karl Kroop's words had reminded them that, in the present volatile atmosphere, they were all, just the tiniest bit, sticking their necks out. Technically they were in violation of Governor Duck's ban on public assemblies on campus.

It all started with my arrest. If it hadn't been for that, I think nothing would have happened. It was Désirée, you see, who bailed me out . . .

'Hallo, is that you Désirée?'

'About time! Have you forgotten I'm supposed to be going out tonight?'

'No, I haven't forgotten.'

'Where in hell are you?'

'I'm in prison, actually.'

'*In prison?*'

'I've been arrested for stealing bricks.'

'Jesus. *Did* you steal them?'

'No, of course not. I mean, I had them in the car, but I didn't steal them . . . It's a long story.'

'Better cut it short, Professor,' said the police officer who was standing guard over him.

'Look Désirée, can you come down here and try and bail me out? They say it will cost about a hundred and fifty dollars.'

'Cash,' said the policeman.

'Cash,' he repeated.

'I don't have that much, and the banks are shut. Will they accept an American Express credit card?'

'Do you accept credit cards?' Philip asked the policeman.

'No.'

'No, they don't.'

'I'll get the money somehow,' said Désirée. 'Don't worry.'

'Oh, I'm not worried,' said Philip miserably. He heard Désirée hang up, and put his own receiver down.

'You're allowed one other phone call,' said the policeman.

'I'll save it up,' he said.

'You got to make it now or not at all. And you better not count on getting bailed out, leastways not till Monday. You're an alien, see? That can complicate things.'

'Oh dear. What happens now?'

'What happens now is that I lock you up. Too bad the misdemeanour cell is full right up with other folk been taking bricks that don't belong to them. I'm gonna have to put you in the felons' cell.'

'Felons?' The word had a dread sound to his ears, and his misgivings were not allayed by the two powerfully built Negroes who sprang to their feet with feral agility as the cell door was opened.

'This here's a Professor, boys,' said the policeman, propelling Philip firmly inside and locking the door. 'So mind you speak nice to him.'

The felons prowled around him.

'What you busted for, Professor?'

'Stealing bricks.'

'Hear that, Al?'

'I heard it, Lou.'

'Like how many bricks, Professor?'

'Oh, about twenty-five.'

The felons looked wonderingly at each other. 'Perhaps they was gold bricks,' said one. The other gave a high-pitched, wailing laugh.

'Any cigarettes, Professor?'

'I'm sorry, no.' It was the only time he ever regretted having given up smoking.

'That's a sharp pair of pants the Professor is wearing, Al.'

'Sure is, Lou.'

'I like a pair of pants that fits nice and snug around the ass, Al.'

'Me too, Lou.'

Philip sat down quickly on the wooden bench that ran round the wall, and didn't move until Désirée bailed him out. 'You came just in time,' he told her as they drove away from police headquarters. 'I should have been raped if I'd stayed the night.'

It was funny in retrospect, but he had no wish to repeat the experience. If a posse of cops were to come rushing through Mather Gate right now to arrest them, he thought he would probably be among the first to break ranks and flee to the sanctuary of his office. Fortunately it was a quiet day on campus and the vigil seemed unlikely to provoke a breach of the peace. Passers-by just stared and smiled. A few made peace signs or Black Power salutes and shouted 'Right on!' and 'Power to the People!' A television team, a reporter and his cameraman, toting the heavy equipment on his back like a bazooka, filmed them for a few minutes, the lens of the camera slowly traversing along the length of the steps, irresistibly recalling the annual school photograph. Sy Gootblatt held a copy of the *Euphoric State Daily* in front of his face. 'How do we know they aren't working for the FBI?' he explained.

To begin at the beginning: I was driving through Plotinus one

*Saturday afternoon – I'd been shopping downtown – and on the way
back I passed the site of a church that was being demolished and
noticed that lots of people, mostly students, were carrying away the
old bricks in wheelbarrows and supermarket trolleys. I overtook a
group labouring along with a load of bricks in paper sacks and
shopping baskets, and recognized one of my own students . . .* Wily
Smith. With two black friends from the Ashland ghetto and
a white girl in a kaftan and bare feet. They accepted his offer
of a lift to the Garden with alacrity, loaded the bricks into
the boot of the Corvair and jumped into the passenger seats.
As Philip drew up at an intersection near the Garden, Wily
Smith suddenly yelled 'Pigs!' three of the car's doors flew
open simultaneously and Philip's passengers fled in four
different directions. The two policemen in the car that drew
up behind him did not bother to pursue them. They homed
in on Philip, sitting at the wheel, paralysed with fright. 'Did
I go through a red light or something?' he quavered.

'Open up your trunk, please.'

'It's only got some old bricks in it.'

'Just open up the trunk.'

He was so flustered he forgot the Corvair was a rear-
engined car and opened the engine cowling by mistake.

'Don't play games with me, Mac, I haven't the time.'

'Terribly sorry!' Philip opened up the luggage compartment.

'Where'd those bricks come from?'

'The, er, there's a building, a church, being demolished
down the road, you must have seen it. Lots of people are
taking the old bricks away.'

'You have written permission to take those bricks?'

'Look, officer, *I* didn't take the bricks. Those students
who were in the car had them. I was just giving them a
lift.'

'What are their names and addresses?'

Philip hesitated. He knew Wily Smith's address, and it was
his habit to tell the truth, especially to policemen.

'I don't know,' he said. 'I assumed they had permission.'

'Nobody had permission. Those bricks are stolen goods.'

'Really? They can't be worth very much, can they? But I'll take them back to the church right away.'

'Nobody's going to church. You got identification?'

Philip produced his Faculty Identity Card and British driver's licence. The former provoked a curt homily against professors encouraging their students to violate property, the latter provoked deep but silent suspicion. Both documents were confiscated. A second police car drew up beside them and the occupants began to unload the bricks from Philip's car and to transfer them into the police cars. Then they all went to police headquarters.

The room they put him in first was small, windowless and airless. He was strongly cautioned against damaging it or defacing the walls with obscenities, frisked for weapons, and left alone for half an hour to meditate on his sins. Then they brought him out and booked him. His faculty identity card and British driver's licence were scrutinized again. The contents of his pockets were itemized and confiscated – a discomfiting experience, which reminded him of a game played long ago on Pythagoras Drive. There was much amusement around the duty-sergeant's desk at the appearance of a marble, belonging to Darcy, in his jacket pocket ('Ho, ho, you're sure losing your marbles now, hey Professor?') turning into moral disapproval mingled with prurient envy when it became evident that the car he was driving and the house he was living in belonged to a woman other than the wife whose portrait was in his wallet. He was photographed, and his fingerprints taken. After that he was allowed his phone call to Désirée and then he was locked up with the felons. Désirée succeeded in bailing him out at seven in the evening, just when he had given up hope of being out before Monday. She was waiting for him in the lobby of the Hall of Justice, cool, crisp and confident in a cream-coloured trouser-suit, her red hair drawn back in a bun. He fell on her neck.

'Désirée . . . Thank God you came.'

'Hey, you look strung out. They been beating you up or something?'

'No, no, but it was . . . upsetting.'

Désirée was gentle, even tender, for the first time in their acquaintance. She stood on her toes to kiss him on the lips, linked arms and drew him towards the exit. 'Tell me all about it,' she said.

He told her in rambling, disconnected sentences. It wasn't just the shock of relief: as once before, the unexpected kiss had melted some glacier within him – unsuspected emotions and forgotten sensations were suddenly in full flood. He wasn't thinking about the arrest any more. He was thinking that it was the first time they had touched one another. And it almost seemed as if Désirée was thinking the same thing. To his disconnected remarks, she gave disconnected answers; driving home, she took her eyes off the road for dangerously long periods to look at him, she laughed and swore a little hysterically. Observing and interpreting these signs he felt still more excited and bewildered. His limbs trembled uncontrollably as he got out of the car, and went into the house. 'Where are the twins?' he asked. 'Next door,' said Désirée, looking at him strangely. She shut the front door, and took off her jacket. And her shoes. And her trousers. And her shirt. And her panties. She didn't wear a bra.

'Excuse me, Phil,' Sy Gootblatt whispered. 'But I think you're having an erection and it doesn't look nice at a vigil.'

At about 12.30, the vigil came to an uneventful end, and the demonstrators dispersed, chattering, for lunch. Philip had a shrimp salad sandwich with Sy Gootblatt in the Silver Steer restaurant on campus. Afterwards, Sy went back to his office to pound out another Hooker article on his electric typewriter. Philip, too restless to work (he hadn't read a book, not a real book, right through, for weeks) took the air. He strolled across Howle Plaza, soaking up the sunshine, past the booths and stalls of student political groups – a kind of ideological fair, this, at which you could join SDS, buy the literature of the Black Panthers, contribute to the Garden Bail Fund, pledge yourself to Save the Bay, give blood to the Viet Cong, obtain leaflets on first-aid in gas attacks, sign a petition to legalize pot, and express yourself in a hundred other interesting ways. On the street side of the plaza, a fundamentalist preacher and a group of chanting Buddhist monks vied with each other for the souls of those less committed to the things of this world. It was a relatively quiet day in Plotinus. Although there were State Troopers stationed on every intersection along Cable Avenue, directing the traffic, keeping the pavements clear, preventing people from congregating, there was little tension in the air, and the crowds were patient and good-humoured. It was a kind of hiatus between the violence, gassing and bloodshed of the recent past and the unpredictable future of the Great March. The Gardeners were busy with their preparations for that event; and the police, having had some bad publicity for their role in the Garden riots, were keeping a low profile. It was business as usual along Cable Avenue, though several windows were shattered and boarded up, and there was a strong, peppery smell of gas in the Beta Bookshop, a favourite gathering-place for radicals into which the police had lobbed so many gas grenades it was said you could tell which students in your class had bought their books there by the tears streaming down their faces. The more wholesome and appetizing fumes of hamburger, toasted cheese and pastrami, coffee and cigars, seeped into the street from crowded bars and cafés, the record shops were playing the latest rock-gospel hit *Oh Happy Day* through their external speakers, the bead curtains rattled in the breeze outside Indian novelty shops reeking of joss-sticks, and the strains of taped sitar music mingled with the sounds of radios tuned to twenty-five possible stations in the Bay area coming from the open windows of cars jammed nose to tail in the narrow roadway.

Philip snapped up a tiny vacant table at the open window of Pierre's café, ordered himself an ice-cream and Irish coffee, and sat back to observe the passing parade: the young bearded Jesuses and their barefoot Magdalenes in cotton maxis, Negroes with Afro haircuts like mushroom clouds and metallic-lensed sunglasses flashing heliographed messages of revolution to their brothers across the street, junkies and potheads stoned out of their minds groping their way along the kerb or sitting on the pavement with their backs to a sunny wall, ghetto kids and huckleberry runaways hustling the parking meters, begging dimes from drivers who paid up for fear of getting their fenders scratched, priests and policemen, bill-posters and garbage collectors, a young man distributing, without conviction, leaflets about courses in Scientology, hippies in scarred and tattered leather jackets toting guitars, and girls, girls of every shape and size and description, girls with long straight hair to their waists, girls in plaits, girls in curls, girls in short skirts, girls in long skirts, girls in jeans, girls in flared trousers, girls in Bermuda shorts, girls without bras, girls very probably without panties, girls white, brown, yellow, black, girls in kaftans, saris, skinny sweaters, bloomers, shifts, muu-muus, granny-gowns, combat jackets, sandals, sneakers, boots, Persian slippers, bare feet, girls with beads, flowers, slave bangles, ankle bracelets, earrings, straw boaters, coolie hats, sombreros, Castro caps, girls fat and thin, short and tall, clean and dirty, girls with big breasts and girls with flat chests, girls with tight, supple, arrogant buttocks and girls with loose globes of pendant flesh wobbling at every step and one girl who particularly caught Philip's attention as she waited at the kerb to cross the street, dressed in a crotch-high mini with long bare white legs and high up one thigh a perfect, mouth-shaped bruise.

Sitting there, taking it all in with the same leisurely relish as he sucked the fortified black coffee through its filter of whipped cream, Philip felt himself finally converted to expatriation; and he saw himself, too, as part of a great historical process – a reversal of that cultural Gulf Stream which had in the past swept so many Americans to Europe in search of Experience. Now it was not Europe but the West Coast of America that was the furthest rim of experiment in life and art, to which one made one's pilgrimage in search of liberation and enlightenment; and so it was to

American literature that the European now looked for a mirror-image of his quest. He thought of James's *The Ambassadors* and Strether's injunction to Little Bilham, in the Paris garden, to 'Live . . . live all you can; it's a mistake not to,' feeling himself to partake of both characters, the speaker who had discovered this insight too late, and the young man who might still profit by it. He thought of Henry Miller sitting over a beer in some scruffy Parisian café with his notebook on his knee and the smell of cunt still lingering on his fingers and he felt some distant kinship with that coarse, uneven, priapic imagination. He understood American Literature for the first time in his life that afternoon, sitting in Pierre's on Cable Avenue as the river of Plotinus life flowed past, understood its prodigality and indecorum, its yea-saying heterogeneity, understood Walt Whitman who laid end to end words never seen in each other's company before outside of a dictionary, and Herman Melville who split the atom of the traditional novel in the effort to make whaling a universal metaphor and smuggled into a book addressed to the most puritanical reading public the world has ever known a chapter on the whale's foreskin and got away with it; understood why Mark Twain nearly wrote a sequel to *Huckleberry Finn* in which Tom Sawyer was to sell Huck into slavery, and why Stephen Crane wrote his great war-novel first and experienced war afterwards, and what Gertrude Stein meant when she said that 'anything one is remembering is a repetition, but existing as a human being, that is being, listening and hearing is never repetition'; understood all that, though he couldn't have explained it to his students, some thoughts do often lie too deep for seminars, and understood, too, at last, what it was that he wanted to tell Hilary.

Because I've changed, Hilary, changed more than I should have thought possible. I've not only, as you know, been lodging with Désirée Zapp since the night of the landslip, I've also been sleeping with her quite regularly since the day of my arrest, and to be honest I can't seem to work up any guilt or regret about it. I should be very sorry,

*naturally, to cause you any pain, but when I ask myself what injury
have I done to you, what have I taken away from you that you had
before, I come up with the answer: nothing. It's not my relationship
with Désirée that has been wrong, it seems to me, but our marriage.
We have possessed each other totally, but without joy. I suppose, in
the thirteen years of our married life, this trip of mine to America has
been the only occasion on which we have been separated for more than
a day or two. In all that time I don't suppose there was one hour when
you didn't know, or couldn't guess, what I was doing, and when I
didn't know, or couldn't guess what you were doing. I think we even
knew, each of us, what the other was thinking, so that it was scarcely
necessary for us even to talk to each other. Every day was pretty much
like the last one, and the next one was sure to be like this one. We
knew what we both believed in: industry, thrift, education, modera-
tion. Our marriage – the home, the children – was like a machine
which we served, and serviced, with the silent economy of two techni-
cians who have worked together for so long that they never have to ask
for the appropriate tool, never bump into each other, never make an
error or have a disagreement and are bored out of their minds by the
job.*

*I see I've slipped unconsciously into the past tense, I suppose be-
cause I can't conceive of returning to that kind of relationship. Which
is not to say that I want a divorce or separation, but simply that if we
are going to go on together it will have to be on a new basis. Life,
after all, should go forwards, not backwards. I'm sure it would be a
good idea if you could come out here for a couple of weeks so that you
could understand what I'm trying to say in context, so to speak, and
make your own mind up about it all. I'm not sure I could explain
myself in Rummidge.*

*Incidentally, as regards Désirée: she has no claims on me, nor I on
her. I'll always regard her with affection and gratitude, and nothing
could make me regret our relationship, but of course I'm not asking
you to come out and join a ménage à trois. I'll be moving into my
own apartment soon . . .*

Yes, that should do it, Philip thought, as he paid his bill. I
won't send it off just yet, but when the time comes, that
should do very nicely.

*

'I think one has to accept,' Philip said earnestly into the QXYZ microphone, 'that those who originally conceived the Garden were radicals looking for an issue on which to confront the Establishment. It was an essentially political act by the radical Left, designed to provoke an extreme display of force by the law-and-order agencies, thus demonstrating the revolutionary thesis that this allegedly democratic society is in fact totalitarian, repressive and intolerant.'

'If I understand you correctly, Professor Swallow,' said the nasal-voiced caller, 'you're saying that the people who started the Garden were ultimately responsible for all the violence that followed.'

'Is that what you're saying, Phil?' Boon cut in.

'In a sense, yes. But there's another sense, perhaps a more important one, in which the thesis has been proved right. I mean, when you have two thousand troops camped in this small community, helicopters buzzing overhead all day, a curfew at night, people shot in the streets, gassed, arrested indiscriminately, and all to suppress a little public garden, then you have to admit that there does seem to be something wrong with the system. In the same way, the idea of the Garden may have been a political stratagem to those who conceived it, but perhaps it's become an authentic and valuable idea in the process of being realized. I hope you don't think I've evaded your question.'

'No,' said the voice in his earphones. 'No. That's very interesting. Tell me, Professor Swallow, has anything like this ever happened at your own University in England?'

'No,' said Philip.

'Thanks for calling,' said Boon.

'Thank you,' said the caller.

Boon flicked the switch that controlled the open line and intoned his station identification into the mike. His left arm was in plaster and bore the legend, 'Broken by Arcadia County Sheriff's Deputies, Saturday May 17th, at Shamrock and Addison. Witnesses needed.' 'Uh, we have time for just one or two more calls,' he said. The red light flashed. 'Hallo and good evening. This is Charles Boon, and my guest, Professor Philip Swallow. What's on your mind?'

This time it was an old lady, evidently a regular caller, for Boon rolled one eye in despair at the sound of her slow, quavering voice.

'Don't you think, Professor,' she said, 'that what young folks need today is some college courses in self-control and self-denial?'

'Well –'

'Now, when I was a girl – that was a while ago, I can tell you, heh heh . . . Would you like to guess how old I am, Professor?'

Charles Boon cut in ruthlessly: 'O K Grandma, what is it you're trying to tell us? A girl's best friend is N-O spells NO?'

After a brief silence, the voice quavered, 'Why, bless my soul Mr Boon, that's exactly what I was going to say.'

'What about that, Phil?' said Charles Boon. 'You got any views on N-O spells NO as a panacea for our times?' He took a swig from the Coke bottle in front of him, and gave a practised silent burp. Through the glass panel to Boon's left Philip could see the sound engineer yawning over his knobs and dials. The engineer looked, ungratefully, rather bored. Philip wasn't in the least bored. He had enjoyed the broadcast enormously. For nearly two hours he had been dispensing liberal wisdom to the audience of the Charles Boon Show on every conceivable subject – the Garden, drugs, law and order, academic standards, Viet Nam, the environment, nuclear testing, abortion, encounter groups, the Underground press, the death of the novel, and even now he had enough energy and enthusiasm left to find a word on the Sexual Revolution for the old lady.

'Well,' he said, 'sexual morality has, of course, always been a bone of contention between the generations. But there's more honesty, less hypocrisy about these matters than there used to be, and I think that must be a good thing.'

Charles Boon couldn't stand any more of this. He cut off the old lady and started to wind up the show. The red light flashed again, and he said OK, they would take one last call. The voice sounded distant, but quite clear.

'Is that you Philip?'

'Hilary!'

'At last!'

'Good God! Where are you?'

'At home, of course. You can't imagine the trouble I've had getting through.'

'You can't speak to me now.'

'It's now or never, Philip.'

Charles Boon was sitting up tensely in his seat, clutching his earphones with his free hand as if he had just picked up a conversation from outer space. The engineer behind the glass screen had stopped yawning and was making frantic signals.

'This is a private call that's been put through by mistake,' Philip said. 'Please disconnect it.'

'Don't you dare, Philip,' said Hilary. 'I've been trying for a whole hour to get through to you.'

'How in God's name did you get the number?'

'Mrs Zapp gave it to me.'

'Did she happen to mention that it was the number of a phone-in programme?'

'Eh? She said you were anxious to get in touch with me. Was it about my birthday?'

'My God, I forgot all about that.'

'It doesn't matter in the least.'

'Look, Hilary, you must get off this line.' He leaned across the green baize table to reach the control switch, but Boon, grinning demonically, fended him off with his plaster cast and made signals to the engineer to turn up the volume. His vagrant eye was shooting in all directions with excitement. 'What is it you want, Hilary?' Philip asked anguishedly.

'You've got to come home at once, Philip, if you want to save our marriage.'

Philip laughed, briefly and hysterically.

'Why do you laugh?'

'I was writing to tell you more or less the same thing.'

'I'm not joking, Philip.'

'Neither am I. By the way, have you any idea how many people are listening to this conversation?'

'I don't know what you're talking about.'

'Exactly, so will you kindly get off the bloody phone.'

'If that's the way you feel about it . . . I just hope you understand that I'm very probably going to have an affair.'

'I'm having one already!' he cried. 'But I don't want to tell the whole world about it.'

That finally stopped Hilary. There was a gasp, a silence and a click.

'Terrific,' Charles Boon said, when the red and green lights went out and the mike was dead at last. 'Terrific. Sensational. Fantastic radio.'

The weather forecast had predicted sunny spells, and the first of them woke Morris early, shining straight on to his face through the thin cotton drapes. Sunny spells. 'Who is casting these sunny spells?' he used to ask his Rummidge acquaintances. 'What kind of a witch wastes her time casting *sunny* spells?' Nobody else seemed to think it was funny, however, and now even he was getting used to the quaint meteorological idiom. 'Temperature about the seasonal average.' 'Rather cool.' 'Scattered showers and bright periods.' The imprecision of these terms no longer bothered him. He accepted that, like so much British usage, it was a language of evasion and compromise, designed to take the drama out of the weather. No talk of 'lows' or 'highs' here: all was moderate, qualified, temperate.

He lay on his back for a while, eyes closed against the sunlight, and against the almost equally blinding floral wallpaper adorning the walls of the Swallows' guest room, listening to the house rousing itself for a new day, the whole structure stretching and groaning like a flophouse full of old men. The floorboards creaked, the plumbing whined and throbbed, doorhinges squeaked and windows rattled in their frames. The noise was deafening. Morris added his quota with a prolonged fart that nearly lifted him off the mattress. It was his customary salute to the dawn; something about Rummidge, the water probably, gave him terrible wind.

His ears twitched at the sound of a footfall on the landing. Hilary? He leapt out of bed, rushed to the window, flung it open and furiously flapped the bedclothes.

All wasted effort. The feet belonged to Mary Makepeace: he recognized her heavy pregnant tread. For a moment he'd thought Hilary had relented and was going to slip into his room for a quick roll in the hay before reveille. He slammed the window shut and hopped shivering back to bed. How close, actually, he'd come to getting into the sack with Hilary last night.

She'd been blue because it was her birthday and Swallow hadn't sent her a gift, not even a goddam card. 'When I don't want them he sends me roses by Interflora, then he goes and forgets my birthday,' she complained with a crooked smile. 'He's hopeless about things like that. Usually the children remind him.' To cheer her up, Morris invited her out for a meal. She demurred. He pressed. Mary supported him, also Amanda. Hilary allowed herself to be persuaded. Took a shower, washed her hair, and changed into a fetching black maxi that he hadn't seen before, with a low-cut neckline that showed off the smooth creamy texture of her shoulders and bosom. 'Hey, you look terrific,' he said sincerely, and she blushed right down to her cleavage. She kept fiddling with her shoulder straps and hitching a shawl round her shoulders until she'd had a second dry martini, after which she leaned negligently forward across the restaurant table and didn't seem to mind his taking long appreciative looks down inside her dress.

He took her to the one tolerable trattoria in Rummidge, and afterwards to Petronella's, a small club in a basement near the station where they usually had decent music and the clientele were not too oppressively adolescent. This evening the entertainment was provided by a so-so folk-blues group called Morte D'Arthur with a wistful girl singer who sang pastiches of recordings by Joan Baez and other vocalists of that ilk; but it could have been worse, a heavy rock band for instance which Hilary wouldn't have liked at all. She seemed to enjoy herself, anyway, looking round at the Tudor-adobe decor wonderingly, and applauding enthusiastically after each song, saying, 'I never knew there were places like this in Rummidge, however did you discover it?' He didn't like to point out that Petronella's and a dozen places like it were advertised every evening in the local paper, it would have seemed like a put-down, but it was a fact that Hilary and her peer group simply didn't see most of what was happening in the city around them. There was, believe it or not, a Rummidge scene of sorts, though you had to search quite hard for parts of it – the gay clubs, for instance, or the West Indian dives in the Arbury ghetto – but there were other parts, almost as interesting, that were accessible enough. For instance, the cocktail bar of the Ritz, Rummidge's best hotel, on a Saturday night, when the car-workers gathered with their wives and girl friends for the conspicuous consumption of alcohol. However high the hotel pegged its prices in an effort to maintain a classy atmosphere, the car-workers could match them. They gathered round the tables or perched at the bar, the women balancing their huge beehive wigs, towering like cumulus cloud above their stocky, broad-shouldered escorts who sat stiffly, calloused horny hands sticking out of their sharp new suits, ordering round after round of daiquiris, whisky-sours, White Ladies, Orange Blossoms, and special inventions of Harold, the prize-winning barman – Mushroom Cloud, Supercharger, Fireball and Rummidge Dew ... 'I'll take you there some time,' he promised Hilary.

'Goodness, you do seem terribly *au fait* with everything, Morris. Anyone would think you'd lived in Rummidge for years.'

'Sometimes it feels like that,' he joked mildly.

'You must be looking forward to going back to Euphoria.'

'Well, I don't know. I'll be sorry to miss the first Rummidge Grand Prix.'

'Surely the climate ... and your family?'

'I'll be glad to see the twins again. But it may be the last time. You know Désirée wants a divorce.'

Hilary's eyes filled with ginny tears. 'I'm sorry,' she said.

He shrugged and put on his stoical, weary, Humphrey Bogart expression. There was a rose-tinted mirror behind Hilary's head in which he was able to make small, unobtrusive adjustments to his face when he wasn't occupied in looking down Hilary's neckline.

'Isn't there a chance of a reconciliation?' she asked.

'I was hoping this trip of mine would swing it. But by the way she's been writing, her mind's made up.'

'I'm sorry,' she said again.

The girl in Morte D'Arthur was singing 'Who Knows Where The Time Goes?' in a very passable imitation of Judy Collins. 'You and Philip ever have any . . . problems?' he risked asking.

'Oh, no, never. Well, I say never –' She stopped, embarrassed.

He reached across the table and covered her hand with his. 'I know about Melanie, you know.'

'I know.' She stared at his big, brown hand, hair luxuriant on the knuckles. It looked like a bear's paw, Désirée used to say, but Hilary didn't flinch. 'That was the first time,' she said.

'How do you know?'

'Oh, I know.' She looked up at him. 'I'm sorry it had to be your daughter.'

If there was a correct formula for accepting this kind of apology, Morris couldn't think of it. He shrugged again. 'And you've forgiven him for that?' he said.

'Oh yes. Well, I think so.'

'I wish Désirée was as understanding as you,' he sighed.

'Perhaps she has more to forgive?' she said timidly.

He grinned rakishly. 'Perhaps.'

The girl vocalist had been joined by the lead and bass guitars and they were singing 'Puff the Magic Dragon' in imitation of Peter, Paul and Mary. The lead guitar was the weak link in the ensemble, Morris decided. Perhaps he was

Arthur. In which case the group's name was a consummation devoutly to be wished. 'Shall we move on to some other place?' he said. Now that the pubs were shut, Petronella's was filling up with less refined customers, heavy drinkers and the odd hooker. Any minute now Morte D'Arthur would finish their set, and a rowdy disco would begin. There was a roadhouse Morris knew that had a juke box loaded exclusively with forties swing records.

'I think we should be going home,' Hilary said.

He glanced at his watch. 'What's the hurry? Mary is baby-sitting.'

'Even so. I'm getting drowsier and drowsier. I'm not used to drinking this much in an evening.'

In the Lotus, she let her head fall back against the head-restraint and closed her eyes. 'It's been a lovely evening, Morris. Thank you so much.'

'It's my pleasure.' He leaned across and kissed her experimentally on the lips. She put her arms round his neck and responded with relaxed enjoyment. Morris decided to take her home after all.

The household was asleep when they got back, and they tiptoed around without speaking. While Hilary was laying the breakfast table ready for the next morning, Morris went to the bathroom, briskly washed his private parts and brushed his teeth, changed into clean pyjamas and silk kimono, and waited expectantly in his room until she mounted the stairs. He gave her a few minutes, then quietly crossed the landing and entered the bedroom. Hilary was sitting at the dressing-table in her slip, brushing her hair. She turned round, startled.

'What is it, Morris?'

'I thought maybe I would sleep in here tonight. Isn't that what you had in mind?'

She shook her head, aghast. 'Oh no, I couldn't.'

'Why not?'

'Not here. Not with all the children in the house. And Mary.'

'Where else? When else? Tomorrow I go back to O'Shea's. The roof is fixed.'

'I know. I'm sorry Morris.'

'Come on, Hilary, let yourself go. Relax. You're all tensed up. Let me give you a little massage.' He moved up behind her, and placed his hands on the back of her neck. He began to work his fingers into Hilary's shoulder muscle. But she did not relax, held her head rigid and averted, so that in the mirror they resembled a tableau of a strangler and his victim. 'I'm sorry, Morris, I just couldn't,' she murmured.

'OK,' he said coldly, and left her, immobile before the mirror.

A few minutes later they met again on the landing, coming and going between their bedrooms and the bathroom. Hilary was in nightdress and dressing-gown, her face shiny with face-cream. He must have looked grim and resentful, because she put a hand on his arm as he passed.

'Morris, I'm sorry,' she whispered.

'Forget it.'

'I wish I could . . . I wish . . . You've been so kind.' She swayed against him. He caught and kissed her, slipped his hand under her gown and was going great when a floorboard creaked somewhere nearby and she tore herself away from him and rushed back into her room. Nobody was around, of course. It was just the goddam house talking to itself as usual. Hilary said it was the central heating that caused the ancient wood to shrink and expand. Could be. There were huge gaps between the floorboards in the guestroom, through which a delicious aroma of bacon and coffee now began to percolate from the kitchen below. Morris decided it was time to get up.

He found Mary Makepeace cooking breakfast for the three children in one of Hilary's button-through overalls that scarcely met across her bulging stomach.

'What did you do to Hilary last night?' she greeted him.

'What d'you mean?'

'No sign of her this morning. You fill her up with liquor?'

'Just a couple of martinis.'

'Eggs with your bacon?'

'Uh, I'll have two, scrambled.'

'What d'you think this is, Howard Johnson's?'

'Yeah, and let me have a side order of golden-crisp ranch-fried potatoes.' He winked at Matthew, open-mouthed over his bowl of cornflakes. The young Swallows were not used to adult repartee over the breakfast table.

'Morris, could you possibly take me to the railroad station on your way to work this morning?'

'Sure. Taking a trip somewhere?'

'You remember I told you I was going to visit my family's grave in County Durham?'

'Isn't that a long way from here?'

'I'll stay overnight in Durham. Be back tomorrow.'

Morris sighed. 'I shan't be here. O'Shea has fixed his roof, so I'll be going back to the apartment. I'm going to miss the cooking here.'

'Aren't you scared to go back to that place?'

'Oh, well, you know what they say: a lump of frozen urine never strikes in the same place twice.'

'Hey kids, hurry up, or you'll be late for school.' Mary put a plate of scrambled eggs and bacon in front of Morris and he tucked in appreciatively.

'You know, Mary,' he said when the children had left the room, 'your talents are wasted as an unmarried mother. Why don't you persuade that priest of yours to become a Protestant? Then you could make an honest man of him.'

'Funny you should say that,' she replied, taking an air-mail envelope from her pocket and wagging it in the air. 'He just wrote to say he's been laicized.'

'Great! He wants to marry you?'

'He wants to shack up with me anyway.'

'What are you going to do?'

'I'm thinking about it. I wonder what's the matter with Hilary? There are some things I have to tell her before I leave.'

Amanda appeared at the door, arrayed in her school uniform – dark maroon blazer, white shirt and tie, grey skirt. The students of Rummidge High School for Girls wore their skirts very, very short indeed, so that they resembled mythical biform creatures like mermaids or centaurs, all prim austerity above the waist, all bare forked animal below. The bus stops in the neighbourhood were a nympholept's paradise at this time of the morning. Amanda blushed under Morris's scrutiny. 'I'm off, Mary,' she said.

'Just run upstairs first, Mandy, and ask your mother if she'd like a cup of tea or something, would you?'

'Mummy's not upstairs. She's in Daddy's study.'

'Really? I must tell her about the meal tonight.' Mary bustled out.

'I see the Bee Gees are giving a concert in town the week after next,' Morris said to Amanda. 'Shall I get tickets?'

Amanda's eyes gleamed. 'Oh, yes please!'

'Perhaps Mary will come with us, or even your mother. D'you dig the Bee Gees?' he asked Mary, who had returned.

'Can't stand them. Amanda, you'd better be on your way. Your mother's tied up on the telephone.'

Hilary was still on the phone when it was time for Mary to leave. She scribbled a note for Hilary while Morris backed the Lotus into the road, its exhaust booming in a deep baritone that rattled the house windows in their frames.

'What time is your train?' he asked as Mary, manoeuvering her belly with care, lowered herself into the passenger seat.

'Eight-fifty. Will we make it?'

'Sure.'

'This car wasn't built for pregnant women, was it?'

'The seat reclines. How's that?'

'That's great. Mind if I practise my relaxation?'

'Go ahead.'

Almost at once they hit a tailback of rush-hour traffic in the Midland Road. A line of people waiting at a bus stop gazed curiously at Mary Makepeace practising shallow breathing in the bucket seat of the Lotus.

'What's that all about?' Morris inquired.

'Psychoprophylaxis. Painless childbirth to you. Hilary's teaching me.'

'You believe in it?'

'Of course. The Russians have been using it for years.'

'Only because they can't afford anaesthetics, I'll bet.'

'Who wants anaesthetics at the most important moment of a woman's life?'

'Désirée wanted the hospital to put her out for the whole goddam nine months.'

'She was brainwashed, if you'll pardon the expression. The medical profession has succeeded in persuading women that pregnancy is a kind of illness that only doctors know how to cure.'

'What does O'Shea think about it all?'

'He just believes in old-fashioned pain.'

'That figures. You know, Mary, I can't understand why you put yourself in that guy's hands. He looks like the kind of doctor who used to take bullets out of gangsters in old "B" pictures.'

'It's the system here. You have to register with a local doctor to get referred to the hospital. O'Shea was the only doctor I knew.'

'I don't like to think of him examining you . . . I mean, he has dirt under his fingernails!'

'Oh, he leaves that kind of thing to the hospital. He only gave me a pre-natal once and it seemed to embarrass hell out of him. He fixed his eyes on this hideous picture of the Sacred Heart on the wall and kept muttering under his breath like he was praying.'

Morris laughed. 'That's O'Shea.'

'It was a kind of spooky occasion all round. There was this nurse of his –'

'Nurse?'

'A black-haired girl with no teeth –'

'That's no nurse, that's Bernadette, the Irish slavey.'

'Well, she was wearing a nurse's uniform.'

'A con trick. O'Shea is just saving money.'

'Anyway, she kept glowering at me from out of the corner of the room like a wild animal. I don't know, perhaps she was smiling at me and it just looked like a snarl.'

'She wasn't smiling, Mary. I should keep out of Bernadette's way if I were you. She's jealous.'

'Jealous of me?'

'She thinks I knocked you up.'

'Good Lord!'

'Don't sound so surprised. I'm perfectly capable of it. What time did you say your train was? Eight-fifty?'

'That's right.'

'We're going to have to break the law a little bit.'

'Take it easy, Morris. It's not that important.'

The traffic appeared to be backed up for nearly a mile from the intersection with the Inner Ring. Morris pulled out and varoomed down the wrong side of the road, scandalized drivers honking protest in his wake. Just before he reached the Inner Ring an invalid carriage, as they were called (more like euthanasia on wheels, he would have said, a frontwheel blowout in one of those crazy boxed-in tricycles and you were a gonner) handily stalled and gave him space to get the Lotus back into line.

'How about that?' he said elatedly. But unfortunately a cop on traffic duty had observed the manner of Morris's arrival. He came across, unbuttoning his tunic pocket.

'Oh dear,' said Mary Makepeace. 'Now you're going to get a ticket.'

'Would you mind going back into that quick-breathing routine?'

The policeman had to bend almost double to peer into the car. Morris gestured with his thumb at Mary Makepeace panting for all she was worth, her eyes closed and her tongue hanging out like a dog's, hands clasping her belly. 'Emergency, officer. This young lady's going to have a baby.'

'Oh,' said the cop. 'Well, all right, but drive more carefully or you'll both end up in hospital.' Smiling at his own joke, he held up the traffic for them to proceed against the lights. Morris waved his thanks. He got Mary Makepeace to the station with five minutes to spare.

Driving back to the University, Morris took the newly opened section of the Inner Ring, an exhilarating complex of tunnels and flyovers that was part of the proposed Grand Prix circuit. He leaned back in the bucket seat and drove with straight, extended arms in the style of a professional racing driver. In the longest tunnel, safe from police observation, he put his foot down and heard with satisfaction the din of the Lotus's exhaust reverberating from the walls. He came out of the tunnel like a bullet, into a long canted curve elevated above roof level. From here you got a panorama of the whole city and the sun came out at that moment, shining like floodlighting on the pale concrete façades of the recent construction work, tower blocks and freeways, throwing them into relief against the sombre mass of nineteenth-century slums and decayed factories. Seen from this perspective, it looked as though the seeds of a whole twentieth-century city had been planted under the ground a long time ago and were now beginning to shoot up into the light, bursting through the caked, exhausted topsoil of Victorian architecture. Morris found it an oddly stirring sight, for the city that was springing up was unmistakably American in style – indeed that was what the local blimps were always beefing about – and he had the strange feeling of having stumbled upon a new American frontier in the most unexpected place.

But one thing was for sure, they had a long way to catch up in music on radio. The clock in the campanile was striking nine and one godawful disc jockey was handing over to another on Radio One as he swept through the main gates of the University. The security man saluted smartly: since his success in ending the sit-in Morris had become a well-known and respected man-about-campus, and the orange Lotus made him instantly identifiable. There was, naturally, no difficulty in finding parking space this early in the morning. The Rummidge faculty liked to complain about timetable clashes, but the real problem was their reluctance to teach before ten o'clock in the morning or after four in the afternoon or in the lunch period or on Wednesday afternoons or any time at weekends. That scarcely left them time to open their mail, let alone teach. Unaware of this gentlemanly tradition, Morris had fixed one of his tutorials at nine am, much to the disgust of the students concerned, and it was to meet this group that he now stepped out to his office – not with excessive haste, for they were invariably late.

The English Department had changed its quarters since his arrival at Rummidge. It was now situated on the eighth floor of a newly built hexagonal block, one of those he had surveyed from the Inner Ring. The changeover had taken place in the Easter vacation amid much wailing and gnashing of teeth. Oy, oy, Exodus was nothing in comparison. With a characteristically whacky, yet somehow endearing tenderness for individual liberty over logic and efficiency, the Administration had allowed each faculty member to decide which items of furniture he would like transferred from his old accommodation to the new, and which he would like replaced. The resulting permutations were totally confusing to the men carrying out the work and innumerable errors were made. For days two caravans of porters could be seen tottering from one building to the other, carrying almost as many tables, chairs and filing cabinets out of the new one as they carried into it. For a new building, the Hexagon had already acquired quite a mythology. It was built on a prefabricated principle and confidence in the soundness of the structure had been undermined by hastily issued restrictions on the weight of books each faculty member was allowed on his bookshelves. The more conscientious members of staff were to be observed in the first weeks of their occupation resentfully weighing their books on kitchen or bathroom scales and adding up long columns of figures on pieces of paper. There were also restrictions on the number of persons allowed into each office and classroom, and it was alleged that the windows on the West side were sealed up because if all the occupants of those rooms were to lean out at the same time the building would fall over. The exterior had been faced with glazed ceramic tiles guaranteed to resist the corrosion of the Rummidge atmosphere for five hundred years, but they had been attached with an inferior adhesive material and were already beginning to fall off here and there. Notices bearing the motto 'Beware of Falling Tiles' decorated the approach to the new building. These warnings were not superfluous: a tile fell in fragments at Morris's feet just as he mounted the steps at the entrance.

All in all, it was hardly surprising that the move was the subject of bitter complaint by members of the English Department; but there was one feature of the new building that entirely redeemed it in Morris's eyes at least. This was a type of elevator which he had never seen before, quaintly named a paternoster, that consisted of an endless belt of open compartments moving up and down two shafts. The movement was slower, naturally, than that of a normal elevator, since the belt never stopped and one had to step into it while it was moving, but the system eliminated all tedious waiting. It also imparted to the ordinary, quotidian action of taking an elevator a certain existential edge of drama, for one had to time one's leap into and out of the moving compartment with finesse and positive commitment. Indeed for the elderly and infirm the paternoster constituted a formidable challenge, and most of them preferred to labour up and down the staircase. Admittedly the notice pasted beside the red-painted Emergency device on every floor did not inspire confidence: 'In case of emergency, pull the red lever downwards. Do not attempt to free persons trapped in the paternoster or its machinery. The maintenance staff will attend to malfunctions at the earliest possible opportunity.' One day there would be a conventional elevator as well, but as yet it wasn't in operation. Morris didn't complain: he loved the paternoster. Perhaps it was a throwback to his childhood delight in fairground carousels and suchlike; but he also found it a profoundly poetic machine, especially if one stayed on for the round trip, disappearing into darkness at the top and bottom and rising or dropping into the light again, perpetual motion readily symbolizing all systems and cosmologies based on the principle of eternal recurrence, vegetation myths, death and rebirth archetypes, cyclic theories of history, metempsychosis and Northrop Frye's theory of literary modes.

This morning, however, he contented himself with a direct journey to the eighth floor. His tutorial students were already waiting, slumped against the wall beside the door of his office, yawning and scratching themselves. He greeted them and unlocked the door, which bore his name on a slip of paper pasted over the nameplate of Gordon Masters. As soon as he got inside, the communicating door opposite opened and Alice Slade inched her way apologetically into the room, clutching a large stack of files.

'Oh,' she said, 'are you teaching, Professor Zapp? I wanted to ask you about these postgraduate applications.'

'Yeah, teaching till ten, Alice, OK? Why don't you ask Rupert Sutcliffe about it?'

'Oh, all right. Sorry I disturbed you.' She backed out.

'Siddown,' he said to the students, thinking to himself that he would have to move back into Swallow's room. On accepting the job of mediator between the Administration and the students he'd asked for secretarial assistance and an outside telephone line – requests which had been promptly and economically satisfied by moving him into the office made vacant by the abrupt departure of Gordon Masters. You could still tell from the marks on the walls where the hunting trophies had hung. Although his work as mediator was virtually finished, it hardly seemed worthwhile moving back into Swallow's room, but in the meantime the Departmental Secretary, conditioned to refer all problems, inquiries and decisions to Masters, had begun to bring them, as though compelled by a deep-seated homing instinct, to him, Morris Zapp, although Rupert Sutcliffe was supposed to be the Acting Head of the Department. In fact Sutcliffe himself was inclined to come to Morris with oblique appeals for advice and approval, and other members of staff too.

Suddenly freed from Masters' despotic rule after thirty years, the Rummidge English Department was stunned and frightened by its own liberty, it was going round and round in circles like a rudderless ship, no, more like a ship whose tyrannical captain had unexpectedly fallen overboard one dark night, taking with him sealed instructions about the ship's ultimate destination. The crew kept coming out of habit to the bridge for orders, and were only too glad to take them from anyone who happened to be occupying the captain's seat.

Admittedly it was a comfortable seat – a padded, tip-back, executive's swivel chair – and for that reason alone Morris was reluctant to move back into Philip Swallow's room. He leaned back into it, put his feet on the desk and lit a cigar. 'Well now,' he said to the three dejected-looking students. 'What are you bursting to discuss this morning?'

'Jane Austen,' mumbled the boy with the beard, shuffling some sheets of foolscap covered with evil-looking handwriting.

'Oh yeah. What was the topic?'

'I've done it on Jane Austen's moral awareness.'

'That doesn't sound like my style.'

'I couldn't understand the title you gave me, Professor Zapp.'

'Eros and Agape in the later novels, wasn't it? What was the problem?'

The student hung his head. Morris felt in the mood for a little display of high-powered exposition. Agape, he explained, was a feast through which the early Christians expressed their love for one another, it symbolized non-sexual, non-individualized love, it was represented in Jane Austen's novels by social events that confirmed the solidarity of middle-class agrarian capitalist communities or welcomed new members into those communities – balls and dinner parties and sight-seeing expeditions and so on. Eros was of course sexual love and was represented in Jane Austen by courtship scenes, tête-à-têtes, walking in pairs – any encounter between the heroine and the man she loved, or thought she loved. Readers of Jane Austen, he emphasized, gesturing freely with his cigar, should not be misled by the absence of overt reference to physical sexuality in her fiction into supposing that she was indifferent or hostile to it. On the contrary, she invariably came down on the side of Eros against Agape – on the side, that is, of the private communion of lovers over against the public communion of social events and gatherings which invariably caused pain and distress (think for instance of the disastrous nature of group expeditions, to Sotherton in *Mansfield Park*, to Box Hill in *Emma*, to Lyme Regis in *Persuasion*). Getting into his stride, Morris demonstrated that Mr Elton was obviously implied to be impotent because there was no lead in the pencil that Harriet Smith took from him; and the moment in *Persuasion* when Captain Wentworth lifted the little brat Walter off Anne Elliot's shoulders . . . He snatched up the text and read with feeling:

' "... *she found herself in the state of being released from him . . . Before she realized that Captain Wentworth had done it . . . he was resolutely borne away . . . Her sensations on the discovery made her perfectly speechless. She could not even thank him. She could only hang over little Charles with the most disordered feelings.*" How about that?' he concluded reverently. 'If that isn't an *orgasm*, what is it?' He looked up into three flabbergasted faces. The internal telephone rang.

It was the Vice-Chancellor's secretary, asking if Morris would be free to see the VC some time that morning. Was the President of the Student Council quibbling about representation on the Promotions and Appointments Committee, Morris inquired. The secretary didn't know, but Morris was willing to take a bet he was right. He'd always been surprised by the readiness with which the Student President had waived representation on Promotions and Appointments: no doubt his militant henchmen had been leaning on him to raise the issue again. Morris smiled knowingly to himself as he scribbled an appointment for 10.30 in his desk diary. Mediating between the two sides in this dispute at Rummidge he often felt like a grandmaster of chess overlooking a match between two novices – able to predict the entire pattern of the game while they sweated over every move. To the Rummidge faculty his prescience seemed uncanny, his expertise in chairing negotiations amazing. They didn't realize that he had seen so many campus disturbances in Euphoria that he knew the basic scenario by heart.

'Where were we?' he said.

'*Persuasion* . . .'

'Oh, yeah.'

The telephone rang again. 'An outside call for you,' said Alice Slade.

'Alice,' Morris sighed. 'Please don't put any calls through until this class is over.'

'Sorry. Shall I ask her to call back?'

'Who is it?'

'Mrs Swallow.'

'Put her on.'

'Morris?' Hilary's voice sounded trembly.

'Hi.'

'Are you teaching or something?'

'No, no, not really.' He covered the mouthpiece with one hand and said to the students, 'Just read through that scene in *Persuasion* will you and try to analyse how it builds up to a climax. In every sense of the word.' He leered at them encouragingly, and resumed his conversation with Hilary. 'What's new?'

'I just wanted to apologize for last night.'

'Honey, it's me that should apologize,' said Morris, taken by surprise.

'No, I behaved like a silly young girl. Leading you on and then backing away in a panic. After all, it's nothing to make a fuss about, is it?'

'No, no.' Morris swung round in his chair to turn his back on the students, and spoke in a low voice. 'What isn't?'

'Anyway, I haven't had such a nice evening for years.'

'Let's do it again. Soon.'

'Could you bear it?'

'Sure. Delighted.'

'Lovely.'

There was a pause, in which he could hear Hilary breathing.

'Is that OK, then?' he asked.

'Yes. Morris . . .'

'Yeah?'

'Are you going back to your flat today?'

'Yeah. I'll come round to pick up my bag this evening.'

'I was going to say, you could stay another night if you wanted to.'

'Well . . .'

'Mary's away tonight. Sometimes I get scared in the night, in the house on my own.'

'Sure. I'll stay.'

'You're sure it's no trouble?'

'No, no. That's fine.'

'All right. See you this evening, then.' She hung up abruptly. Morris swung round in his chair to replace the receiver and rubbed his chin thoughtfully.

'Shall I read my paper or not?' said the bearded student, with a trace of impatience.

'What? Oh, yeah. Read it. Read it.'

While the boy drawled on about Jane Austen's moral awareness, Morris pondered the implications of Hilary's surprising call. Could she possibly mean what he thought she meant? He found it difficult to concentrate on the paper, and was relieved when the clock in the campanile struck ten. As the students shuffled out through the door, Rupert Sutcliffe shuffled in, a tall, stooped, melancholy figure, with ill-fitting glasses that kept slipping to the end of his nose. Sutcliffe was the Department Romantics man, but he was short on joy, and being made Acting Head on Masters' departure hadn't apparently raised his spirits.

'Oh, Zapp. Could you spare a minute?'

'Can we discuss it over a cup of coffee?'

'I'm afraid not. Not in the Senior Common Room. It's a rather delicate matter.' He closed the door conspiratorially behind him and tip-toed towards Morris. 'These post-graduate applications –' He placed a stack of files (the same that Alice Slade had brought in earlier) on to Morris's desk. 'We've got to decide which ones to put forward for approval by the Faculty Committee.'

'Yeah?'

'Well, one of them is from Hilary Swallow. Swallow's wife, you know.'

'Yes, I know. I'm one of her referees.'

'God bless my soul, are you really? I hadn't noticed. You know all about it then?'

'Well, something. What's the problem? She was halfway through a Master's course when she got married and quit. Now her kids are growing up and she'd like to get back into research.'

'That's all very well, but it puts us in a rather awkward position. I mean, the wife of a colleague . . .'

He was a bachelor, Sutcliffe, a genuine old-fashioned bachelor, as distinct from being gay or hip – and women scared him to death. The two on the Department staff he treated as honorary men. If his colleagues had to have wives, he intimated, the least they could do was to keep them at home in decent obscurity. 'I think Swallow might at least have discussed the matter with us before letting his wife make a formal application,' he sighed.

'I don't think he knows anything about it,' said Morris carelessly.

Sutcliffe's glasses nearly jumped off his nose. 'You mean – she's *deceiving* him?'

'No, no. She wants to be considered on her own merits, without any favouritism.'

Sutcliffe looked doubtful. 'That's all very well,' he grumbled. 'But who's to supervise her, if she does come?'

'I think she was rather hoping you would, Rupert,' Morris said mischievously.

'God forbid!' Sutcliffe picked up the files and made for the door, as if fearing that Hilary might jump out of a cupboard at him and demand a supervision. He paused with his hand on the doorknob. 'By the way, will you be coming to the Departmental Meeting this morning?'

'Can't be sure, Rupert,' said Morris, rising from his executive's chair and shrugging on his jacket. 'I have an appointment with the V C at ten thirty.'

'That's unfortunate. I was hoping you would chair the meeting. We've got to discuss next session's lecture programme, and there's bound to be a lot of disagreement. They will argue so, since Masters left . . .'

He drifted out. Morris followed him and was locking the door of his office when Bob Busby came running down the corridor, money and keys jingling in his pockets.

'Morris!' he panted. 'Glad I caught you. You're coming to the meeting?'

Morris explained that he probably wouldn't be able to make it. Busby looked glum. 'That's too bad. Sutcliffe will take the chair, and he's hopeless. I'm afraid Dempsey is going to try and force through some proposal about compulsory linguistics.'

'Is that bad?'

Busby stared. 'Well, of course it's bad. I thought from the way you tore into Dempsey's paper at the staff seminar . . .'

'I was attacking his paper, not his discipline. I have nothing against linguistics as such.'

'Well, for practical purposes Dempsey *is* linguistics around here,' said Busby. 'Compulsory linguistics means compulsory Dempsey for the students and I don't think even they deserve that.'

'You may have something there, Bob,' said Morris. He had ambivalent feelings about Robin Dempsey. In one sense he was the nearest thing the Department had to a recognizable professional academic. He was industrious, ambitious and hard-headed. He had no quirks or crotchets. He was, apart from being necessarily less brilliant, very much what Morris himself had been at the same age, and indeed had made some overtures of friendship, or at least collusion, with Morris in the course of his visit. Morris, however, had found these advances surprisingly resistible. He did not feel inclined to join Dempsey in patronizing the rest of the Rummidge faculty. Even if they were in many respects a bunch of freaks, he found them easy to get along with. Never in his academic career had he felt less threatened than in the last five months. 'Look, Bob,' he said. 'I've got an appointment with the VC.'

'Yes, I must be on my way, too,' said Busby. He jog-trotted off in the direction of the Senior Common Room. 'Get to the meeting if you can!' he shouted over his shoulder. Morris had no intention of attending the meeting if he could possibly avoid it. Staff meetings at Rummidge had been bad enough under Masters' whimsically despotic regime. Since his departure they made the Mad Hatter's Tea Party seem like a paradigm of positive decision-making.

He stepped with a lithe, well-timed movement into the paternoster and subsided gently to the ground floor. As he emerged into the bright air (another sunny spell was in progress) the clock in the campanile struck the half hour and he accelerated his pace. It was as well he did so, for another tile sprang from the wall above his head with a resounding crack like a bullet ricocheting and scattered in fragments just behind him. This isn't even funny any more, he thought looking up at the façade of the building, now beginning to look like a gigantic crossword puzzle. Before long somebody was going to get seriously killed and sue the University for a million dollars. He made a mental note to mention it to the Vice-Chancellor.

'Ah, Zapp! Awfully good of you to drop in,' the Vice-Chancellor murmured, half-rising from his desk as Morris was ushered in. Morris waded through the deep-pile carpeting and shook the hand limply extended to him. Stewart Stroud was a tall, powerfully built man who affected a manner of extreme languor and debility. He seldom spoke above a whisper, and moved about with the caution of an elderly invalid. Now he sank back into his chair as if the effort of rising and shaking hands had exhausted him. 'Do pull up a chair, old man,' he said.

'Cigarette?' He made a feeble attempt to push a wooden cigarette box across his desk in Morris's direction.

'I'll have a cigar, if you don't mind. Will you join me?'

'No, no, no.' The VC smiled and shook his head wearily. 'I want to ask your advice concerning one or two little problems.' He propped his elbows on the arms of his chair and, by interlacing his fingers, formed a shelf on which to rest his chin.

'Promotions and Appointments?' Morris queried.

The shelf collapsed, and the VC's jaw sagged momentarily. 'How did you know?'

'I guessed the students wouldn't let you get away with excluding them from that committee.'

Stroud's face cleared. 'Oh, it's nothing to do with the *students*, dear fellow.' He permitted himself an almost vigorous gesture of dismissal. 'All that unpleasantness is over and done with, thanks to you. No, this is something exclusively concerning academic staff, and absolutely confidential. I have here –' he nodded at a manilla file reposing on his otherwise immaculate desk – 'a list of nominations from the various Faculties for Senior Lectureships, due to come before the Promotions and Appointments Committee this afternoon. There are two names from the English Department. Robin Dempsey, whom you probably know, and your opposite number, now in Euphoria.'

'Philip Swallow?'

'Precisely. The problem is that we have fewer Senior Lectureships to play with than we thought, and one of these men will have to be unlucky. The question is, which one? Who is the more deserving? I'd like to have your opinion, Zapp. I'd really value your opinion on this ticklish question.' Stroud slumped back in his seat and closed his eyes in fatigue after this uncharacteristically long speech. 'Do have a look at the file, old chap, if that would help,' he murmured.

The file merely confirmed what Morris knew already: that Dempsey was much the stronger candidate on grounds of research and publication, while Swallow's claim was based on seniority and general service to the University. As teachers there was no evidence on which to discriminate between them. Normally, Morris wouldn't have hesitated to back brains and recommend Dempsey. Service, after all, was cheap. The laws of academic *Realpolitik* indicated that if Dempsey didn't get quick promotion, he might leave, whereas Swallow would stay on, doing his job in the same dull, conscientious way whether he got promoted or not. Furthermore, if Morris had no great personal warmth for Dempsey, he had several good reasons for positively disliking Philip Swallow, who had screwed his daughter, butchered his work in the *TLS* and, for all he knew, filled that cupboard with empty cans as a booby trap. It was a strange and should have been a satisfying twist of circumstance that had placed the fate of this man in his hands. Yet Morris, mentally fingering the executioner's axe and studying the bared neck of Philip Swallow held out on the block before him, hesitated. It wasn't, after all, only Swallow's happiness and prosperity that were at stake here. Hilary and the children were also involved, and for their welfare he felt a warm concern. A rise for Swallow meant more bread for the whole family. And, he couldn't help thinking, whatever it was that Hilary had meant to imply by the invitation to stay an extra night, her welcome could only be made warmer by the news that Philip was to get a promotion partly through his (Morris's) influence, right? Right.

'I'd say, promote Swallow,' Morris said, handing back the file.

'Really?' Stroud drawled. 'I thought you'd favour the other man. He seems the better scholar.'

'Dempsey's publications are OK, but they've more show than substance. He's never gonna really make it in linguistics. The senior class at MIT could run rings round him.'

'Is that so?'

'Also, he's not popular in the Department. If he gets promoted over so many older people, all hell will break out. The Department is already drifting into collective paranoia. No point in making things worse.'

'Very true, I'm sure,' Stroud murmured, making a tiny, fatal stroke on the list of names with his gold fountain pen. 'I'm much obliged to you, my dear fellow.'

'You're welcome,' said Morris, getting to his feet.

'Don't go yet, old chap. There's something else I wanted to –'

The VC broke off and stared indignantly at the door which connected with his secretary's office and had suddenly opened. The secretary hovered timidly at the threshold. 'Yes? What is it, Helen? I said I was not to be disturbed.' Irritation made his manner almost brisk.

'I'm sorry Vice-Chancellor. But there are two gentlemen . . . and Mr Biggs of Security. It's very important, they say.'

'If you would just ask them to wait until Professor Zapp has left –'

'But it's Professor Zapp they want to see. A matter of life and death, they said.'

Stroud lifted an eyebrow in Morris's direction. Morris shrugged his incomprehension, but felt a twinge of apprehension. Had Mary Makepeace given birth on the 8.50 to Durham?

'Oh, very well, you'd better let them come in,' said the Vice-Chancellor.

Three men entered the room. One was the superintendent of the campus security force. The other two introduced themselves as a doctor and a male nurse from a private psychiatric clinic somewhere in the sticks. They came quickly to the point of their intrusion. Professor Masters had escaped from their care the night before and it was thought that he would probably make for the University. Unfortunately, there was reason to believe that he might be intending violence to certain parties, in particular Professor Zapp.

'Me?' Morris exclaimed. 'Why me? What have I ever done to the old guy?'

'It appears from notes made by one of our staff,' said the doctor, looking curiously at Morris, 'that he associated you with certain recent disturbances at the University. He feels that you conspired with the students to weaken the authority of the senior staff.'

'You was a Quisling, was how he put it, sir,' said the male nurse, with a friendly grin. 'Said you plotted to get him removed.'

'That's ridiculous! He resigned of his own free will,' Morris exclaimed, looking appealingly to Stroud, who coughed and lowered his eyes.

'Well, we did have to use a little persuasion,' he murmured.

'Professor Masters is of course a sick man,' said the doctor. 'Subject to delusions. But I noticed, Professor Zapp – we looked for you in the English Department first – that you're occupying Professor Masters' old room –'

'That's just chance!'

'Quite so. But just the sort of thing to confirm Professor Masters in his delusion, should he discover it.'

'I'll move back into my old room directly.'

'I think, Professor Zapp, for your own safety, you should stay away from the University altogether until Professor Masters is traced and safely returned to the clinic. You see, we're afraid he may have obtained a weapon . . .'

'Oh, come now, doctor,' said the Vice-Chancellor. 'Don't let's be too alarmist.'

'Well, it is alarming, sir,' said the Superintendent of Security, speaking for the first time. 'After all, Professor Masters is an old soldier, and a sportsman. A crack shot, I was always given to understand.'

'Jesus,' said Morris, trembling with backdated fear. 'Those tiles.'

'What tiles?' said the VC.

'Twice today I've been shot at and I didn't realize. I thought it was just your lousy new building shedding tiles. Jesus, I might have been killed. That crazy old man's been sniping at me, you dig? I'll bet he's been up on the clock tower with telescopic sights. I thought this was supposed to be a peaceful country! I've lived forty years in the States and never once heard a shot fired in anger. I come over here and what happens?' He became aware that he was shouting.

'Steady on, Zapp,' the VC murmured.

'Sorry,' Morris mumbled. 'It's just the shock of discovering that you've been near death without knowing it.'

'Quite natural I'm sure,' said Stroud. 'Why don't you go straight home and stay safely indoors until this little problem is solved?'

'I think that's the wisest thing you could do,' said the doctor.

'You talked me into it,' said Morris, making for the door. He slowed down when he realized that he was not being accompanied, and turned. The four men, grouped around the desk, smiled encouragingly at him. Too proud to ask for an escort, Morris made a gesture of farewell, stalked purposefully out through the secretary's office, and only as he descended the stairs of the Administration Block remembered that he had left his car keys in his office and would have to return to the Hexagon before leaving the University. He made a complicated detour which kept cover between himself and the campanile, and entered the Hexagon from the rear at the lower ground floor. He boarded the paternoster, here at its lowest accessible point, and was borne silently aloft to the eighth floor. As he stepped out on to the landing, the first thing he saw was Gordon Masters ripping from his office door the temporary paper slip bearing Morris's name. Morris froze. Masters looked up from grinding the paper under his heel and stared at Morris with puzzled half-recognition: both his eyes were bright with lunacy. He took a pace forward, gnawing and tugging at his unkempt moustache. Morris retreated rapidly into the paternoster and was borne upwards. He could hear Masters galloping up the staircase that spiralled round the shaft of the paternoster. Each time Masters arrived on a landing, Morris was just moving out of sight. On the eleventh floor Morris, thinking to trick his pursuer, jumped out of the elevator and boarded a downward-moving compartment, but not before Masters glimpsed the manoeuvre. Morris heard a heavy thump above his head as Masters leapt into the next compartment. On the fifth floor Morris hopped out and boarded a rising compartment. He was preparing to get out at the eighth floor again when he saw Masters' feet coming into view, upon which he quickly turned to face the rear wall and continued his upwards journey. Numb with fright he passed the ninth, tenth, eleventh and twelfth floors and then entered the limbo of grinding machinery and flashing lights that was at the top of the shaft. The cabin he was in lurched sideways and then began its descent. Morris hopped out at the twelfth floor to meditate his next move. As he stood pondering on the landing Masters appeared before him moving slowly downwards, standing on his head. They gazed at each other in mutual puzzlement until Masters sank from Morris's sight. It was only much later that Morris deduced that Masters, having been carried upwards beyond the top floor of the paternoster's circuit, and being under the impression that the compartment turned over to make its descent, had performed a handstand in the belief that he would drop harmlessly from ceiling to floor when his compartment was inverted.

Now Morris could hear him running indefatigably up the stairs towards the twelfth floor. Morris jumped into the paternoster on the down side. As he passed the tenth floor, Masters whizzed past on foot, glimpsed him out of the corner of his eyes, skidded to a halt, and jumped into the compartment above Morris. Morris went down to the sixth floor, crossed the landing and travelled up to the ninth, walked across, went down past the eighth checking that the coast was clear, decided that it was, and got out on the seventh floor to re-ascend. Leaping across the landing to board the paternoster going up, he brushed against Masters agilely transferring himself in the opposite direction.

Morris went up to the ninth floor, across and down to the sixth, up to the tenth, down to the ninth, up to the eleventh, down to the eighth, up to the eleventh, down to the tenth, up and over the top, and got out on the twelfth, going down.

Masters was standing there, with his back to Morris,

226

looking into the shaft of the upward-moving side of the paternoster. With a hard, well-aimed thrust, Morris bundled him into the paternoster and he was borne aloft into limbo. As Masters' feet disappeared from view, Morris broke the seal on the safety device embedded in the wall and pulled the red lever. The moving chain of compartments suddenly jerked to a halt, and a bell began to ring shrilly. Very faintly, muffled shouts and the hammering of fists could be heard coming from the top of the shaft.

Hilary wore a preoccupied frown as she opened the door. When she recognized Morris she went pale, then blushed. 'Oh,' she said faintly. 'It's you. I was just going to phone you.'

'Again?'

She let him in and closed the door. 'What have you come for?'

'I don't know, what are you offering?' He waggled his eyebrows like Groucho Marx.

Hilary looked distressed. 'Aren't you teaching today?'

'It's a long story. D'you want to hear it in the lobby or shall we sit down?' Hilary was still lingering by the front door.

'I was going to say that after all I don't think it would be a good idea for you to stay the night.' She spoke very quickly, averting her eyes from his.

'Oh? Why's that?'

'I just don't think it would be a good idea.'

'OK. If that's the way you want it. I'll take my bag round to O'Shea's now.' He moved towards the stairs.

'I'm sorry.'

'Hilary,' Morris said, in a tone of fatigue, stopping on the first stair, but not turning round. 'If you don't want to sleep with me, that's your privilege, but for Christ's sake don't keep saying you're sorry.'

'I'm –' She choked back the word. 'Have you had lunch?'

'No.'

'There's nothing in the house, I'm afraid. I should have gone shopping this morning. I could open a tin of soup.'

'Don't bother.'

'It's no bother.'

He went up to the guest room to get his suitcase. When he came downstairs, Hilary was in the kitchen, stirring cream of asparagus soup in a saucepan and frying croutons. They ate at the kitchen table. Morris recounted his adventures with Masters, to which Hilary reacted with a suprising lack of excitement – indeed she scarcely seemed to be listening, politely murmuring, 'Really?' 'Goodness me,' and 'How terrifying,' just a little late on cue.

'Do you believe what I'm telling you?' he said at last. 'Or d'you think I'm making it all up?'

'*Are* you making it up?'

'No.'

'Then of course I believe you, Morris. What happened next?'

'You seem to be taking it pretty coolly. Anyone would think this kind of thing happened every week. I don't know what happened next. I phoned security to tell them Masters was trapped in the top of the paternoster and got the hell out of the place . . . Hey, this is good.' He slurped the soup greedily. 'By the way,' he said, 'your husband is going to get promoted.'

'What?' Hilary laid down her soup spoon.

'Your husband is going to get a Senior Lectureship.'

'Philip?'

'That's right.'

'But why? He doesn't deserve it.'

'I'm inclined to agree with you, but I thought you'd be pleased.'

'How do you know?'

Morris explained.

'So really,' said Hilary slowly, 'you fiddled this for Philip.'

'Well, I wouldn't say it was entirely my doing,' said

Morris modestly. 'I just gave Stroud a nudge in the right direction.'

'I think it's perfectly foul.'

'What?'

'It's corrupt. To think that people's careers can be made or marred like that.'

Morris dropped his spoon with a deliberate clatter, and appealed to the kitchen walls. 'Well, that's gratitude –'

'Gratitude? Am I supposed to feel grateful, then? It's like the films, what do they call it, the casting couch. Do you have a promotions couch in your office in America?' Hilary was on the verge of tears.

'What's gotten into you, Hilary?' Morris expostulated. 'How many times have you said that Philip would have done better in his career if only he'd pushed, like Robin Dempsey? Well, I pushed for him.'

'Bully for you. I just hope it's not wasted effort.'

'What d'you mean?'

'Suppose he doesn't come back to Rummidge?'

'What are you talking about? He's got to come back, hasn't he?'

'I don't know.' Hilary was crying now, great big tears that plopped into her soup like raindrops into a puddle.

Morris got up and went round to the other side of the table. He put a hand on each of her shoulders and shook her gently. 'What is this all about, for Chrissake?'

'I phoned Philip this morning. After last night . . . I wanted him to come home. Straight away. He was horrible. He said he was having an affair –'

'With Melanie?'

'I don't know. I don't care who it is. I felt such a fool. There I was, tortured with guilt because I kissed you last night, because I wanted to sleep with you –'

'Did you, Hilary?'

'Of course I did.'

'Then what are we waiting for?' Morris tried to pull her to her feet, but she shook her head and clung to the chair.

'No, I don't feel like it now.'

'Why not? What did you ask me to stay over for anyway?'

Hilary blew her nose on a Kleenex. 'I changed my mind.'

'Change it again. Seize the moment. We have the house to ourselves. Come on, Hilary, we both need some loving.'

He was standing behind her now, gently kneading the muscles of her neck and shoulders, as he had offered to do the night before. This time she did not resist, but leaned back against him and closed her eyes. He unfastened the buttons of her blouse and slid his hands down over her breasts.

'All right,' said Hilary. 'Let's go upstairs.'

'Morris,' said Hilary, shaking him by the shoulder. 'Wake up.'

Morris opened his eyes. Hilary, rosy-complexioned and demure in a pink dressing-gown, was sitting on the edge of the bed. Two cups steamed on the bedside table. He detached a wiry pubic hair from his lower lip. 'What time is it?' he said.

'Gone three. I've made a cup of tea.'

Morris sat up and sipped the scalding tea. He met Hilary's eyes over the rim of the cup and she blushed. 'Hey,' he said softly. 'That was terrific. I feel great. How about you?'

'It was lovely.'

'You're lovely.'

Hilary smiled. 'Don't overdo it, Morris.'

'I'm serious. You are one lovely piece of ass, you know that?'

'I'm fat and forty.'

'Nothing wrong with that. So am I.'

'I'm sorry I hit you about the head when you started, you know, that kissing stuff. Not very sophisticated, you see.'

'I like that. Now Désirée –'

Hilary lost a little of her radiance. 'Could we not talk about your wife, please? Or Philip. Not just now.'

'OK,' said Morris. 'Let's neck instead.' He pulled her down on to the bed.

'No, Morris!' she protested, struggling feebly. 'The children will be home soon.'

'There's plenty of time,' he replied, delighted to find himself capable of making love again. The telephone began to ring downstairs in the hall.

'Telephone,' Hilary moaned.

'Let it ring.'

But Hilary wrenched herself free. 'If something had happened to the children, I'd never forgive myself,' she said.

'Be quick.'

Hilary soon returned, her eyes wide with surprise.

'It's for you,' she said. 'It's the Vice-Chancellor.'

Morris took the call standing in the hall in his underpants.

'Ah, Zapp. Terribly sorry to bother you,' the VC murmured. 'How are you feeling after your adventures?'

'I'm feeling terrific right now. What happened to Masters?'

'Professor Masters, I'm glad to say, is back in the care of his doctors.'

'I'm glad to hear that.'

'Remarkably quick thinking on your part, old man, to trap him in the lift. Very neat. Allow me to congratulate you.'

'Thanks.'

'Reverting to our conversation of this morning: I've just come from the Promotions and Appointments Committee. Swallow's Senior Lectureship went through without a hitch, you'll be glad to know.'

'Uhuh.'

'And you may remember that I was on the point of asking you something else when we were interrupted by Doctor Smithers.'

'Yeah?'

'You haven't guessed what it is?'

'No.'

'Quite simply, I've been wondering whether you've given any thought to applying for the Chair of English.'

'You mean the Chair here?'

'Precisely.'

'Well, no. It never crossed my mind. You wouldn't want an American as Head of the Department. The staff wouldn't stand for it –'

'On the contrary, my dear fellow, all the members of the English Department who have been sounded out on the subject suggested your name. I don't say there may not be something of the better-the-devil-you-know attitude behind it, but obviously you've impressed them as someone capable of running the Department efficiently. I need hardly say that, after your part in resolving the crisis over the sit-in, you would be highly acceptable to the University community at large, staff and students alike. And personally I should be delighted. Not to put too fine a point on it, old friend, if you want the job, it's yours.'

'Thank you very much,' said Morris. 'I'm very honoured. But I'd never sleep easy. Supposing Masters escaped again? He might well think his suspicions of me had been justified.'

'I shouldn't let that worry you, old man,' Stroud murmured soothingly. 'I think you must have imagined that Masters was shooting at you today. There was no evidence that he'd been armed, or that he was intending any violence to you personally.'

'What was he chasing me all over the Hexagon for, then?' Morris demanded. 'To kiss me on both cheeks?'

'He wanted to talk to you.'

'*Talk* to me?'

'It appears that a long time ago he reviewed one of your books very unfavourably in *The Times Literary Supplement*, and he thought you might have found out about it and be bearing a grudge. Does that make any kind of sense?'

'I guess it does, yes. Look, Vice-Chancellor, I'll think about the Chair.'

'Yes, do, my dear fellow. Take your time.'

'What would the salary be?'

'Well, that is open to negotiation. The University has funds at its disposal for discretionary supplementary awards in special cases. I'm sure this would be regarded as a very special case.'

Morris tracked Hilary down in the bathroom. She was lying in the huge, claw-footed Victorian tub and, as he burst in, covered her breasts and pubis with washcloth and loofah.

'Come, come!' he said. 'This is no time for prudery. Move up and I'll get in behind you.'

'Don't be absurd, Morris. What did the V C want?'

'I'll scrub your back.' He slipped off his underpants and climbed into the tub. The water rose dangerously high and began to run out of the overflow outlet.

'Morris! You're mad. I'm getting out.'

But she didn't get out. She leaned forward and wriggled her shoulders ecstatically as he scrubbed.

'Did Philip ever borrow books from Gordon Masters?' he asked.

'All the time. Why?'

'It doesn't matter.'

He pulled her back between his knees and began to soap her big melon-shaped breasts.

'Oh, Lord,' she moaned. 'How are we ever going to get out of this before the children come home?'

'Relax. There's plenty of time.'

'What did the V C want?'

'He offered me the Chair of English.'

Trying to turn round to look at him, Hilary skidded on the bottom of the bath and nearly went under the water. 'What – Gordon Masters' Chair?'

'That's right.'

'And what did you say?'

'I said I'd think about it.'

Hilary rinsed herself and climbed out of the tub. 'What an extraordinary thing. Could you face settling in England?'

'Right now, the idea has great attractions,' he said meaningfully.

'Don't be silly, Morris.' She covered herself modestly with a bath towel. 'You know very well this is just an episode.'

'What makes you say that?'

She shot him a shrewd glance. 'How many women have there been in your life?'

He stirred uncomfortably in the tepid water, and ran some more into the tub. 'That's an unfair question. At a certain age a man can find satisfaction in one woman alone. He needs stability.'

'Besides, Philip will be coming back soon.'

'I thought you said he wasn't?'

'Oh, that won't last. He'll be back, with his tail between his legs. Now *there's* someone who really does need stability.'

'Maybe we could fix him up with Désirée,' Morris joked.

'Poor Désirée. Hasn't she suffered enough?' The telephone began to ring. 'Please hurry up and get dressed, Morris.' She pulled on her dressing-gown and went out.

Morris lay half-floating in the deep tub, fondling his genitals and pondering Hilary's question. *Could* he face settling in England? Six months ago, the question would have been absurd, the answer instantaneous. But now he wasn't so sure . . . It would be a solution, of sorts, to the problem of what to do with his career. Rummidge wasn't the greatest university in the world, agreed, but the set-up was wide open to a man with energy and ideas. Few American professors wielded the absolute power of a Head of Department at Rummidge. Once in the driver's seat, you could do whatever you liked. With his expertise, energy and international contacts, he could really put Rummidge on the map, and that would be kind of fun . . . Morris began to project a Napoleonic future for himself at Rummidge: sweeping away the English Department's ramshackle Gothic syllabus and substituting an immaculately logical course-system that took some account of developments in the subject since 1900; setting up a postgraduate Centre for Jane Austen Studies; making the use of typewriters by students obligatory; hiring bright American academic refugees from student revolutions at home; staging conferences, starting a new journal . . .

He heard a tinkle as Hilary replaced the telephone receiver, and pulled the plug out by its chain with his big toe. The waters gradually receded, making islands, archipelagos and then continents of his knees, belly, cock, chest and shoulders. As regards his domestic life, he had nothing to lose by staying in England. If Désirée insisted on leaving him and taking the twins with her, Rummidge, after all, was no further from New York than Euphoria. Possibly she might even be coaxed into giving their marriage another chance in Europe. Not that Rummidge was exactly what Désirée had in mind when she thought of Europe, but still, you could fly to Paris in fifty minutes from Rummidge airport if you wanted to . . .

The last water gurgled away, tugging at the hairs on his legs and buttocks, and he lay on the bottom of the tub, damp and naked, like a stranded castaway. Gulliver. Crusoe. A new life?

Hilary came in.

'OK, OK,' he said. 'I'm getting out.' Then he noticed she was looking at him strangely. 'What's the matter?'

'That phone call . . .'

'Yeah, who was it? The V C had second thoughts?'

'It was Désirée.'

'*Désirée!* Why didn't you fetch me?' He leaped out of the bath and grabbed a towel.

'She didn't want to speak to you,' said Hilary. 'She wanted to speak to me.'

'You? What did she say, then?'

'The woman Philip has been having an affair with . . .'

'Yeah?'

'Is her. Désirée.'

'You're kidding.'

'No.'

'I don't believe it.'

'Why not?'

'Why not? I know Désirée. She hates men. Especially weak-kneed men like your husband.'

'How do you know he's weak-kneed?' Hilary demanded, with some irritation.

'I just know. Désirée is a ball-breaker. She eats men like your husband for breakfast.'

'Philip can be very gentle, and tender. Perhaps Désirée likes that for a change,' Hilary said stiffly.

'The bitch!' Morris exclaimed, slapping the side of the tub with his towel. 'The double-crossing bitch.'

'I thought she was being remarkably straightforward, myself. She said she heard my conversation with Philip this morning – I don't know quite how, because when I phoned your house she gave me a different number ... But anyway, she knew all about it, and she thought it only fair to put me in the picture, since Philip hasn't had the courage to tell me what's been going on. Naturally I felt I had to be equally honest.'

'You mean you told her about ... this afternoon?'

'Of course. I particularly wanted Philip to know.'

'What did Désirée say?' he asked almost fearfully.

'She said,' Hilary replied, 'that perhaps we ought to meet somewhere to talk the situation over.'

'You and Désirée?'

'All of us. Philip too. A sort of summit conference, she said.'

6. Ending

*Exterior: BOAC VC 10 flying from left to right across screen –
afternoon, clear sky. Sound: jet engines.*
    Cut to:
Interior: VC 10 – afternoon.
Angle on MORRIS *and* HILARY *seated halfway down cabin.
Sound: muted noise of jet engines.*

HILARY is turning pages of *Harper's*, nervously and
inattentively. MORRIS yawns, looks out of window.
*Zoom through window. Shot: eastern seaboard of America.
Long Island, Manhattan.*
    Cut to:
*Exterior: TWA Boeing 707 flying from right to left across
screen – afternoon, clear sky. Sound: noise of jet engines.*
    Cut to:
*Interior: TWA Boeing 707 – afternoon. Sound: cool instru-
mental version of 'These Foolish Things'.*
Close-up: PHILIP, *asleep, wearing headphones, his
mouth slightly open. Draw back to reveal* DÉSIRÉE
sitting next to him, reading Simone de Beauvoir's The
Second Sex. DÉSIRÉE *looks out of the window, then at
her wristwatch, then at* PHILIP. *She twists the knob
above his head which controls the in-flight entertainment. Sound changes abruptly to narration of 'The Three
Bears'.*

RECORDED VOICE: And the Daddy Bear said, 'Who's been
sleeping in MY bed?' and the Mummy Bear said, 'Who's
been –'

PHILIP wakes with a guilty start, tears off his earphones.
Sound: muted noise of jet engines.

DÉSIRÉE : (*smiles*) Wake up, we're nearly there.

PHILIP : New York? Already?

DÉSIRÉE : Of course, you never know how long you're going to be stacked at this time of the year.

    Cut to:

    Interior : VC 10 – afternoon.

MORRIS : (*To* HILARY) I hope to hell we aren't stacked for hours over Kennedy.

    Cut to:

    Exterior : VC 10 – afternoon. We see the plane head-on. It begins to lose height. Sound : jet engines changing note.

    Cut to:

    Exterior : Boeing 707 – afternoon. We see the plane head-on. It begins to bank to the right. Sound : jet engines changing note.

    Cut to:

    Interior : Flight deck, VC 10 – afternoon. BRITISH CAPTAIN, *scanning the sky, looks to his right. Close-up:* BRITISH CAPTAIN *registers alarm.*

    Cut to:

    Interior : Flight deck, Boeing 707 – afternoon. Close-up: AMERICAN CAPTAIN *registers horror.*

    Cut to:

    Interior : Flight deck, VC 10 – afternoon. Looking over the BRITISH CAPTAIN*'s shoulder we see the Boeing 707, terrifyingly near, cross the path of the VC 10, banking in an effort to avoid collision. The* BRITISH CAPTAIN *manipulates the controls to bank in the opposite direction.*

    Cut to:

    Interior : Boeing 707, passengers' cabin – afternoon. Alarm and confusion among passengers as the plane tilts violently. Sound : screams, cries etc.

    Cut to:

    Interior : VC 10 passengers' cabin – afternoon. Alarm and confusion among passengers as the plane tilts violently. Sound : screams, cries etc.

    Cut to:

    Interior : Flight deck, VC 10 – afternoon.

BRITISH CAPTAIN: (*coolly into microphone*) Hello Kennedy
Flight Control. This is BOAC Whisky Sugar Eight. I
have to report an air miss.
> *Cut to:*
> *Interior: Flight deck, Boeing 707 – afternoon.*

AMERICAN CAPTAIN: (*enraged, into microphone*) What the
fuck do you think you guys are doing down there?
> *Cut to:*
> *Interior: VC 10 passengers' cabin – afternoon. Sound:
> babble of conversation – 'Did you see that?' ' Must have missed
> us by inches', 'Sure was a near thing' etc.*

MORRIS: (*mopping his brow*) I always said, if God had meant
us to fly he'd have given me guts.

HILARY: I feel sick.
> *Cut to:*
> *Interior: Boeing 707 passengers' cabin – afternoon. Sound:
> babble of conversation.*

DÉSIRÉE: (*shakily, to* PHILIP) What was that?

PHILIP: I think we nearly collided with another plane.

DÉSIRÉE: Jesus Christ!
> *Fade out.*
> *Fade in on interior: hotel room in mid-town Manhattan, blue
> decor – late afternoon. Sound: TV commentary on baseball
> game, turned low.* There are two suitcases open, but
> not unpacked. HILARY is lying, fully dressed but
> without her shoes, on one of the twin beds, her
> eyes closed. MORRIS, in shirt sleeves, is crouched in
> front of the TV, watching a ball game, drinking
> Scotch on the rocks which he has fixed from a tray
> with bottle, ice, glasses etc. on the dressing table.
> There is a knock on the door. *Shot:* HILARY's eyes flick
> open.

MORRIS: Yeah? Come in.

DÉSIRÉE: (*entering, followed by* PHILIP) Morris?
> HILARY sits up quickly, swings her feet to the floor.

MORRIS: Désirée! (*sets down his drink, comes to door with open
arms*) Honey!
> DÉSIRÉE catches MORRIS's wrists deftly and brings him

to a dead stop. She kisses him demurely on the cheek, then releases him.

DÉSIRÉE: Hallo, Morris.

MORRIS: (*rubbing his wrists*) Hey, you've gotten awfully strong.

DÉSIRÉE: I've been taking karate lessons.

MORRIS: Ve-ry good! You should go into the Park tonight and practise on the rapists. (*He extends hand to* PHILIP) You must be Philip.

    Shot: PHILIP staring, speechless, across the room at HILARY. Zoom in on HILARY, sitting bolt upright on the bed, staring across at PHILIP.

MORRIS: Well, if you're *not* Philip, things are even more complicated than I thought they were. (*He takes* PHILIP's *hand and shakes it*)

PHILIP: Sorry! How do you do. (PHILIP *looks back at* HILARY)

HILARY: (*faintly*) Hello, Philip.

PHILIP: Hello, Hilary.

DÉSIRÉE: (*walks across to* HILARY) Hilary – I'm Désirée. (HILARY *rises*) Don't get up.

HILARY: (*apologetically, putting on her shoes*) I was just lying down . . .

    HILARY and DÉSIRÉE shake hands.

DÉSIRÉE: How was your flight?

MORRIS: Great! We nearly collided with another plane.

DÉSIRÉE: (*wheels round*) So did we!

MORRIS: (*gapes*) *You* nearly collided . . . ?

PHILIP: Yes, just coming into New York. One wonders how often it happens.

MORRIS: (*soberly*) I think it can only have happened once this afternoon.

PHILIP: You mean . . . ?

MORRIS: (*nods*) We were nearly introduced in mid-air.

PHILIP: Phew!

HILARY: (*sits down quickly on the bed*) How frightful!

DÉSIRÉE: It would have solved a lot of problems, of course. A spectacular finale to our little drama.

HILARY: Oh don't!

MORRIS: But we escaped. Perhaps God isn't angry with us after all.

PHILIP: Who says he is?

MORRIS: Well, Hilary ...

PHILIP: (*To* HILARY) Do you?

HILARY: (*defensive*) Of course not. It's Morris who's afraid of God, only he won't admit it. I just want to get things sorted out.

DÉSIRÉE: Sure. That's what we're here for.

PHILIP: (*To* HILARY) How are the children?

HILARY: They're all right. Mary is looking after them. You've put on weight, Philip.

PHILIP: Yes, a little.

HILARY: It suits you.

MORRIS: (*To* DÉSIRÉE) I like the pants suit. How are the twins?

DÉSIRÉE: They're fine. How about a drink for the rest of us?

MORRIS: Sure. (*hastens to pour drinks*) Hilary? Philip? Scotch?

HILARY: No thanks, Morris.

MORRIS: About rooms. Shall Désirée and I take this one?

DÉSIRÉE: Who says I'm sharing with you?

MORRIS: (*shrugs*) OK, honey. You and Philip have the other room. We'll stay here.

HILARY: Either way, isn't it rather prejudging the issue?

MORRIS: (*spreads hands*) OK. What do you suggest?
  Cut to:
  Interior: blue hotel room – night.
  PHILIP and MORRIS are in the twin beds. PHILIP, wearing pyjamas, is apparently asleep. MORRIS, bare-chested, is awake, one hand behind his head, the other under his sheet.

MORRIS: We shouldn't have let them get away with it.
  (*pause*)
It's ridiculous.
  (*pause*)
I get so goddam horny in hotel rooms.
  (*pause*)
Philip.

PHILIP: Mmm?

MORRIS: How d'ya make out with Désirée?

PHILIP: Very nice.

MORRIS: I mean, in the sack.

PHILIP: Very nice.

MORRIS: Hard work, though, isn't it?

PHILIP: I wouldn't have said so.

(pause)

MORRIS: Uh, ever get her to, uh, blow you?

PHILIP: No.

MORRIS: *(sighs)* Neither did I.

(pause)

PHILIP: I never thought of asking.

(pause)

PHILIP sits up suddenly, wide awake.

PHILIP: Did you ever ask Hilary?

MORRIS: Sure.

PHILIP: What happened?

MORRIS: Nothing.

PHILIP relaxes, sinks back on to the bed, closes eyes.

(pause)

MORRIS: She didn't know what I was talking about.

Cut to:

Interior: hotel room, pink decor – night.

DÉSIRÉE and HILARY asleep in the twin beds. Telephone on bedside table between them. Telephone rings. DÉSIRÉE gropes, picks up receiver.

DÉSIRÉE: *(half asleep)* Hallo.

Intercut close-ups of MORRIS *and* DÉSIRÉE.

MORRIS: Hallo, sweetheart.

DÉSIRÉE: *(annoyed)* What do you want? I was asleep.

MORRIS: Uh ... Philip and I were wondering *(looks across at Philip)* if we couldn't come to some more comfortable arrangement ...

DÉSIRÉE: Like what?

MORRIS: Like if one of you girls would like to change places with one of us ...

DÉSIRÉE: You mean *either* of us? With either of you? You don't have any preference?

MORRIS: (*laughs uneasily*) We leave it to you.

DÉSIRÉE: You're despicable. (*Puts down receiver*)

MORRIS: Désirée!

MORRIS rattles the receiver.

(*gloomily*) Bitch!

Cut to:

Interior: pink hotel room – night.

HILARY: Who was that?

DÉSIRÉE: Morris.

HILARY: What did he want?

DÉSIRÉE: Either of us. He wasn't fussy.

HILARY: What?

DÉSIRÉE: Philip too. I'm afraid Morris is a bad influence.

HILARY: (*sits up*) I'd like to talk to Philip.

DÉSIRÉE: *Now?*

HILARY: I'm wide awake.

DÉSIRÉE: Please yourself. (*turns over*)

HILARY: Don't you want to talk to Morris on your own?

DÉSIRÉE: No!

Cut to:

Interior: hotel corridor – night.

HILARY, in dressing-gown, emerges from door on left, leaving it ajar, crosses corridor and knocks on door to right. It opens. HILARY goes in, door shuts. After a short interval, door on right opens and MORRIS, in dressing-gown, comes out, closes door behind him, crosses corridor, enters door left, closes it behind him.

Cut to:

Interior: blue hotel room – night.

HILARY: (*nervously*) I only came in here to talk, Philip.

Cut to:

Interior: pink hotel room – night. Sound: door clicks shut.

DÉSIRÉE: (*levelly*) You lay a finger on me, Zapp, and you'll regret it.

Cut to :

Interior : blue room – early morning.

PHILIP and HILARY asleep in each other's arms in one
of the beds.

Cut to :

Interior : pink room – early morning.

Pan slowly round room, which is in a mess – chairs
overturned, lamps knocked over, bedclothes ripped
from beds etc. There is no sign of MORRIS and DÉ-
SIRÉE until they are discovered on the floor between
the two twin beds, naked, tangled together in a heap
of pillows and bedclothes. They are fast asleep.

Cut to :

Interior : coffee-shop in hotel – morning.

MORRIS, DÉSIRÉE, PHILIP and HILARY are
finishing breakfast. They are sitting in a booth, men on
one side of the table, women on the other.

MORRIS: Well, what are we going to do this morning?
Shall we show these two hicks the town, Désirée?

DÉSIRÉE: It's gonna be hot. In the nineties, the radio said.

HILARY: Shouldn't we have a serious talk? I mean, that's
what we've come all this way for. What are we going to
do? About the future.

MORRIS: Let's consider the options. Coolly. (*prepares to
light cigar*) First: we could return to our respective homes
with our respective spouses.

MORRIS lights cigar, and examines the tip. HILARY
looks at PHILIP, PHILIP looks at DÉSIRÉE, DÉSIRÉE
looks at MORRIS.

DÉSIRÉE: Next option.

MORRIS: We could all get divorced and remarry each other.
If you follow me.

PHILIP: Where would we live?

MORRIS: I could take the Chair at Rummidge, settle down
there. I guess you could get a job in Euphoria . . .

PHILIP: I'm not so sure.

MORRIS: Or you could take Désirée to Rummidge, and I'd go back to Euphoria with Hilary.

    HILARY rises to her feet.

Where are you going?

HILARY: I don't wish to listen to this childish conversation

PHILIP: What's wrong? You started it.

HILARY: This is not what I meant by a serious talk. You sound like a couple of scriptwriters discussing how to wind up a play.

MORRIS: Hilary, honey! There are choices to be made. We must be aware of all the possibilities.

HILARY: (*sitting down*) All right, then. Have you considered the possibility that Désirée and I might divorce you two and *not* remarry?

DÉSIRÉE: Right on!

MORRIS: (*thoughtfully*) True. Another possibility is group marriage. You know? Two couples live together in one house and pool their resources. Everything is common property.

PHILIP: Including, er . . .

MORRIS: Including that, naturally.

HILARY: What about the children?

MORRIS: It's great for children. They amuse each other, while the parents . . .

DÉSIRÉE: Screw each other.

HILARY: I never heard of anything so immoral in my life.

MORRIS: Oh, come on Hilary! The four of us already hold the world record for long-distance wife-swapping. Why not do it under one roof? That way you get domestic stability plus sexual variety. Isn't that what all of us want? I don't know how you two made out last night, but Désirée and I really had a –

DÉSIRÉE: OK, OK, that's enough of that.

PHILIP: I must say it's an intriguing idea.

DÉSIRÉE: In theory I'm sympathetic – I mean as a first step towards getting rid of the nuclear family, it has possibili-

245

ties. But if Morris is in favour there must be a twist in it somewhere.

HILARY: (*sardonically, to* MORRIS) As a matter of academic interest: in this so-called group marriage, what happens if the two men both fancy the same woman at the same time?

DÉSIRÉE: Or the two women want to sleep with the same man?

(*Pause*) MORRIS rubs his chin thoughtfully.

PHILIP: (*grins*) I know. The one who's left out watches the other three.

MORRIS and DÉSIRÉE crack up laughing. HILARY joins in despite herself.

HILARY: But can't we be serious for a moment? Where is this all going to *end*?

Cut to:

Interior: blue hotel room – afternoon.

The door opens and in come MORRIS, DÉSIRÉE, HILARY and PHILIP. They carry packages and carrier bags with Manhattan store names on them. They look hot and sweaty, but relaxed. They flop down on chairs, beds.

MORRIS: We made it.

DÉSIRÉE: Jesus, I'd forgotten what a New York heatwave was like.

PHILIP: Thank God for air conditioning.

MORRIS: I'll go get some ice.

MORRIS goes out. PHILIP sits up suddenly.

PHILIP: Désirée.

DÉSIRÉE: What?

PHILIP: D'you realize what day this is . . . The day of the March!

DÉSIRÉE: The march? Oh, yeah, the March.

HILARY: What's that?

PHILIP: (*excitedly*) The educational network is carrying it.

PHILIP goes over to TV, turns it on.

DÉSIRÉE: It was this morning, wasn't it? It's all over by now.

PHILIP: It's still morning in Euphoria. Pacific time.

DÉSIRÉE: That's right! (*to* HILARY) Have you heard about the trouble at Plotinus? Over the People's Garden?

HILARY: Oh that. You missed a lot of excitement at Rummidge this term, you know, Philip. The sit-in and everything.

PHILIP: Somehow I can't think of anything seriously revolutionary happening at Rummidge.

HILARY: I hope you're not going to turn into one of these violence snobs, who think that nothing's important unless people are getting killed.

DÉSIRÉE: 'Violence snobs', I like that...

PHILIP: Well, as a matter of fact people *could* be killed today in Plotinus, quite easily.

DÉSIRÉE: You have to make allowances, Hilary. Philip got very involved with the Garden and all that. He even went to jail.

HILARY: Good God! You never told me, Philip.

PHILIP: (*crouching over set as it begins to warm up*) It was only for a few hours. I was going to write to you about it but... it was connected with other things.

HILARY: Oh.

A Western film comes up on the TV screen. PHILIP switches channels until he hits the transmission of the Plotinus March.

PHILIP: Ah! (*tunes TV. Sound: chanting, cheers, bands etc.*)

MORRIS enters with ice and soft drinks.

MORRIS: What's that?

DÉSIRÉE: The big March at Plotinus.

MORRIS: No kidding?

VOICE OF COMMENTATOR: And it certainly looks as though the great March is going to pass off peacefully after all...

MORRIS watches with interest as he prepares the drinks. *Close-up* of TV screen. We see the column of marchers passing the fenced-in Garden. It is a warm sunny morning in Plotinus. The crowd is festive, good-humoured. The marchers carry banners, flags, flowers and sod. Inside the fence, National Guardsmen stand at ease. The camera zooms in on various sections of the crowd. We see trucks with rock bands and topless dancers performing on them, people dancing in the spray from hosepipes, marching arm-in-arm etc. We can recognize various familiar faces among the marchers. Over these pictures, the voice of the COMMENTATOR and the comments of MORRIS, PHILIP, HILARY and DÉSIRÉE.

VOICE OF COMMENTATOR: A lot of people feared blood would run in the streets of Plotinus today, but so far the vibrations are good . . . The marchers are throwing flowers instead of rocks . . . they're weaving flowers into the mesh of the hurricane fence . . . they're planting sod on the sidewalk outside the Garden . . . that's how they're making their point . . .

PHILIP: I say, there's Charles Boon. And Melanie!

MORRIS: Melanie? Where?

DÉSIRÉE: Next to that guy with his arm in plaster.

HILARY: She's very pretty.

VOICE OF COMMENTATOR: So far, nobody has tried to scale the fence. The guardsmen, as you can see, are standing at ease. Some of them have been waving to the marchers . . .

PHILIP: And there's Wily Smith! D'you remember, Hilary, I told you about him. In the corner of the picture in the baseball cap. He was in my writing class. Never wrote me a single word.

VOICE OF COMMENTATOR: Sheriff O'Keene and his men, the blue meanies as the students call them, are well out of sight . . .

DÉSIRÉE: Hey, look at the topless dancers!

PHILIP: That's Carol and Deirdre, surely?

DÉSIRÉE: I think you're right.

VOICE OF COMMENTATOR: The column has been going past for about thirty minutes now, and I still can't see the end of it.

PHILIP: And there's the Cowboy and the Confederate Soldier! Everybody in Plotinus must be on this march.

VOICE OF COMMENTATOR: I think these pictures say it all.

HILARY: (*a little wistfully*) You sound as if you wish you were there yourself, Philip.

DÉSIRÉE: You bet he does.

PHILIP: No, not really.

> PHILIP turns down the volume of the TV but leaves the vision on. *Draw back* to reveal the four of them gathered round the TV, drinks in hand.

PHILIP: 'That is no country for old men . . .'

MORRIS: Come now, Philip, let's have no defeatism.

PHILIP: I'd be an imposter there.

DÉSIRÉE: Explain yourself.

PHILIP: Those young people (*gestures at TV screen*) really care about the Garden. It's like a love affair for them. Take Charles Boon and Melanie. I could never feel like that about any public issue. Sometimes I wish I could. For me, if I'm honest, politics is background, news, almost entertainment. Something you switch on and off, like the TV. What I really worry about, what I can't switch off at will is, oh, sex, or dying or losing my hair. Private things. We're private people, aren't we, our generation? We make a clear distinction between private and public life; and the important things, the things that make us happy or unhappy are private. Love is private. Property is private. Parts are private. That's why the young radicals call for fucking in the streets. It's not just a cheap shock-tactic. It's a serious revolutionary proposition. You know that Beatles' song, 'Let's Do It In The Road' . . . ?

DÉSIRÉE: Bullshit.

PHILIP: Eh?

DÉSIRÉE: Absolute bullshit, Philip. You've been brainwashed by the Plotinus Underground. You've been reading too many copies of *Euphoric Times*. Who's going to get fucked in the streets when the revolution comes, tell me that?

PHILIP : Who?

DÉSIRÉE : Women, that's who, whether they like it or not. Listen, there are girls getting raped every night down at the Garden, only *Euphoric Times* doesn't recognize the word rape, so you'd never know it. Any girl who goes down to help with the Garden is caught in a sexual trap. If she won't put out the men will accuse her of being bourgeois and uptight and if she complains to the cops they'll tell her she deserves everything she gets by simply being there. And if the girls aren't being screwed against their will, they're slaving over the stewpot or washing dishes or looking after kids, while the men sit around rapping about politics. Call that a revolution? Don't make me laugh.

HILARY : Hear, hear!

PHILIP : Well, you may be right, Désirée. All I'm saying is that there *is* a generation gap, and I think it revolves around this public/private thing. Our generation – we subscribe to the old liberal doctrine of the inviolate self. It's the great tradition of realistic fiction, it's what novels are all about. The private life in the foreground, history a distant rumble of gunfire, somewhere offstage. In Jane Austen not even a rumble. Well, the novel is dying, and us with it. No wonder I could never get anything out of my novel-writing class at Euphoric State. It's an unnatural medium for their experience. Those kids (*gestures at screen*) are living a film, not a novel.

MORRIS : Oh, come on, Philip! You've been listening to Karl Kroop.

PHILIP : Well, he makes a lot of sense.

MORRIS : It's a very crude kind of historicism he's peddling, surely? And bad aesthetics.

HILARY : This is all very fascinating, I'm sure, but could we discuss something a little more practical? Like what the four of us are going to do in the immediate future?

DÉSIRÉE : It's no use, Hilary. Don't you recognize the sound of men talking?

MORRIS : (*To* PHILIP) The paradigms of fiction are

essentially the same whatever the medium. Words or images, it makes no difference at the structural level.

DÉSIRÉE: 'The structural level', 'paradigms'. How they love those abstract words. 'Historicism'!

PHILIP: (*To* MORRIS) I don't think that's entirely true. I mean, take the question of endings.

DÉSIRÉE: Yeah, let's take it!

PHILIP: You remember that passage in *Northanger Abbey* where Jane Austen says she's afraid that her readers will have guessed that a happy ending is coming up at any moment.

MORRIS: (*nods*) Quote, 'Seeing in the tell-tale compression of the pages before them that we are all hastening together to perfect felicity.' Unquote.

PHILIP: That's it. Well, that's something the novelist can't help giving away, isn't it, that his book is shortly coming to an end? It may not be a happy ending, nowadays, but he can't disguise the tell-tale compression of the pages.

HILARY and DÉSIRÉE begin to listen to what PHILIP is saying, and he becomes the focal point of attention.

I mean, mentally you brace yourself for the ending of a novel. As you're reading, you're aware of the fact that there's only a page or two left in the book, and you get ready to close it. But with a film there's no way of telling, especially nowadays, when films are much more loosely structured, much more ambivalent, than they used to be. There's no way of telling which frame is going to be the last. The film is going along, just as life goes along, people are behaving, doing things, drinking, talking, and we're watching them, and at any point the director chooses, without warning, without anything being resolved, or explained, or wound up, it can just . . . end.

PHILIP shrugs. The camera stops, freezing him in mid-gesture.

THE END

Also by David Lodge

SMALL WORLD

A marvellous sequel to *Changing Places*. Philip Swallow and
Morris Zapp cross paths once again but this time in the areas of
the academic conference. Fast and funny, it involves romantic
conquests and disappointments, in-fighting and the pursuit of
achievement. It all goes to prove it's only a small world ...

HOW FAR CAN YOU GO?

Winner of the Whitbread Book of the Year Award for 1980

How far could they go? On one hand there was the traditional
Catholic Church, on the other the siren call of the permissive
society. And what with the advent of COC (Catholics for an
Open Church), the social lubrication of the Pill and the disap-
pearance of Hell, it was difficult for Polly, Dennis, Angela and
the others not to rupture their spiritual virginity on the way to
the seventies ...

'Hilarious ... a magnificent book' Graham Greene

THE BRITISH MUSEUM IS FALLING DOWN

While Adam Appleby's thesis awaits its birth in the British
Museum, back at home, the 'Vatican Roulette' has failed them
again and a fourth little faithful is apparently on the way. A
serpent tempts Adam towards the chemists ... and the author
of *How Far Can You Go?* opens up a brilliant comedy on the
absurd dilemma of Catholics in the days before the Pill.

'Hilarious without being vulgar' – *Daily Telegraph*

GINGER, YOU'RE BARMY

'David Lodge is a perfectionist. This novel has all the ring of
complete authenticity' – A. N. Wilson in the *Spectator*

'This is a remarkable novel on many levels, vivid, funny and
with a compassion made all the more moving by the harshness
of its military setting' – Selina Hastings in the *Daily Telegraph*

Also published

OUT OF THE SHELTER

A CHOICE OF PENGUINS

☐ *Stanley and the Women* **Kingsley Amis**   £2.50

'Very good, very powerful . . . beautifully written . . . This is Amis
père at his best' – Anthony Burgess in the *Observer*. 'Everybody
should read it' – *Daily Mail*

☐ *The Mysterious Mr Ripley* **Patricia Highsmith**   £4.95

Containing *The Talented Mr Ripley*, *Ripley Underground* and
Ripley's Game. 'Patricia Highsmith is the poet of apprehension' –
Graham Greene. 'The Ripley books are marvellously, insanely read-
able' – *The Times*

☐ *Earthly Powers* **Anthony Burgess**   £4.95

'Crowded, crammed, bursting with manic erudition, garlicky puns,
omnilingual jokes . . . (a novel) which meshes the real and personal-
ized history of the twentieth century' – Martin Amis

☐ *Life & Times of Michael K* **J. M. Coetzee**   £2.95

The Booker Prize-winning novel: 'It is hard to convey . . . just what
Coetzee's special quality is. His writing gives off whiffs of Conrad, of
Nabokov, of Golding, of the Paul Theroux of *The Mosquito Coast*.
But he is none of these, he is a harsh, compelling new voice' –
Victoria Glendinning

☐ *The Stories of William Trevor*   £5.95

'Trevor packs into each separate five or six thousand words more
richness, more laughter, more ache, more multifarious human-ness
than many good writers manage to get into a whole novel' – *Punch*

☐ *The Book of Laughter and Forgetting*
  Milan Kundera   £3.95

'A whirling dance of a book . . . a masterpiece full of angels, terror,
ostriches and love . . . No question about it. The most important
novel published in Britain this year' – Salman Rushdie

A CHOICE OF PENGUINS

☐ *Small World* **David Lodge**

A jet-propelled academic romance, sequel to *Changing Places*. 'A new comic débâcle on every page' – *The Times*. 'Here is everything one expects from Lodge but three times as entertaining as anything he has written before' – *Sunday Telegraph*

☐ *The Neverending Story* **Michael Ende**

The international bestseller, now a major film: 'A tale of magical adventure, pursuit and delay, danger, suspense, triumph' – *The Times Literary Supplement*

☐ *The Sword of Honour Trilogy* **Evelyn Waugh**

Containing *Men at Arms, Officers and Gentlemen* and *Unconditional Surrender*, the trilogy described by Cyril Connolly as 'unquestionably the finest novels to have come out of the war'.

☐ *The Honorary Consul* **Graham Greene**

In a provincial Argentinian town, a group of revolutionaries kidnap the wrong man . . . 'The tension never relaxes and one reads hungrily from page to page, dreading the moment it will all end' – Auberon Waugh in the *Evening Standard*

☐ *The First Rumpole Omnibus* **John Mortimer**

Containing *Rumpole of the Bailey*, *The Trials of Rumpole* and *Rumpole's Return*. 'A fruity, foxy masterpiece, defender of our wilting faith in mankind' – *Sunday Times*

☐ *Scandal* **A. N. Wilson**

Sexual peccadillos, treason and blackmail are all ingredients on the boil in A. N. Wilson's new, *cordon noir* comedy. 'Drily witty, deliciously nasty' – *Sunday Telegraph*